JACOB

VH NICOLSON

B

Boldwood

First published in 2022. This edition published in Great Britain in 2025 by Boldwood Books Ltd.

Copyright © VH Nicolson, 2022

Cover Design by Lori Jackson

Cover Images: Depositphotos and Shutterstock

The moral right of VH Nicolson to be identified as the author of this work has been asserted in accordance with the Copyright, Designs and Patents Act 1988.

Every effort has been made to obtain the necessary permissions with reference to copyright material, both illustrative and quoted. We apologise for any omissions in this respect and will be pleased to make the appropriate acknowledgements in any future edition.

A CIP catalogue record for this book is available from the British Library.

Paperback ISBN 978-1-83678-616-0

Large Print ISBN 978-1-83678-617-7

Hardback ISBN 978-1-83678-615-3

Ebook ISBN 978-1-83678-618-4

Kindle ISBN 978-1-83678-619-1

Audio CD ISBN 978-1-83678-610-8

MP3 CD ISBN 978-1-83678-611-5

Digital audio download ISBN 978-1-83678-612-2

This book is printed on certified sustainable paper. Boldwood Books is dedicated to putting sustainability at the heart of our business. For more information please visit https://www.boldwoodbooks.com/about-us/sustainability/

Boldwood Books Ltd, 23 Bowerdean Street, London, SW6 3TN

www.boldwoodbooks.com

For my family

AUTHOR'S NOTE

Please note this book comes with a content warning. This book is intended for over 18s.

My books all come with the guarantee of a happily ever after but sometimes the journey to get there can be hard fought. The main focus of my books is love, romance and happiness.

Please keep that in mind.

1

SKYE

Tapping the stop button on my music app, the sound of Adele's soulful voice immediately stops.

I let out a sigh of satisfaction, giving the buns in my hair a quick squeeze to relieve the pressure. They've been in all day, and I'm desperate to get home and unravel my platinum-silver locks. I've been a graphic designer here at Baxter and Bain Branding in my hometown of Castleview Cove since I left art college, but sitting at a desk all day is beginning to take its toll on my shoulders.

Stretching my stiffened neck to ease the tension from sitting hunched over a desk for the last—I check the clock— five hours, I whip off my noise-canceling headphones and lay them on my messy desk. I jolt when a muffled groan echoes across the deserted office, making the beat of my heart shift up a gear.

I sit as still as a statue and dart my eyes around the dark-ened space.

Nothing.

I must have imagined it.

Turning my attention back to the project management software, it glows back from my computer screen in vivid green, confirming I have completed yet another two projects four days ahead of schedule.

I can't wait to pour myself a celebratory crisp glass of wine as soon as I get back home.

The same muffled moan echoes again but much louder this time.

A shiver of panic runs down my spine.

I slowly roll my chair away from my desk. Security is watertight at Baxter and Bain, so they would know if an intruder was in the building... wouldn't they?

I leap to my feet when the chilling sound of a woman sighing floats hauntingly toward me.

Another low moan drifts my way from the managers' corridor.

I creep quietly toward the noise.

A yellow glow from Jacob's office, our account executive—and my boss—makes my shoulders sag with relief.

My friend since high school and my ex-boyfriend's best friend, Jacob doesn't ever work nights. I know this because I am the only one that does.

What the hell is he doing here?

Now only a couple of feet away from his office, the distinctive sound of a high-pitched feminine moan is more obvious.

Oh my God, is Jacob watching porn in the office?

Curiosity gets the better of me and I move toward the sound.

I have to cover my mouth to silence a gasp when I reach Jacob's office, his door wide open.

He's fucking a girl over his desk from behind. Her ice-white hair covers her cheek-to-desk face, making it impossible for me to make out her features.

I don't recognize her silver-white locks that are weirdly similar to mine.

I stand in the doorway, unable to tear my eyes off him as he drives into her with wild abandon while she groans with pleasure.

A faint sheen of perspiration covers his glorious, athletic chest. His torso is covered in tattoos I've never seen before. My eyes dip lower toward his defined abs and chiseled V pointing downward, tempting me to catch a glimpse of his cock, but I can't see it from this angle.

I want to see.

He presses the girl's shoulders firmly against the hard surface with one hand and with the other, he digs his fingertips into the pale skin of her hips.

"Ah, Jacob," she moans.

"I told you. No talking," Jacob scolds through his clenched jaw.

His buzz cut and matching beard length make him look more of a rebel than he really is.

My feet are glued to the floor.

I want to watch.

I shouldn't. He's my ex-boyfriend's best friend.

But I've never realized how utterly drop-dead gorgeous he is before.

Tonight, I'm seeing him in a whole new light.

Warmth spreads between my thighs and my breathing becomes labored. I'm so turned on.

His gruff voice commands the girl currently being fucked into oblivion, "You are not to come. Do you hear me?"

"Yes, sir," the faceless girl replies.

Holy shit! My fingers twitch at the hem of my short white sweater dress.

I want to touch myself.

Jacob lets out a low moan as he thrusts into her. "Skye," he groans with his head slightly dipped.

I gasp at my name on his lips. My shock echoes around the otherwise silent corridor.

Jacob's head snaps up, finding me standing in the doorway. He doesn't react, his face fixed and expressionless.

"What was that?" the nameless girl breathlessly asks, her cheek still pressed firmly against the desk.

"Nothing," Jacob lies with a devilish smirk. "Touch yourself."

On his instruction, the girl underneath him lifts one of her hands from the desk and places it between her legs.

Unblinking, he keeps staring at me. "Do it for me." Dripping with desire, his voice rumbles in his chest.

On autopilot, my hand glides along the sliver of skin between my black over-the-knee socks and the hem of my mid-thigh dress. Before I know what's happening, I've pulled my dress around my waist and I am holding it in place, not caring that I'm flashing my G-string or that my hand is inside the now-soaked white lace.

I'm so wet. For him.

"Now make yourself come for me, Skye." His emerald eyes turn darker, making me feel like I'm lost in a forest.

My fingertips dance across my swollen clit and I almost let out a moan. But I don't. I don't want the girl he's screwing to know I am here. The only eyes I want on me are his.

"I wish you wouldn't call me Skye," the girl below him whines.

"I told you to be quiet." His thrusts become brutal. "Show me." He lowers his gaze to my pussy.

Without hesitation, I pull my panties to the side, giving him what he wants.

"Bare. Smooth," he gasps. "So fucking beautiful." He licks his bottom lip.

The girl below him huffs. "Jacob, what is with you tonight? You're acting weird." But she doesn't stop him as he continues to fuck her.

I slide my finger between my pussy lips again and circle my clit. My chest heaves as a moan fights desperately to leave my chest. I rub harder, feeling my impending orgasm begin to take over my body.

"Do you need to come?" he growls.

I nod submissively.

"Come for me, Skye."

His teeth sink into his plump bottom lip as he continues to watch me pinch, then circle my clit through hooded eyes.

The girl's moans become louder, as do his, and when I push a finger inside my wet pussy and press my thumb against my swollen bud, I come—the force of my silent orgasm making my legs tremble and my heart hammer.

This pushes him over the edge, and he comes too.

Never losing eye contact with me, he calls out my name in a gruff, harsh tone.

I'm transfixed.

Breaking us from our spell, he blinks slowly, as if not believing what we just did.

I release my dress from my tight grip, removing my hand from between my legs at the same time.

Eyes widening, I stifle a cry of shock.

I feel so ashamed.

What have I done?

* * *

Jacob

My name is Jacob Baxter.

I'm thirty years old, and I'm in love with Skye McNairn.

The girl I grew up with. The woman I can't have.

The incredibly distracting woman I have an unhealthy secret obsession with. The woman currently staring at me through the open doorway of my office as I fuck another girl from behind on my desk while imagining it's her.

It's catastrophically wrong on so many levels, but I can't stop myself.

As I keep railing the girl below me, I'm pretty sure I'm blowing any minuscule chance I ever had with Skye out of the water too, although she has never shown any interest in me.

She has only ever seen me as a *friend*, which sucks.

Look, don't touch. Those have always been the rules because she's my best friend's ex.

She's off limits, so it's wrong for me to want her the way I do.

But she consumes my thoughts twenty-four-seven.

It doesn't help that I'm her boss and spend hour after hour, day after day, with her gorgeousness. It's hideously torturous.

From her smile and sweet giggle to her cute space buns that she wears every day. Her platform shoes and tiny multi-colored print dresses, and don't get me started on the over-the-knee socks that make my cock so fucking goddamn hard the private bathroom in my office has become my one-man wank tank.

I should rewrite her employee contract with a clause outlining that she's forbidden to wear them.

Being so close to someone you know you can't touch or even tell how you feel is fucking painful. I feel it every day and I'm pretty certain she doesn't even know I exist.

But right now, she's here watching me, and I intend on making the most of it. Consequences be damned.

She grabs a fistful of her dress, gripping it tight as her breathing quickens.

"Do you like to watch?" I ask her.

Below me, Verity answers, but I'm not asking her.

Skye nods.

"Touch yourself." My eyes stay fixed on her. I'm going to fucking blow my load if she obeys.

Skye hesitates momentarily.

"Do it for me," I coax.

I try to mask my shock as she pulls her dress up to her waist, then pushes her hand inside her white lace panties.

"Now make yourself come for me, Skye." She better come quick; I'm not going to last. She's making the dreams I've had about her for years a reality.

Skye shows me her pussy, and it's more beautiful than I could ever have imagined—pink, swollen, and I can see from here how wet she is for me.

She slides her fingers between her pussy lips, then circles her clit.

"Come for me, Skye," I urge again.

She silently comes, taking me with her as she lets go, and I blow my load.

Her eyes grow wide, brows pinched, and before I know what's happening, she vanishes.

What the fuck have I done?

2

SKYE

Four weeks ago

"We are over, Owen."

He stares at me in disbelief.

I repeat myself, ensuring he gets the message. "Did you hear me? I said, we are over, Owen."

"What do you mean, over?" He pulls his shoulders up toward his ears to prevent the rain from entering the neckline of his jacket.

Crossing my arms across my chest, I spell it out for him. "O.V.E.R. Over, Owen. We are through. Kaput. Finito. I am so done with your... shit." I hate swearing, but he's annoying me.

"My shit?"

"Yes, your shit. Your lack of interest in me. That *shit*." I let out an exasperated sigh, angry at myself now for swearing three times in about ten seconds. "Tonight was your last chance. You made me a promise to try harder, but you broke it." The shadow from my outside light shines down on his face, highlighting the deep circles under his eyes. He looks tired. "I spent four hours preparing dinner for you. Where have you been?"

"I'm sorry, baby. Please. I lost track of time. You're the only good, normal part of my life. Please don't do this. I'm fucking begging you, Skye. Don't end us." He sounds desperate.

"We can't keep doing this," I sigh, slowly shaking my head back and forth. "We need to stop kidding ourselves that this is what we both want." I bite my lip, considering if I should say what I've been holding in, but decide he deserves my honesty. "We were just kids when we started dating, but we've become each other's comfort blanket and that's not healthy. There is no passion or love. Where is the spark? The wining and dining? The thoughtfulness? There is nothing between us other than friendship, Owen, and you know that."

"Please, please. Don't do this to me." His hand clutches his chest as if I'd physically wounded him with my words. "I am genuinely sorry. I just have fuck tons of crap going on at the moment with my mom and dad."

"But how am I supposed to know that if you never talk to me, Owen?"

Stuffing his hands into the pockets of his jeans, he lets out a deep, long defeated sigh.

"I'm worried about you, but I can't help if you refuse to open up to me. You've had years to talk to me. I've been right here."

His mouth draws into a thin line as if he's fighting to keep the words inside.

"Fine," I huff frustratedly. "If you won't tell me, it shows me you don't trust me or care for me, if you ever did."

"Skye, you've got me all wrong. I do care for you. I'm always here for you."

I laugh. "On Monday, you stood me up at the gym. The

gym, for Christ's sake. You barely remembered it was my birthday this year until Jacob reminded you."

Owen grinds his teeth, making his jaw twitch as I continue to deliver my list of grievances.

"You failed to pick me up from work when my car was in for a service yesterday." At least he's consistently crap; I'll give him ten out of ten for that.

"You should have called me." He frowns.

"I did," I say matter-of-factly. "Five times."

He never answers his phone when I call him, and he very rarely texts me back. I never seem to be worthy of his time, even though he's never off his phone.

"You only turn up when you want to sleep with me or when your friends are busy."

"It's not like that," he sighs sadly, as if he can sense the weight of my words and the finality of my decision.

Feeling my patience wear thin, my voice raises a few octaves. "Yes, it is. You made every excuse to wriggle yourself out of coming to my nana's eightieth birthday party last month. You have never come to my parents' house for Sunday dinner, and we've been dating, if that's what you can call it, on and off for fourteen years." I bang my hand against the wall, making him jump. "You don't care about me or my family. And why did my invitations to your parents' fancy parties stop? I'm clearly not what they want for you, but you have never had the balls to tell me." I suck in a deep breath. "Be honest with yourself. You know it's over. I deserve better."

"Shit," he sighs breathlessly and tips his head toward the night sky, letting the rain bounce off his handsome face. "I blew it with you, didn't I?" His shoulders deflate. "I let my parents get into my head."

"You did. But it's over."

He shakes his head and then grabs the back of his neck. "Fuck." His frustration echoes around the empty cobbled street.

"You had better go home before you catch a chill."

"Can I not come in? For five minutes, please? Just to chat?" His eyes plead with me.

"Just go home." I fake-smile. "You're not the only one at fault here, and it wasn't all bad. We did have lots of laughter and fun when we were younger, but it's done... whatever this has been between us, it's over. You need to leave. Night, Owen. See you around, yeah?"

3

SKYE

I'm nervously biting my nails and realize, if I don't stop, I'm going to nibble them down to the cuticle. Pulling my finger from my mouth, I rub my clammy hands down the fabric of my dress.

As Jacob stands at the front of the conference room, leading our weekly meeting, I can't stop looking at him and now that I know what's under his crisp white dress shirt, I can almost make out the faint abstract outlines of ink that cover his body. He's a living, breathing work of art, making me want to explore every inch of him.

"So that wraps up our Monday morning project briefing." He scratches the scruff on his face, then pushes his hands into the pockets of his dress trousers. "Any questions?"

He looks around the conference room table, continuing to act like I don't exist.

I should have used a sick day.

While jealousy is not an emotion I'm familiar with, it's a feeling I've become best friends with over the past two nights.

I'm jealous of the way he touched that girl, the way he fucked her.

I want that to be me.

Conflicted, pure desire has taken up permanent residency in my veins, messing with every thought I'm now having about Jacob.

It's pure carnal need and want.

That one night seems to have changed everything.

I sit straighter in the boardroom chair, feeling hot all over. Uncomfortably so. He's the one I fantasized about as I got myself off last night in the shower, and whose eyes, tattoos, and muscular body I saw as I finally drifted off to sleep at five o'clock this morning.

If I could slap some sense into myself right now, I would. Because he's not just my ex's best friend. He's my boss.

And now it feels... awkward?

Plus, Jacob's attitude to me this morning is making it worse.

"Okay. We are done. Thank you all. And Pete?" Jacob addresses our account manager. "Can we schedule a meeting with finance to discuss the JoJo and Crow account?"

Pete salutes Jacob. "On it. I'll calendar that in for next week. That way, we are prepared, as I know you and Skye are going to London for that meeting next month."

Are we?

I love London, but last year Jacob and I went to New York, and it was one of the most incredible business trips I've been on.

Once our meeting with our client was over, Jacob extended our visit by two days. It was a complete sightseeing whirlwind, but unforgettable. He took me to the Museum of the City of New York, where they were exhibiting David

Carson's work. I freaked out when our cab pulled up out the front of the museum. I mean, it was David Carson—only the most freaking well-known graphic designer in the world.

Jacob told me how cute my mini freak-out was, as he proceeded to hire a dedicated curator to show us around, and to top the trip off, he even took me to the theater to see *Wicked*.

I still can't fathom out how he knew it was my favorite musical.

He's so thoughtf—

Shattered fragments of my thoughts begin piecing themselves together, and it suddenly dawns on me. The bicycle tire repair kit he bought me in case I got a puncture on the way to work, the secret Santa gift last year—a program of *Wicked* the musical signed by Idina Menzel—his interest in the books I read, his texts to make sure I am safe when I cycle home from work...

I think Jacob likes me.

Not just as a friend. But more.

No, that can't be right. Can it? I mean, it's Jacob.

But everything he's done for me... It all begins to make sense.

And he's never said anything.

How long has he liked me? Did he like me in New York?

Or am I wrong? Am I overthinking the whole situation after Saturday night's events?

Events? It was more than an event. He made me come. It doesn't matter that it was my fingers. It was all him. And I wanted every second of it.

But was it more than a moment? Was it something bigger? Is it something he's wanted for longer than I've realized?

I massage my fingertips into my temples, trying desperately to think of anything else that could prove I am on the right path.

Did it start at school? I mean, he spoke to me all the time at school and *always* walked me home.

Oh. My. God.

No way. That's impossible.

I flinch when Jacob says my name. "Skye. Are you listening?"

My fingers drop from my temples and I stutter, "Eh, yeah, no, sorry, what? I was thinking about the printing problems I needed to resolve today."

"Printing problems?" Jacob questions me, his eyebrows rising.

"Not anymore, no. Sorry. We did *have* problems. It's all sorted." I manage a tense smile as my heart beats uncontrollably. "Sorry, what were you saying?" I push my shoulders back, suddenly aware of my appearance.

Not one to become obsessional about boys or any boy for that matter, I have become *that* girl. The girls at school I used to roll my eyes at. The giggling, flirting and planning what outfit to wear each day to impress the boy they had their heart set on that week.

I've turned into the dumbass that cares about what I wore today and how I look right now, behind this boardroom table. For a boy. A man. Definitely a man.

A gorgeous, tattooed devil in a white shirt.

Jacob finally makes eye contact with me, and my heart skips a beat. "I was asking if you had time to read the email I sent you this morning and if you are able to attend London with me next month for five days? I need you."

He needs me.

He adds, "Frankie can't make it."

He doesn't need me at all. Not personally. It's strictly business. *Stupid girl.*

"Oh."

"Is that a yes or a no, Skye?" His brow wrinkles as he waits for me to answer.

I clear my throat. "Yes, I can attend."

Five days. Alone. With Jacob.

Goddammit.

"Good," he says curtly. "Okay, thank you, everyone. You can all go." He stays rooted to the spot.

As if a veil has been lifted from my eyes, I'm seeing him in a whole new light.

My brain is working overtime, and I need to get out of here.

I push my seat back to leave along with everyone else, but Jacob stops me. "Skye, stay seated please," he barks, making it sound much more like a demand than a request.

My breath hitches in my chest. If he mentions Saturday night, I might die.

"Someone's in trouble." Shona, Jacob's personal assistant, squeezes my shoulder as she passes me.

"Shut up, Shona," I hiss and she laughs back at me.

Jacob storms over to the frosted glass door and bangs it shut, making me jump.

He lets out a heavy breath and swivels on the balls of his feet. Walking back toward the table, he lays his hands flat against the tabletop, arms spread wide, and glares at me. "Do you mind explaining this shit, Skye?"

"Explaining what?" I feign innocence.

"This." He lifts a piece of paper and dangles it in front of me before ripping it into pieces and throwing it in the trash can.

I clear my now fossil-dry throat and croak, "I can't stay here, not after..." I look up at him as he storms toward my chair.

I suddenly feel tiny in comparison to his six-foot-two, broad-shouldered frame.

"You're not resigning, Skye." Displeasure bounces off of him, filling the room with tension.

When I wrote that letter last night, it seemed like such a good idea, although in hindsight, it feels like I've made the worst decision. I love my job, but how can I stay after what happened between us?

"I must apologize for my behavior and for..." I struggle to grit the words out. "Watching you." I whisper my last two words and turn my head the other way, unable to look at him. "It was very unprofessional of me."

"We both crossed a line. A line that we won't cross again. We scratched an itch. End of story."

I sneak a cheeky glance his way as he straightens to his full height, folding his thick arms across his broad chest. *He's gorgeous.*

"Skye?"

"Sorry." I bow my head and fiddle with the hem of my dress. "I just, I'm... You make me nervous and I'm a wee bit embarrassed about what happened," I mumble. "I'm confused about Saturday, and now there's everything else." I lift my head, my eyes connecting with his. "You. Us. High school."

"High school? What the hell has that got to do with your resignation?" His brows dip low, causing his forehead to wrinkle.

"Nothing."

And everything.

"I mean, I've probably got it all wrong. Just forget everything I said. Saturday... it was a lot. It's got me all in a spin."

"You're not resigning. I won't let you go." He runs his bear-sized hand back and forth across his buzz cut.

His jaw tics a couple of times as he clenches it, as if holding in what he *really* wants to say.

"Do you even have a job to go to, Skye?"

I shake my head.

He points to the shredded pieces of my resignation letter. "So why?"

"I've told you... because of Saturday. I'm sorry for what happened," I whisper then bow my head again.

He lowers his voice to a gentle murmur that soothes my anxiety. "Skye. I'm sorry too. I was out of order the other night. You can sue me for sexual harassment."

I scoff, lifting my eyes to meet his. "I would never do that."

"But you can if you want to. I'm giving you permission. I seriously breached our employer contract. And as my employee, it's my duty to make sure your well-being is taken care of."

I'd like him to take care of me.

He pushes his hands into his pockets. "I messed up and I will not have you punish yourself for my behavior."

He continues, "Blame me. Not yourself. I take full responsibility for my inappropriate actions the other evening. If I hadn't asked you to..."

"Make myself come while I watched you with that girl in your office," I blurt out.

He clenches his jaw harder this time, forcing his nostrils to flare while ignoring what I've said. "You have two choices. Sue me, I leave and you stay, or you accept my apology and stay. Whatever you choose, you are staying. End of story."

"I would never raise a formal complaint against you. You're my friend." My eyes soften as I shake my head in disbelief at his suggestion.

"I'm your *boss*." His words drive a nail through my heart.

"Is that all you are to me?" I ask breathlessly.

Tilting his head back, he stares at the ceiling, before resting his hands on his hips and when he finally looks back at me, his green eyes are dancing with something I can't explain. "Don't," he warns.

Disappointed he's not taking the bait, I ask, "Can I go now?"

He nods then reaffirms our agreement. "Yes. But just so we're clear. Forget what happened over the weekend. You are not resigning. Promotion is on the horizon for you, Skye. This place is your life. You love it here and you're shit-hot at your job. I won't let Saturday change that. Andrew is leaving. He's moving to Edinburgh with his new wife, so you will slot straight into his position as creative director," Jacob informs me.

"Director?" I repeat, stunned by the news.

"We have to interview you first as a formality, but it's yours if you want it."

"I want it," I say far too quickly.

His familiar warm smile returns. "Then it's yours. But please tell me I didn't fuck this up." Jacob motions to the space between us. "You're staying, right?"

I can't help the gigantic smile that breaks free from my lips, too. "Yes," I confirm.

"Thank fuck for that. My father would never forgive me if we lost you." He lets out an audible breath.

I push my chair back and pull myself to full height to face him, but I'm still tiny by comparison.

"What were you doing here on a Saturday night, Skye? Should you not have been out at a bar crying into your cocktails over Owen? That's what Owen's been doing over you."

"I had no plans on Saturday and I had a great idea for a logo." I pause to study his face. He seamlessly pulls off looking moody and handsome at the same time, which is no mean feat. "And I'm not sad about Owen."

Jacob's forehead furrows in confusion. "You're not?"

"No." I shrug. "We were coasting, and you know it." I close the space between us. "I didn't love Owen. Not romantically."

"You didn't?" His Adam's apple slowly moves as he takes an audible gulp.

"It was fun to begin with, but when the fun ended, there was no foundation to our relationship. We ended up being friends with benefits."

He winces as if he's in physical pain.

I continue, "I'm not sad or mad." I bite my lip teasingly, circling the focus back to him and me. "And I'm glad I was here on Saturday night, or I would have missed the show."

"Did you like it?" he asks, leaning in so close I can feel his breath on my cheek.

Unblinking, I reply in a whisper, "Every minute."

He doesn't respond, but his breathing becomes heavier.

"You have a beautiful body, Jacob. I like your new tattoos," I murmur as I trace my fingers over the buttons on his shirt, knowing that I am skating on very thin ice and this could backfire badly but I'm desperate to see if he reacts.

He clenches his jaw, making the veins in his neck strain, highlighting his pounding pulse.

"I'm trying to be fucking good here, Skye. You aren't making it easy."

I look down to discover his dress trousers working hard to conceal his huge erection.

I sweeten up my voice, playing with him to get an answer. "You called her Skye."

He pauses, letting his eyes drop down my body and then back up to my face. "I did."

"Why?"

"I can't answer that," he replies, sounding almost pained.

"Do you like me, Jacob?"

He blows out a long, slow breath. "We could never happen."

"That didn't answer my question. Do you have feelings for me?"

Every inch of him smells like desire and sin, and his face looks like he's fighting a battle with his conscience. Finally, he speaks. "You are Owen's ex-girlfriend, and I have an agreement with my boys."

"Is that the stupid pact you three made when you were fourteen?" I scoff.

"Yes. And it's not stupid."

"And all these years later, it's still in place?" I lay my hand on his chest, trying to soothe the stress and anger that seems to surge through his body. He hisses as if I've burned him.

"Yes, our bro code still stands. So, I suggest you take your hand off me." He grits his jaw. "And you have never been interested in me, so we have nothing to worry about here." The hunger in his eyes tells me a different story.

"But what if I am interested now?" I skim my fingers around his shirt collar. To a passerby, I look like I'm straightening it, but they can't see my fingertips skimming over his neck or hear the way his breathing reacts to my touch.

He grabs my wrist. "Enough," he says, instantly releasing

me as if I scorched his skin. "I can't touch you," he hisses through clenched teeth.

I take a step back. "Well, that's a shame because I really enjoyed the other night. It's all I've thought about."

"You've no idea who you're playing with, Butterfly." He looks as shocked with his words as I am.

"Oh, I think I know, Jacob. Remember, I've known you since we were teenagers. I'm playing with the guy who's hiding his feelings for me. Who fucked a girl over his desk while pretending it was me and then made me come on his demand. And it's also the guy who won't break his stupid 'bro code'." I wrap finger air quotes around his stupid agreement. "To be with the girl he likes. But what he doesn't know is that, since Saturday, all I've thought about is him. How he fucked that girl, how much I wanted it to be me, and how much I want him to touch me right now." I clear my throat, feeling brave. "It's the same guy I imagined last night when I made myself come." I almost blush. I've never been a dirty talker before, but I want him to know what he's doing to me.

"Fuck," he groans.

"I know exactly who I am playing with, Jacob. The question is whether he's going to play the game too."

4

JACOB

If anything, it's me who should resign. She's too much of a temptation and I no longer trust myself around her.

But if I leave, I won't get to see her every day. And if I can't touch her, I need to continue this sadistic torture of breathing the same air as her at least.

Like clockwork, at 3 p.m., I watch Skye make her way to the restroom to touch up her lip gloss. She's beautifully predictable.

I leap to my feet and storm in her direction. Time is fucking with me. I've been patiently waiting for her to appear, but every tick of the clock has dragged since she left me standing in the boardroom with an aching cock, surrounded by her heady scent.

Pushing the bathroom door open, I quietly shut it behind me, then turn the lock.

She's too busy humming to herself to notice me. With her head buried in her makeup bag, she rummages around trying to find her lip gloss—the one that makes her lips look all pouty and wet and makes me want to kiss her so fucking bad.

I stand directly behind her and admire her delicate features, considering what she'd look like completely naked, in my bed with her thighs around my ears, screaming my name.

She lifts her head, spotting my reflection in the mirror, and lets out a surprised gasp.

Seeing us like this—reflected in the mirror—we look great together: her fresh innocent face, the opposite of my dark features. For a second, I have visions of us together on Christmas mornings, birthdays, and weekends, living life together. But then the heartbreaking realization hits me hard —I can't have a future with her. No matter how much I want one.

She fumbles about with her earbuds, removing them. The airy music continues playing from them as I bow my head down and whisper in her ear. "So, you want to play?"

She doesn't answer.

My mouth moves closer to her nape, like a magnet; my lips ghost her skin.

"Jacob," she whispers.

"Shh, Butterfly." Placing my hands on the counter either side of her, I press my chest to her back, closing her in. "You had your say earlier. Now it's my time to talk."

This is the closest we've ever been. I've resisted her for so fucking long. Since the day she walked into my English lesson at school as the new girl and sat down beside me.

"As your boss, I am telling you that you are going to stop wearing these sexy little dresses and tempting knee-high socks to work every day because it makes my cock hard for you, and if I have to jerk off in my bathroom for yet another day, I'm going to rub him away."

Her mouth hangs open.

"Oh, don't make out you're all sweet and innocent now, Skye." My lips almost touch her ear, making her eyes blow wide. "You've already worked out that I want to fuck you. Even more, since you showed me what was underneath those little dresses you wear. It's such a pretty pussy, but I can't touch you. Won't. I meant what I said; you are off limits. I slipped up on Saturday. I took it too far."

I press myself closer to her body.

"You and me." I meet her bewildered gaze in the mirror. "We can never happen. You will always be Owen's girl. It can't go any further. No matter how much we want to."

Her expression doesn't change.

"So, Butterfly, we'll forget what happened. We'll go back to being Jacob and Skye. I'll be your boss. You'll be my employee and Owen's ex."

She coughs as if finding her voice, then whispers, "How long have you liked me, Jacob?"

I sway my head slowly back and forth, not answering her.

"How long?" she pushes, her voice more demanding now.

I tut then say, "Don't go searching for something that doesn't exist, Skye."

She catches me off guard when she turns in my arms to face me and I have to grip the vanity unit tighter to stop me from running my knuckles across her jaw. "Don't. Push. Me," I almost growl, desperate to hide the need for her burning through me.

She cups my face with her tiny hands, and for a moment, I stop breathing.

"Tell me. How long?" she urges as she tilts her head toward me slightly.

My breath hitches when I think she's about to kiss me.

"Nothing to tell," I grit out as I pull her hands off my face and move back, ending our moment.

I walk in the direction of the door to exit this self-inflicted misery.

I unlock it, pausing but not turning back to look at her, because I'm not sure I have the restraint to walk away if I do. "There is no game to be played. There is nothing between us. And as of tomorrow, new rule: no more knee-high socks. Or I will fire your ass."

She giggles.

Almost an entire week with her in London. *How will I survive?*

I slam the bathroom door behind me.

May the torment continue.

5

JACOB

One month later

Owen's cheek rests heavily against the breakfast bar in my kitchen. With his eyes closed and his mouth hanging open, he's drooling all over it. "I should go and see Skye tonight," he slurs.

That's a bad fucking idea, but I don't say that; instead, I say, "You need to go to bed." I knock back a huge glug of my protein shake.

Owen never deserved her. *My Skye.*

I add, "No woman on planet Earth will go within a mile of you because you smell like a pig swamp."

"I don't stink." He pops one eye open.

"You fucking do. I can smell you from the front door," Lincoln announces as he swaggers in.

Lincoln pulls a stool from my breakfast bar and makes himself at home as he grabs a handful of grapes from my fruit bowl, popping one in his mouth.

"Fuck off, pony boy," Owen mumbles.

"Well, at least someone's getting pussy around here." Lincoln grins.

"I don't struggle for pussy," I lie. Well, I don't normally struggle, but for some reason, since that night in my office, I can't bring myself to call Verity to hook up again.

I'm lying to myself, too. There is a reason.

Skye.

"Verity?" Lincoln asks, chuckling to himself. "Just date her already."

I roll my eyes, dismissing him.

"I'm the odd man out? No pussy for Owen," he grumbles to himself.

"You don't need pussy, Owen. You need to sober the fuck up and get your shit together. Have you been drinking all day? Why were you not at work?" Lincoln's brow wrinkles with what looks like worry.

Owen holds his head in his hands. "I hate my life."

"Oh, here we go. Poor little rich boy syndrome." My jesting gains another chuckle from Lincoln as he pats Owen's shoulder.

"It's hard being a single playboy, with only a historic castle to live in and flash sports cars to drive." Lincoln's voice is laced with irony.

"Fuck off," Owen slurs. Leaning over too far in an effort to swat Lincoln's arm away, he loses his balance, and as if in slow motion, he falls sideward off the bar stool, taking my designer Perspex chair with him.

With an enormous echoing clatter, he lands in a heap on the floor.

"Shit." Lincoln leaps off his chair as I run around the breakfast bar to help.

I swiftly untangle Owen's trapped leg from beneath the tall

chair and stand it upright while Lincoln checks his head for any injuries.

Owen groans in pain.

"You alright, bud?" I bend down to check him over as well.

He rubs his temples. "I'm not alright. My whole body hurts," he moans, slurring his liquor-fueled words. "And my heart. And my feet."

"Did he walk here?" Lincoln looks at me for an explanation for his weird reply. I honestly don't know. Judging by his usually immaculate white sneakers, he's walked across the fields to get here. They are filthy.

"My head," Owen grumbles again.

Lincoln grabs a cushion from my sofa, and lays it under Owen's head, where he still lies on my kitchen floor.

"What are we gonna do with you, Owen?" I sit my ass on the floor beside him and pat his chest.

Owen snaps his eyes open. "Euthanize me. I'm not marrying her," he spits out before his eyes flutter closed again.

I look at Lincoln. "What's he talking about?" I question.

"Fucked if I know."

"You're not marrying Skye, Owen. You broke up two months ago," I remind him. My heart will fucking die if he marries her. The very idea causes shooting pains in my chest.

Owen groans again. "Not Skye. You dumbassssss," he slurs. "Evangeline."

Lincoln blurts out what I'm thinking. "Who the hell is Evangeline?"

"My wife-to-be." He raises his hands to the ceiling.

"What?" Lincoln and I both shriek at the same time.

"I have to marry her because of some sort of fucked-up agreement between her family and mine. It's all arranged. Mom and Dad are a pair of selfish assholes. I hate them." He lets his hands fall back to the floor, making them slap against the marble. "I have a sore head."

"It'll be worse in the morning," Lincoln helpfully points out.

"And I will lose Skye forever," he moans as he rubs his temples clumsily.

Lincoln tilts his head to the side in pity and delivers Owen the brutal truth. "You lost her years ago, buddy. If you loved her the way I love Violet, you would have put a ring on it long before now, no matter what your parents said. You were never right for Skye. You fucking messed her about, and your mother never approved of your relationship. It was doomed from the start."

Owen covers his face with his hands. "You're a fucking know-it-all. I hate it when you're right," he says into his cupped hand, muffling his words. "I'm going to run away."

"Good for you. Where to?" Lincoln teases.

"I'll decide in the morning," he replies.

"Well, be sure to tell us where you are going, so we know you're not dead in a ditch or drinking yourself into a coma somewhere."

"I'm not telling you where I'm going. That's the whole point of running away," he moans.

I push to my feet. "Run away tomorrow, but for now, buddy, you are going to sleep the booze off in my spare room. C'mon."

Lincoln and I take an arm each, and slowly drag an unco-operative Owen to the spare room.

"Shit, you weigh a ton," Lincoln complains as he struggles to keep him upright.

"Been working out. Nothing else to do." He belches and I have to turn my head to avoid the alcohol fumes.

We lay Owen down on the bed and as we're walking away, Lincoln asks, "Do you reckon what he's saying is true?"

"Fucked if I know. I'll ask when he's sobered up."

"Do you think he'll really run away?" Lincoln looks concerned as he glances back to where Owen lies unconscious and snoring, then walks to my front door.

"Not a fucking chance. That boy has it too comfortable here. He's talking shit."

Lincoln nods as if satisfied with my reassurance, then stuffs his hands in his pockets. "How's work been? I haven't seen you for a few weeks," Lincoln enquires.

"Fine. Same old same old," I lie.

"Do you want to hit the nightclub on Saturday night?"

"Can't. I'm off to London with Skye on business."

"Skye, huh?"

I clear my throat, ignoring his implication.

It's not the first time Lincoln has questioned me about my feelings for Skye. I tried to deny it, but he was so persistent, I eventually gave in and admitted how I felt. Well, I admitted I felt something, but I didn't mention the fact that I'm completely in love with her and have been since I was sixteen.

"She's not with Owen anymore. So...?" His mouth pulls to the side in a boyish smirk.

"Bro code," I remind him.

"We are thirty years old now. We made that pact when we were virgins, for Christ's sake. I'm certain if you spoke to him, he—"

"It's a no-go."

Lincoln waves his hand dismissively as he steps out of my house and walks toward his black Porsche. "Keep telling yourself that. But if you want any chance with her, then now is the time. You missed your shot the last time, Jay. You've waited long enough."

"Shut up, Linc," I hiss, hoping Owen is too out of it to hear this conversation.

He spins around, holding his hands up in mock surrender, walking backward as he laughs at my icy stare. "Okay. I won't mention it again. But you know the danger you're putting yourself in... being alone with her, in a hotel. I mean, you're asking for trouble. Make sure you call me if you're feeling tempted. Although you know what I think—"

"I told you, it's never going to happen. She's his fucking high-school sweetheart."

"You know that's bullshit. There is no love lost between those two. He went with other girls every time they split up."

"Bro code." I sound like a broken record.

"Speak to him."

"She'll have a new boyfriend soon," I say unconvincingly, finding myself clenching my fists at the thought.

Lincoln spots my distress. "Alright, caveman. Whatever. I look forward to hearing from you while you're in London wanting me to talk you out of knocking on her hotel door and fucking her senseless." He chuckles, swinging his car door open and sliding into the driver's seat. "Call me when Owen sobers up and you find out who the hell Evangeline is?" He slams his door shut.

Firing up his stunning sports car, he gives me a brief wave before he drives carefully down my gravel drive and slips out onto the country road. Lincoln opens his baby up, disappearing with loud pops and bangs from his Porsche 911 exhaust into the cold night.

I sigh, my hot breath evaporating in a huge puff of smoke. He's right, I should speak to Owen. But I don't know how.

Where do I even start?

Closing my front door, I lock us in for the night and head back along the glass corridor that divides the living spaces of my home from the bedrooms.

I move my tired-from-the-gym body into the bedroom, snick my door shut and wander into my adjoining bathroom then peel off my gym kit and throw everything into my hamper, including my sneakers. I've been working out so much lately that they need a good wash, or they are likely to walk themselves to the washing machine.

Before jumping in the shower, I admire my new tattoos in the bathroom mirror. I'm still getting used to how different my body looks, covered in black ink, and my hard work at the gym has really paid off. I'm bigger and broader now than I have ever been. I don't look anything like the slim, lanky boy I used to be.

I only joined the gym to pummel Skye out of my system and make myself feel better. That was a big fat fail. However, the by-product of all the workouts has my body in the best shape of my life... My head and my heart? Now that's another story.

Turning slightly, my eyes linger on the black and aqua-blue clouds with multiple interwoven symbols across my back. Only I know what they signify, and that's the way it will stay.

Freshly showered, I jump into my king-sized bed, pull the navy-blue comforter up to my waist and rest my weary bones.

Sliding my phone off the nightstand, I set a reminder alarm to check on Owen every hour. I'm a fucking babysitter for a thirty-year-old who weighs over two hundred pounds of solid muscle.

But he needs me, and he would do the same for me.

Opening the video app on my phone, I click on my subscribed channels and do what I've been doing every night since she started her hand lettering channel. I watch her.

Selecting her latest video, I turn the volume down to the lowest setting so Owen can't overhear and gaze at the screen. "Hi and welcome to another *Hand lettering with Skye* tutorial."

While the hand lettering she creates is oddly hypnotic, my eyes focus on her ocean blues and kind smile on the small inset video on the bottom right-hand side of the screen.

I wish I could make it bigger.

She bites her soft pink lips, sticking her tongue out as she concentrates. What I wouldn't give to have a taste of that tempting mouth. I pause the video at the point when she lifts her head and looks straight down the camera lens.

"Shit," I mutter to myself before closing down the app, and slap my phone face down on the bed.

Rolling over onto my side, I close my eyes with the hope that maybe tonight I can get a couple of hours of sleep at least, in between Owen-sitting, but my mind is plagued with thoughts of her.

6

JACOB

Wheeling my suitcase into the kitchen, I get the fright of my life when a voice calls out, "Morning."

Skye.

"What are you doing here?" My voice comes out gruffer than expected. I didn't hear the doorbell ring.

Owen steps through the sliding glass doors from the back garden. "Sorry, I went to get some fresh air." He runs his hands through his disheveled hair. He looks wrecked. I was up every hour to check on him and twice I found him with his head in the toilet. "Skye says you're off to London?" He grips his hand to his stomach, presumably because he feels sick again.

"I arranged to meet you at the airport." I look at Skye and almost moan out loud. She's wearing my favorite skirt. The black and teal plaid pleated one and those fucking socks.

Motherfucker.

"I thought I could leave my car here instead and we could travel together. I had Shona change my arrangements." She smiles cheekily.

You're playing with fire, Butterfly.

She turns to Owen. "You don't look so good. You've turned a funny shade of green again."

"I feel horrendous." He belches, making Skye's nose scrunch. She looks cute when she does that.

"When was the last time you ate? You look dreadful. You need a haircut and a shave." She looks him up and down. "Your mother will not be impressed if she sees you looking less than her Brodie standards."

Owen snarls, "You think I don't know that, Skye?"

Not deterred, she continues, "Fine, whatever, Owen. I am only trying to help." She waves her hand casually through the air. "You are no longer my problem." She turns to me and smiles. "Are you ready to go? Your car is outside waiting."

I catch Owen's attention. "You can stay here for as long as you want."

He bobs his head in acknowledgment.

Walking slowly toward Skye, he stuffs his hands into the pockets of his jeans. "Can we talk, just for a minute, please?" he practically begs.

I don't want to listen to this.

"We really do have to go," she replies quickly, not giving him a chance to speak. "We have a flight to catch and we've said all there is to say, you know that." She looks down and plays with her fingers. "Oh, I just realized." She lifts her head. "I have your tee shirt on." She pulls the faded black fabric, looking sadly at Owen. "I'll have to give you it back."

Owen clears his throat. "It's not mine, actually. It's Jacob's. I stole it from him when we were about sixteen." He points to the now faded, tatty top that looks vintage on Skye. "Funny, I've just noticed that she sort of looks like you." Owen gently smirks.

Skye looks down again at the barely there print of a girl

with blonde pigtails licking a lollipop with a butterfly tattoo on her arm. It's Crazy Town's *The Gift of Game* album cover. One of the songs on that album I would listen to over and over again. It was my song about her.

She lifts her head, and her eyes slide to mine. "Oh."

"Keep it." My voice sounds short and clipped as I head to the front door. "See you when I get back and we need to talk," I shout over my shoulder at Owen. I didn't get the chance to speak with him because I didn't realize he was awake. "When and if you do leave, remember to lock up."

"Thanks for last night," he replies.

I wave over my shoulder.

Skye's little steps quickly appear behind me. "Bye, Owen." She scuttles into the hallway. "Oh, I just remembered."

I look back around, but she's addressing Owen.

"Do you have the receipt for my tablet and stylus pen you bought me for my birthday? They're not working for some reason so I can't use them. They're both still under warranty, but I can't go back to wherever you bought it from without the receipt. Could you find it for me, please?"

Fuck. Fuck. Fuck.

Owen points at me. "I didn't buy it for you. Jay did. I still owe you for those." He laughs. Fucking laughs. Not realizing he probably just hurt her feelings because he couldn't even be bothered to get her a birthday present.

He left that up to me to organize. Again.

I clench my jaw.

Skye's eyes widen in disbelief, while I feel like all the oxygen was just sucked from the room.

"I have the receipt." As soon as my feet hit my gray gravel drive, the driver takes my case. I climb into the car and pull my phone out of the inside pocket of my jacket to check my emails.

Skye moves into the back beside me and slams the door shut and I keep my head down as the driver pulls away.

I try to focus on my phone, but it's not long before I find myself stealing a sly glance down Skye's toned legs. The tiny amount of exposed flawless skin between her pleated skirt and knee-high socks is, yet again, calling out to me.

Fingers crossed on her lap, she fidgets with her thumbs as if they are having a wrestling match. Eventually, she says, "Do you want to talk about any of that?"

"No."

"You don't want to talk about the fact that I'm wearing a tee shirt that belongs to you with an illustration on that apparently looks like me?"

"No."

She grabs her phone from her rucksack. The one I helped Owen buy for her because I saw her swooning over it one lunchtime. She loves it because it has multiple hidden pockets, it fits her laptop, converts to a purse with a top handle, and *looks cute*. It's Parisian chic. Supposedly.

She taps her phone as if in a crazed frenzy.

"Is that why you call me Butterfly?" Her voice remains steady as she pushes it under my nose.

And there on the screen is the track listing of that entire album and a little inset picture of the cover. I rest my head against the headrest, watching the countryside swoosh by in a blur. My stomach feels like a washing machine on the fastest spin cycle.

I'm the guy that pushes everything deep down into the pit of my soul because I've had to. I've had to hide my feelings for all these years, not only from my best friend, but also from her. She has no idea just how engrained into my heart she is.

But the last few weeks have changed everything, and my hidden emotional filing cabinet has been unlocked and flung open with such force that everything has slipped out around me and I have no idea how to start packing it away again... or whether I even want to try. It's too much. I can't deal with all of her questions and my emotions at the same time. I'm not dealing with any of it well at all. I feel sick to my stomach that I'm being a complete jerk around her.

Perspiration beads across my forehead. I remove my dress jacket, carefully laying it on the seat opposite me before I loosen my tie and undo my top button. Nausea bubbles in my stomach like a boiling cauldron.

"And the tablet and pen? You bought that too?" She's persistent, I'll give her that.

Balls to the wall, I go down the full-disclosure route when I reply, "And the rucksack you're using." I raise my eyes to meet hers. I've got nothing to lose because I've already lost her. I lost her the minute she started dating Owen. "Your phone cover. Wallet. Earrings last Christmas," I add.

I stare into her *why have you never told me* eyes, for what seems like an eternity.

Her shocked face softens. "Right," she eventually mumbles, then she starts chewing her top lip.

Breaking our gaze, she reaches over to the drinks storage and grabs a bottle of water. Almost finishing its contents in one go, she screws the top back on and rests it in her lap. And for the rest of the car ride, the hour-long private plane journey, and our transfer to the hotel, we don't say anything to one another.

7

JACOB

"Two room key cards to the penthouse." The hotel receptionist looks back and forth between me and Skye as she slides the keys across the reception desk.

"Penthouse? I didn't book the penthouse." My voice raises an octave.

"I'm sorry, sir, there was a mix-up with the rooms. Unfortunately, our reservation software overbooked the hotel's capacity, and we had no rooms to offer you other than the penthouse. You could try elsewhere, but I don't think you'll find anything else—I know all the other hotels nearby are fully booked tonight as well. It's a complimentary upgrade, sir. It has two double rooms, a lounge, private elevator, luxury bathroom as well as an outdoor patio area with a hot tub. It's all we have left." The hotel receptionist tensely smiles.

"But my assistant booked two double rooms." I grip the edge of the black marble check-in desk. "I have the email confirming the booking."

I can *not* share a suite with her.

The receptionist taps one long manicured fingernail

against the hotel computer then looks up. "I really am very sorry, sir. It's the only room we have available for the next four nights."

Skye leans forward and slides the keys off the cool marble. "We'll take it. Thank you."

"Skye," I warn her.

She moves closer to me then whispers, "So, we have to share the penthouse. Big deal. I'm hardly going to jump your bones now, am I? You're. My. Boss." Skye smiles sweetly. "Unless you want me to, Jacob?" She wraps her finger around my silk tie and gives it a playful tug.

I swat her hand away and smooth my tie back down.

"Loosen up, big guy. I'm kidding." She rolls her eyes before making a beeline for the elevator.

"Looks like we're taking the room." I fake a smile at the hotel receptionist, who tucks her lips into her mouth to hide her amusement.

Grabbing the handle of my suitcase with force, I roll it in Skye's direction.

When the elevator arrives and the doors slide open, I storm into the steel box as Skye elegantly strides in beside me. I hit the penthouse button and tap my key card against the security reader, instructing that we are ready to move. I want to get out of this small space.

I open my mouth to say something, but the elevator bell pings, and the doors glide open to reveal the most incredible penthouse I have ever stayed in.

Skye lets out an audible gasp. "This is beautiful."

Too distracted by her surroundings, she forgets her suitcase, so I remove it from the elevator and locate the bedrooms.

Ensuring she gets the biggest one, I drop her bright pink

case onto the luggage rack. When I walk back into the living area, she's almost running toward me.

"Oh, my God, we really do have a rooftop with a hot tub," she squeals. "And come and see this." She grabs my hand and pulls me into an enormous bathroom.

Stop touching me.

"We have a rainforest shower with color-changing lights. Look." She turns the oversized knob on the wall, making the water flow from the suspended shower. At the same time, the lights on the large waterfall roof panel change from soft green to blue to purple and back again. "Cool, huh?" She squeezes my hand. "I've always wanted a big house. Big enough to have a shower like that. Maybe when I get promoted, I can start saving more money and I can finally buy my own place. I hate renting." Her eyes sparkle under the changing lights as she looks around in awe.

I stare at her profile.

I love you.

Turning her attention to me, she closes the small distance between us, before reaching up and running her fingertip along the skin of my cheek, causing my heart to hammer in my chest. I have to remind myself to breathe.

"You look tired, Jay." She never calls me that anymore, not since high school.

"Didn't get much sleep last night," I confess.

"No?" When she cups her hand around my jaw, I lean into her soft touch. I can't help myself.

I shake my head. "I can't stop thinking about you," I whisper, afraid of what chaos speaking my truth might create.

Skye lets out a whimper before she replies, "Same."

"But we can't happen, Skye." *And all I want to do is kiss you until my dying breath.*

"I know."

I force my eyes closed when she runs her hand to the back of my neck and pulls my forehead to meet hers.

I squeeze her other hand that's still wrapped in mine tighter.

"How long have you liked me, Jacob?" she asks softly, her breath dancing over my lips as she speaks.

I groan. This is getting dangerous. She's too close. It would be too easy to lean in and take what I've been desperate for all these years. A taste of her. A moment where my lips press to hers...

I release her hand and wrap my arm around her waist, pulling her in. My cock is now at full salute. Unable to find the words I want to say, I rub it against her hip, making sure she knows exactly what she does to me.

"Jay." She groans, and it's a sweet melody that lights up all my senses. "Touch me."

The devil on my shoulder tells me to give in while the angel on the other screams at me to put a stop to this stupid infatuation.

I move my mouth to the shell of her ear. "We have a meeting to attend. I'll leave you to freshen up." I bolt for the door.

Too close.

Too fucking close.

8

JACOB

"Do I look okay?" Skye raises her foot flamingo-style off the floor, pushing her hands out to the side like a Charleston dancer. My eyes land on the cream-colored knee-high socks she's changed into.

My cock twitches in my boxers as my eyes drift from her toned legs up to her glossy peach-covered mouth that matches her outfit. The silver of her hair makes her eyes look even bluer today.

"You look fine." *She looks perfect.*

I turn to unlock the elevator, then push my hands into my pockets and rearrange my cock so she can't see how hard I am again. This is becoming ridiculous. I need relief, preferably now, but it'll have to wait.

When the elevator doors open, I step in and hold the door for her.

She stands next to me. "I have a great idea for how we do this meeting today." She seems more chipper this afternoon.

"I trust you," I announce.

"I know you do. Oh…" She starts wriggling about. "That is itchy."

"What's up?" I hold my breath when she pulls up the side of her short skirt, revealing the taut skin of her outer thigh.

"I think I left the price tag on my skirt. I can't reach it." She turns her back to me. "Can you get it for me?"

Tentatively, I reach out to the top of her skirt.

"You'll be better to go up rather than down." She looks over her shoulder at me. Reaching around to demonstrate she can't get her hand down the back of her waistband, she says, "It's too tight."

I clench my eyes shut to prevent myself from looking at her and move my hand under the fabric of her skirt. Not close enough to reach, I step closer. When the hem of the fabric touches my wrist, I stop as the enormity of how close I am to her ass dawns on me.

"Can you feel it?"

I wish I could, Butterfly.

"Not yet." I push my hand further up her skirt and I stop breathing when my fingertips touch the bare skin of her round ass.

"Are you wearing a fucking thong?" I grit my teeth.

"Nope."

"Are you not wearing anything at all? We are going to a business meeting." My voice grows loud in the tiny space.

"No, silly." She giggles. "See." My eyes pop open because I need to know what she wants me to look at… although as soon as I do, I wish I hadn't. She pulls her skirt up, giving me a full view of her beautiful smooth ass, and nestled there, between her cheeks, is a barely-there sliver of peach-colored string that leads to an equally thin waistband.

"It's a G-string. Thongs have a triangle to the back and

front. G-strings only have a triangle at the front." She swivels on the balls of her feet to show me, but I grab on to her naked hips.

"Stop," I demand as I press my front to her back, not even trying to hide my now hard cock, and growl in her ear, about to turn feral.

"Don't fucking move." I dig my fingertips into her hip bones. "I don't know what you're playing at, but this ends now. I've warned you already."

My mouth says one thing, while all I can think about is how much I want to rip her fucking clothes off.

She tilts her head back onto my shoulder, and one of her little space buns hooks around the back of my neck. Our eyes connect in the elevator's mirrored walls.

As she arches her back, it forces her ass against my crotch, and I fight to stifle my moan.

"I said stop moving." I'm surprised why my voice comes out sounding almost strangled.

I slide my fingertips across the swell of her little belly to hold her still, but it makes her squirm more.

I've dreamed about a moment like this. I'm so close to dipping my pointer finger into the tiny mesh triangle of her G-string and touching her. But my hands remain still.

Her hips tilt, as if she's begging me for more.

But still, I resist.

With every rise and fall of her chest, all I can hear is ringing in my ears and the thumping of my heart as if it's pounding out the conflict that's raging in my body right now.

I press my lips hard against the shell of her ear. "We are never going to happen." I release my hold on her and pull the price tag off her skirt roughly, before easing it back into place. She lets out a little yelp, the heat between us turning frosty.

"Nice try, but I won't be touching you, Skye. Not now, not ever." I select the ground floor button, making the doors glide shut.

"You are so mean." She grips the hem of her skirt to straighten it out, then huffs and puffs as if annoyed with me.

She'll be more annoyed when I say what I have to, but I can't stop the next words from leaving my mouth. "And remember, you made your choice. You chose him, not me."

She lets out a shocked gasp. "It was never like that, Jacob. I never chose him over you. We were sixteen, for Pete's sake. And I didn't even know you liked me. You can't blame me."

"Skye, I'm fucking begging you. You have to let this go. Please. Leave. Me. Alone."

A small piece inside of me dies when her blue eyes turn glassy.

"You don't mean that."

I look her straight in the eyes and lie. I'm used to it. It's what I've been doing for years. "Yes, I do. After our meeting, I have a date. We matched on the MeetMe app." I'm not on that app, I'm not signed up to any of them, but I need to create space between us.

"No, you didn't."

"Yes, I did. So don't wait up." Fuck, what am I doing to her? *I never want to hurt you, Butterfly.*

Steadying my nerves, I dust the imaginary lint from my suit collar.

"I don't know who you are right now," she whispers.

I don't know who I am either. My whole world flipped upside down a month ago, and it's yet to return to its axis.

Uncomfortable silence stretches between us. I can't bring myself to even look at her because all it will make me want to do is pull her into my arms and kiss her soft lips until she doesn't hate me anymore.

As the elevator door finally opens, I storm through the hotel reception out into the street and inhale a deep breath of fresh air.

What a fucker of a day this is turning out to be.

And what a fucking jerk you are, Jacob Baxter.

9

JACOB

Stepping out into the bustling street outside the JoJo and Crow offices, I take a moment to inhale a deep breath, glad that our first meeting is finished. Deal done.

I still can't believe she pulled off that proposal and tricked them into wanting a brand that doesn't even exist. It was a genius and bold move. Although it's Skye, and everything she touches turns to gold.

"You played a really risky game back there." I try sounding like her boss but it comes out more awe-inspired and playful.

"I know. Worth it though." I expected her to be ecstatic, but instead, she sighs, looking sad as her eyes skim the busy dockside. She continues to avoid eye contact with me as she slips her backpack onto her shoulders.

"Are you not excited? You did a phenomenal job back there, Skye. I am honored to have you on my team."

"Thank you."

"When did you pull that proposal together?"

"A few weeks ago, but I didn't finish it until late last night."

"You need to put in overtime for those hours. Email me and I will approve them with people operations."

She whispers a small, "Thanks."

Yet again, awkward silence stretches between us.

"Look, Sk—"

"Oh great, I'm glad I caught you both." An out-of-breath Austin, our new client, flies out of the entrance of the building we've just left. "We want to take you out for a drink to celebrate. We are so excited." He clutches his chest, smiling. He's almost wheezing. Poor guy needs to work on his cardio.

"We would love to," Skye answers for us both.

Fuck that, she's not going out with him and his business partner. Austin was overly flirty with her throughout the meeting, making me want to rearrange his face.

She adds, "But it will just be me. Jacob has a *date*."

My heart sinks. Why the fuck did I say that earlier? I now have to stand by my lie. I rock on my heels. "I can easily cancel."

He holds up his hand. "Oh no, don't let me stop you from finding love," he chuckles. "Come on, Skye. We're going to take you to our flagship restaurant, where everything is sustainably sourced and tastes divine." Austin ushers her back toward the doors. "Next time, Jacob." He lifts his eyebrows. "And I'll have those papers signed for you tomorrow."

They both disappear and I'm left standing on the curbside.

This is the way it's meant to be.

I pull my phone from my jacket pocket and scroll down my contacts to find the name I am looking for and hit call.

It rings for a few seconds before the familiar English accent drifts down the phone. "Jacob, darling." Joanna almost purrs down the phone. "Am I getting to see you, after all?"

A wicked smile curves my lips. "Yes, you are."

10

SKYE

Lying in the bubbling water, I watch the steam from the penthouse hot tub billow out into the chilly London night air.

I let the bubbles take the weight of my weary bones and starfish on the surface. I submerge my ears in the water and my eyes close as the meditative rumbling of the hot tub gurgles surround me, vibrating the tension from my body, allowing me to feel more relaxed than I've done in weeks.

But despite the way my body feels generally, I feel weird. Like, off-kilter parallel-universe weird.

If only Jacob would talk to me about his feelings, tell me everything without me having to fill in the gaps for myself. I know for sure it would clear the air between us.

What is wrong with me? He's out on a godforsaken date... I need to forget about him.

But I can't.

He's all I see, all I hear, and all I think about... broad body, sinewy muscles, abs... thank the Lord for washboard abs.

Long gone is the thin-as-a-drainpipe, cute boy I met back on my first day at Castleview Cove High.

Thinking back to that day, a smile curves my lips as I recall our first encounter. We were just sixteen...

* * *

"Everyone, this is Skye McNairn. Our new student here at Castleview Cove High and also the headmaster's daughter."

Oh crap, why did my new English teacher, Mrs. Clark, have to say that? Now no one will want to speak to me. And the last thing I want is to be singled out or given any special privileges. Or for the other kids to bully me because of who I am. Fudgenuggets.

"Make her feel welcome," Mrs. Clark instructs my new class-mates with a stern glare.

Her face instantly changes when she looks at me and, with a warm smile, she points to the seat at the back of the classroom, urging me to fill it.

This is the moment I have been dreading all summer: my first day at a new school. The looks, the attention. The headmaster's daughter. Urgh.

I feel so sick and the nervous flutter of butterflies hasn't stopped swirling in my tummy.

I slowly make my way up the aisle between the desks as a sea of curious stares follows my every move to my seat.

Palms sweaty, I remove my backpack from my shoulder and chuck it on the floor, before parking my backside on the wooden chair, pushing myself down to avoid eye contact with anyone.

"Hey."

I snap my head to the side when a gentle voice startles me and I'm greeted with a beaming smile from a cute skinny guy. His green eyes shine back at me when I smile and mouth a soft, "Hi" in return.

"Are you okay?"

Don't cry, don't cry.

A minute passes before he says, "You can sit with me and my friends at lunch if you want. That way, you'll know some friendly faces and you won't have to eat by yourself."

"That would be nice, thank you," I whisper.

"I'm Jacob. But my friends call me Jay." When I look up again, his smile quickly grows wider, instantly making me feel better.

"I'm Skye," I murmur then drag my attention back to my teacher and listen intently as she starts the lesson.

"You have a really pretty name," Jacob whispers again. "It matches your blue eyes. Sky blue."

I glance sideways, being careful not to get caught talking. I don't want to get into trouble on my first day. "Thanks."

Mrs. Clark taps the electronic whiteboard behind her. "What do we learn about Dill's character in chapter one? Pay attention. This question appeared in last year's examination paper." She lifts her brows knowingly. "Discuss this with your table partner."

My new classmate taps his book cover. "Want to share my book?"

"I have a copy." I reach down, unzip my floral backpack and pull out my dog-eared copy of To Kill a Mockingbird.

"Wow, how many times have you read that?" he laughs.

"A few." I smile. "I love reading."

He considers my reply. "What's your favorite book?"

It takes less than a heartbeat to reply. "The Princess Bride."

"The film?" His mouth drops open as he looks confused by my answer.

I roll my eyes. "It was adapted into a film in 1987. It's a book, and it was written in 1973."

"Smarty pants."

"That's mean," I reply, nudging my elbow against his.

"Hey, I was kidding. I didn't mean to offend you, Ms. Sassy-pants." He smirks. "I love that film."

Oh, I like this guy. He's got the kindest of eyes. "The book is better. It's the greatest love story ever told."

"Isn't it a comedy?"

"It is. But it's also a fantasy book with heaps of adventure and, of course, there's a huge dollop of romance. It's the best type of fairy tale." *The tone of my voice goes all swoony. I love that book and have read it like fifty times.* "It gets me every time... loving someone from afar because the hero was too afraid to tell her. The way Westley uses his own code words to tell Buttercup he loves her..."

"He loves her whatever, however, forever."

"Look at you, making up your own secret code words." *I tease him then pull my hands to my swollen heart.* "Can you imagine meeting someone and falling in love with them at first sight, but never thinking you are good enough for them, so you never tell them?"

"Do you believe in all of that?" *His cheeks pink up.* "The love at first sight thing?"

"I believe there is someone who is made perfectly for every one of us. But fate dictates whether you find them or not," *I reply easily, having spent many an hour thinking about this.*

"Fate."

"Yes."

"Well, I feel like it's fate that you moved here."

"You do?" *I question, my heart hammering.*

"Yeah, and I'm glad you sat down beside me."

"Why?"

"Because who would have told me The Princess Bride was a book? I could have spent the rest of my life not learning that interesting, but very important fact, then I would look like a complete dumbass for passing English Lit without ever knowing." *He lifts his elbow against the table and rests his head on his hand.* "Maybe you should teach this class."

I chuckle.

"Do you have a copy of The Princess Bride *I can borrow?" he asks.*

"You read?"

"Rude, but yeah, of course I read."

I dip my hand into my backpack, and pull out my copy. "Guard this with your life."

He reaches for it, but I pull it back. "Promise me you won't lose it."

He draws an imaginary X over his heart.

"If you do, you will die a painful death by dragon fire."

I lay my book out for him to take and he says, "I will guard it with my life."

"You had better."

We spend the rest of the lesson focused on the work and when the bell rings, I start packing my things back into my backpack as a shadow appears by my side, blocking Jacob from my view. "Hey, I'm Owen."

* * *

My trip down memory lane quickly bursts into a million jagged pieces as soon as Owen appears in it.

I'd forgotten that day until now... well, forgotten that Owen was there when I first met Jacob.

Remembering it now, I think Jay liked me from the first moment we met, but like always, Owen railroaded his way in. Taking what he wanted. Not caring about who he hurt in the process. I didn't see it then, but I see it now.

With my ears submerged under the water, a distorted voice startles me, making my eyes spring open.

Standing on the side of the sunken hot tub, in all of his six-foot-two broad and dark glory, is Jacob.

Subconsciously moving as far away from him as I possibly can, I ease my feet to the floor of the tub. Pushing my hair back off my forehead, I glide back and park my backside on the lip of the underwater seat.

"Are you enjoying yourself?" he asks, standing with his legs wide, hands in his pockets, and dominating the outdoor space.

"Yes, thank you."

"I've never seen you with your hair completely down before." He rolls his tongue over his top teeth.

"Do you like it?"

"I do." He loosens his tie and then undoes the knot before sliding it slowly out of his shirt collar, then proceeds to undo the top button of his white shirt. "You should wear it down more often."

"Your date didn't last long. I thought you'd be out all night with her." My voice is laced with sarcasm.

"I didn't have a date," he confesses, his honesty knocking the wind from me.

"Where did you go then?" I ask, trying to sound like I don't really care.

"I met my cousin, at The Ritz for dinner. She's a cardiothoracic surgeon at Great Ormond Street children's hospital. She's just moved back from New York."

"Wow. That's impressive."

He looks troubled, wrapping his tie around his shovel-sized hands, when he says, "Joanna talked some sense into me. She said I needed to open up."

What I would like him to do with that tie...

"You and me." He gestures to the space between us. "We need to talk. Get out."

"Hop in," I counter, trying not to overthink all the reasons this is a bad idea.

His jaw twitches once, then twice, as he considers my invitation.

"Jacob, as my friend, I'm asking you to get in."

He tilts his neck back as he inhales a deep breath, forcing his wide chest to puff out.

Without another word, he begins unbuttoning his shirt. When the last one is undone, he peels his shirt off, providing me a better look at him.

He's a solid wall of muscle and his skin is a work of art. My mouth salivates at the thought of licking all his delicious divots.

Eyes connected, he toes his black dress shoes off before he unbuckles his belt, leisurely teasing me with the slow tempo of his movements.

Watching him, with my pulse racing, I have to dip my mouth below the surface of the water to stop myself from moaning, unable to tear my eyes away from him.

He grants me a rare knock-out grin and my eyes dip to watch him unzip his suit trousers. Pushing them past his hips, he lets them fall to the wooden deck.

I sit up straighter, my mouth rising out of the water, exposing my lips to the cold air, and an unexpected high-pitched gasp leaves my throat.

I drink in his tall, lean body and it's like something out of a men's fitness magazine. Thick thighs, solid calves, laddered abs I'd like to climb, and, Lord have mercy, the outline of his thick, long cock is obvious beneath his stupidly tight boxers.

I raise my eyebrows, stunned at his surprising choice of

underwear. "Do you have a yellow duck pattern on your boxers?"

"Yes. Why?"

"No reason." I dip my mouth back in the water to hide my amusement.

He leans to the side and pulls his socks off.

Squinting my eyes in the low light, I try to get a better look at the vast expanse of tattoos across his wide shoulders, arms, collar, and chest, as he moves to step into the hot tub, submerging his gorgeous body from my viewing pleasure.

As he sits across from me, tension grows between us.

Growing impatient, I flick water at him, the droplets hitting his chest and running down, making me wish I could follow them with my tongue. "Start talking."

"What do you want to know?" he lets out with a sigh, stretching his arms wide along the sides of the hot tub, his hands clenching the lip of it tight.

"Why did you never tell me you had a thing for me, Jacob?"

He looks around the huge outdoor space before saying, "Because, within the first six months of moving to Castleview Cove, you were all about Owen."

"No, I wasn't," I reply defensively.

"Yes, you were," he scoffs.

"He asked me out, and I said yes. That's different."

"Is it?"

"Yes. I'm not sure if you know this, but I wanted you to ask me out. Properly. Officially. But you never did."

I had prayed to the heavens above for Jacob to ask me out on a date back then. As our friendship blossomed over the weeks, we grew closer, laughed more, and spent so much time together. Most of the time it was just the two of us, but no matter how much I wanted him to, Jacob never tried to kiss me. I guess I stopped wishing he would see me as more than just a friend. I didn't think I had a chance at more with him.

"Then Owen asked me out to the movies and the only reason I said yes was because I didn't think you were interested in me like *that*, Jay."

His head snaps back at my news, his brow wrinkling. "Are you serious? How could you not have known? I spent every single free minute with you. Who was the one that walked you home? Who asked you to go to the ice cream parlor on weekends? Who read to you and joined you in the library? Sat with you inside the castle waiting around as you filled your sketchbooks to the brim?"

I whisper, "You."

"Me." He pokes his chest. "And never, not once, did you ever look at me the way you looked at Owen."

That's not true. I did see him. Every day. "But you never gave me any indication that you even so much as liked me romantically. You never made it seem like you wanted anything more than friendship between us."

His nostrils flare, and the timbre of his voice drops a few levels. "Have you forgotten who made sure you got home before curfew? Or who looked after you when you got tipsy? Who took you home when you ripped your dress at prom, and who helped you fill out your art college application?"

It was always Jacob. Owen was always too busy *having fun*.

And I only just learned that Jacob even bought my Christmas and birthday presents, all lovingly disguised and labeled up from Owen.

"Why didn't you say anything?" I ask, rubbing my water-wrinkled fingers into my temples. Recalling our teenage memories is giving me a headache.

He takes his time considering what he says next. "I was waiting. I don't know what for, but I waited." Every muscle tensed, reminding me of a sixteen-year-old Jacob who was uncomfortable talking about his feelings. "I was a skinny kid, who wasn't good at chatting with girls romantically. Especially girls that look like you."

"Look like me?" I repeat, wondering if I'm dreaming all this right now.

"Have you seen you, Skye? Even when you were sixteen, you were fucking beautiful." He stands up suddenly, causing the bubbles to slosh over the sides. "You would never have gone with a skinny, dorky dude like me."

"I did like you." I stand up, furious that he saw himself that way. "I loved who you were, and I wanted you to ask me out or kiss me."

He steps forward, closing the space between us, but standing far enough away that I can't reach him.

"But the night you went to the movies and kissed Owen, I lost you."

"We were sixteen," I cry, anger bubbling up inside me at a situation I can't change.

"And that kiss sealed our fate."

"You sound like a parrot." I move closer, prodding him in his solid chest. "So you can't go after what you want because of some stupid promise you made when you were fourteen? Am I hearing this correctly?"

"We had a verbal agreement. No touching, dating, or kissing ex-girlfriends. I've never broken it."

"And do you think Owen kept his promise?"

"I don't know. I've never thought about it." He shakes his head. "He's my best friend." He sounds pained.

"And he treated me like shit."

"And you let him." He clenches his fists into tight balls by his sides.

A wave of furious heat scalds my skin as our conversation turns sour. "I did not *let* him."

"You fucking did. Every time he split up with you, he went with other girls, and you took him back again and again. Did he show you he loved you? Not just with words, but actions?"

The facts are difficult to hear because he's right. "He couldn't even be bothered to get you a fucking birthday present!" he roars. "And if you'd looked closely enough, you would have realized it was me who bought you those gifts. Who else would have known about the rucksack you love or the earrings from the New Zealand jewelry designer?" He points his finger into his chest, his voice booming. Dropping his gaze, he runs his hand over his face before looking at me again, his voice softer as he delivers his next line. "I pay attention to every little detail about you because I'm in love with you."

As if not quite believing the confession that just left his lips, his eyes bulging, he stumbles backward, almost falling over.

Hot tears spring up in my eyes.

"Love me?" The words catch in my throat.

He spins around to leave the hot tub.

"Please don't go," I beg, moving quickly and resting my hand on his tattooed shoulder. Goosebumps cascade across his skin and I hope it's from my touch and not the falling outside temperature.

"You were too blind to see it," he says, but he doesn't turn back to face me as he speaks.

"And you were too scared to admit how you feel." I keep my voice low and calm.

He shrugs. "Doesn't matter now." His voice is almost inaudible.

"Jacob, look at me."

His body remains facing away from me as if he's too scared of what might happen if he turns fully, but he twists his head, looking at me over his shoulder.

"All these years?" I'm almost too astonished for words.

His broad shoulders sag. "From the first day you walked into class, I knew then."

Fourteen years.

"And we can't ever be together because of a stupid rule all three of you made up when you were just kids?"

"Exactly."

"And what if I want more?" My hand is still on his shoulder and I run my finger over the black ink that sits beneath my thumb.

He stops my movement and lifts my palm from his skin, releasing his grip quickly. "I can't keep saying this over and over, Skye. It's too late."

"Did Owen know you had a crush on me?"

The sound of the city below, the honking of the horns, and the emergency service sirens fill the air as I wait for him to answer.

"He did." He pauses as we let the weight of this conversation settle around us. "That's what's fucking with my head. I'm mad at myself for not stepping up and being the man I am now, but Owen knew. I stopped sharing the names of the girls I liked at school and university when Owen was around. When you two would split up, he seemed to make a competitive sport out of trying to get the girl before me. And he always did."

His sad emerald eyes have lost all their sparkle. "I need to learn how to fall out of love with you. You have to let me." His voice sounds almost strangled as he speaks.

"Please don't say that." The tears I've been holding back since this conversation started break free, running down my cheeks.

"C'mon, Butterfly, don't cry." Jacob reaches up and thumbs them away. "I didn't mean to upset you and I didn't mean what I said about you letting Owen treat you like shit. I just want you to know you are worth more. You deserve better. Unfortunately, like I keep saying, I can't be that man."

I watch him walk back inside the penthouse, the bright light of the living space illuminating the delicate sky-blue butterfly tattoos covering his back and shoulders. They move across his sculpted frame as if fluttering through the vivid blue clouds branded into his skin. I've never seen his tattoos in detail before, so I gasp as I take in the decorative words cleverly threaded among his artwork that I missed before. The words he said to me years ago.

'Whatever, however, forever.'

He loves me.

11

SKYE

I fidget awkwardly with the handle of my coveted backpack. The one I now know Jacob bought for me.

Everything makes sense now.

This whole time it was really Jacob who was behind Owen's thoughtful gifts.

I was right all along. Owen didn't care for me the way I craved.

Leaning against the wall, Jacob continues to tap away on his phone, like he has done all day, every day since the night in the hot tub, trying to avoid the elephant in the room.

That elephant is me... well, us.

It's been strained all week. We've filled awkward moments discussing projects and nothing more. I miss Jacob, my friend and confidant.

Barely sleeping a wink since our first night here, I'm so exhausted and every client interaction has required a hundred and ten percent of my attention.

All I want to do is go home so I can at least get away from

Jacob for just a minute to wallow in the unfairness of us. If I'm this stressed and unhappy, then I can't imagine what it must feel like for him: loving me from afar for all these years and having to watch me with his best friend.

That word. Love. It feels like a knife to my heart every time I think about his words.

He tipped my world upside down when he said it, and I'm not sure how things will ever feel *normal* again.

"Would it be easier for us if I left Baxter and Bain, Jacob?" I blurt. I think it's the only solution.

"No." His attention is still locked firmly on his phone.

"We can't keep going like this."

"Stop talking."

"Austin, and his partner, Topher, our new clients, offered me an in-house branding position. They are considering setting up a new team," I confess.

That gets his attention. "You are not leaving Baxter and Bain. We've already discussed this, and I made my feelings very clear."

I don't look his way. "They offered me a great package. Health, resettlement, rent for a year, I get to recruit my own team. Seven weeks' vacation and an assistant." I finally throw him a glance.

He looks like an angry bull about to charge the red flag. "Topher only wants to sleep with you."

I roll my eyes. "They asked me to be a surrogate for them too," I say cooly.

"What the fuck?" Heat bounces off him. Face reddened, veins pulsing in his neck, he's about to blow.

"They are *together* together, Jacob. They are partners in every way."

Ding. The elevator alerts us to our destination, and the metal doors glide open.

"You are not taking that job and you are not agreeing to be a fucking surrogate mom for two people you barely know." He bangs the side of the elevator with his clenched fist as his anger spirals out of control, making me glad there is no one to witness his outburst.

"Forget I said anything," I mutter, stepping into our suite.

He's hot on my heels. "Forget?" He charges after me. "What the fuck, Skye?"

I swing back around, throwing my backpack onto the sofa. "Oh, so you *do* remember my name?"

"Don't," he fires out, his voice sounding strained.

"Don't what?"

"Just. Don't do this."

"So, should I continue to pretend you're invisible? Like I am to you now? One minute you confess loving me, then the next you're ignoring me."

He storms across the room, rubbing his buzz cut back and forth frantically.

"Well, now you know how it feels," he spits out bitterly. "I've been doing it for years. I've always been invisible to you. I watched on while you kissed him. Held his hand. Paraded around like you two were fucking couple goals when really it was a complete sham." He holds his stomach as if that very thought makes him want to vomit. "I watched him take advantage of your innocence and sweet nature. I sat on the sidelines listening to him talk about how he had you wrapped around his little finger. Watched him leave you at parties like you didn't matter and ogle other women when he had the most perfect fucking woman to go home with. It made me sick to my stomach. I fucking hate how he treated you."

He pulls his black overcoat off with force and flings it across the chair. "So, yes, Skye, I will continue to act like none of it matters to me because that's my default setting I've become oh so familiar with. You can't expect me to change a habit I've been perfecting for fourteen years because you've decided to open your eyes and see what's been happening in front of you for all that time."

He storms across to the bar, pours himself a large scotch, and downs the two inches of the amber liquid.

I jump when he slams the thick-bottomed glass against the black marble counter. Laying his hands on top of the bar, he dips his head.

I've never seen him so angry and all I want to do is soothe him.

"I feel like I've caused you so much pain. I didn't know, Jay. I promise you, I didn't. I would never want to hurt you. Ever." My voice is laced with so much remorse and I move closer to the bar, needing to be closer to him.

He lifts his head. With his jaw tense, I hear him grinding his teeth together as he glares at me.

"I'm so sorry," I apologize, wanting to help stop the hurt I can see etched onto his face.

He closes his eyes, hunching his shoulders as he breathes deeply.

Oh God, I feel like I'm going to cry. Seeing him look so dejected physically hurts.

Standing on the other side of the bar, I lay my hand over his. "Would it make you feel better if I told you that I see you now, Jacob? I see all of you. I can't stop thinking about you and my heart hurts from how consumed I feel with the idea of you." I pause to let my words sink in, but he doesn't respond. Respecting his need for space, I turn and walk away, twisting to look back at him as I reach the doorway. "I know what the tattoo on your back symbolizes. I can't believe you did that for me but I like that I'm etched into your skin. It's like I can't touch you because of your pact with Owen, but a part of me is carved into you for a lifetime."

12

JACOB

ME

I messed up.

LINCOLN

Shit. Please tell me you didn't sleep with her without speaking to Owen first.

ME

Of course not!

LINCOLN

So what happened then?

ME

I told her.

LINCOLN

About?

ME

How I feel about her.

LINCOLN

And?

ME

I feel worse.

LINCOLN

Unreciprocated love is never going to feel good.

ME

She caught me fucking Verity on my desk in the office a month ago, and I was calling her Skye.

LINCOLN

You're a kinky fucker.

ME

Then Skye made herself come as she watched.

ME

And now Skye thinks she has feelings for me.

My phone rings.

I press accept and instant laughter fills my eardrum. "Fuck, man. You have a way better playboy lifestyle than anyone I know. I need all the fucking details," Lincoln demands.

Even though Skye's been in her room for the last hour with the door shut, I step outside into the cool night air and close the sliding doors behind me, ensuring she doesn't hear my conversation.

I plonk myself down on the outdoor sofa and stretch my legs out in front of me, then proceed to fill Lincoln in on the last crazy week of my fucked-up, self-inflicted, drama-filled love life. Or lack of.

When I finish, I run my finger around the rim of my whiskey glass and wait for Lincoln to say something.

"And she said she sees you now?"

"Yes," I sigh.

"She never loved Owen?"

"Nope."

"Why did she keep getting back with him, then?"

I pinch my nose. "Familiarity. Routine, I guess."

"Better with the devil you do, than the devil you don't."

"Exactly."

"But she's made it clear she's interested in you now?" Seeking clarity on the situation, he keeps firing questions my way.

"Yes."

"And she enjoyed watching you."

"She told me I had a beautiful body."

"She's not wrong. I'd bang you if I was that way inclined."

"Fuck off." My brows pinch together. "She told me that she got herself off in the shower after she watched me and the whole time, she was thinking about me."

"Fuck, that's hot, Jay. Sweet Skye is not so sweet after all." He pauses. "And she knows all the presents were from you?"

"Yeah." Then I confess, "She saw the tattoo I dedicated to her across my back when we were in the hot tub together."

"So that's what your tattoo means? You're a fucking mess."

"Helpful."

"C'mon, Jay. You gotta admit that if you'd just fucking told her all those years ago, then you wouldn't be in this position."

If only I'd been brave enough to stand up for what I wanted. "I know. So what do I do?"

"You're the one I come to for advice because I am shit at this relationship malarkey. If it wasn't for Violet, I would still be one lonely fuck-up myself."

"Dig deep. Tell me what to do, Lincoln."

"Let me help." Violet's voice startles me.

"I maybe should have said you're on speakerphone." Lincoln clears his throat, as if he's trying to hide the laughter in his voice.

"What the fuck, man?" I yell, annoyed that he didn't tell me Violet was there.

"We share everything. So let her help."

I don't get a chance to respond as Violet's California accent appears again. "Was she upset when she went to bed, Jacob?"

"Yes."

"Then apologize. You should do that first. Then be honest with her and tell her exactly how you feel. Explain to her it's not some high-school crush anymore. Then ask her what she wants. You're so wrapped up in your own feelings, but have you considered hers?" Violet keeps throwing me advice. "Then explain how your loyalty lies with Owen. He's your boy at the end of the day. Linc and Owen both are. You've always been tight and I know from speaking with Linc, Owen hasn't had the most loving upbringing and he's troubled right now. As soon as you get back to Castleview Cove, you need to speak to him. Not over the phone either, it needs to be a face-to-face conversation. Man to man."

That makes so much sense.

"Understood?" she asks.

"Got it." My heart is fucking racing. "Do you think Owen will punch me in the nuts when I tell him how I feel?"

"Aw, fuck, yeah, but it'll be worth it if you win the girl of your dreams." I hear a smacking noise, then Lincoln whines, "Christ, for a wee thing, you're strong. That hurt."

"It was only a light smack on your shoulder. Stop being such a big baby," Violet says firmly.

They make me chuckle.

Violet's reassuring voice sings down the earpiece. "He won't punch you in the nuts, Jacob, because you're going to be honest. Okay? Full disclosure."

She makes it sound so simple.

"Feel better?" she asks.

"Yeah. I actually do."

"Well, I don't." Lincoln fake-huffs. "I think you broke my shoulder."

"Oh, shut up, Lincoln." Violet laughs.

"Thanks, guys."

"You know we love you, Jacob. Both you and Owen," Violet says. "We won't pick sides, but you have to do the honorable thing and tell him first before you even think about making moves."

"I know."

"Good luck," they both say in harmony.

"Fix it, Jay," Lincoln says, then hangs up.

First thing to do: apologize.

13

SKYE

Almost drifting off, my body tilts slightly when the mattress dips on the other side of the bed.

Panicked, I shoot up and fumble about, desperately trying to locate the switch for my nightstand lamp and flick it on.

My pulse stops racing when I realize it's just Jacob.

But wait, what?

Lying fully clothed, still in his dress shirt and trousers from earlier, fingers laced together over his hips, he's lying on his back, staring at the ceiling.

"Everything okay?" I turn onto my side to face him.

Pulling the pillow into my neck, not knowing what comes next, I make myself comfortable.

"I'm sorry for shouting at you, Skye."

"It's okay," I whisper.

"It's not okay. I've behaved like an asshole this week," he answers miserably.

I reach out and wrap our pinky fingers together and he gives mine a little squeeze.

"Jay," I start. "Neither of us knows what we are supposed to say or do, or how to behave now. This is new territory for us both."

Our entwined hands land on top of the bedcovers when he turns to face me. The warm, low light of the room makes him look even more gorgeous. I've always admired how handsome he is, but the sex appeal and dominance he exudes suddenly feels overwhelming, making it difficult not to eat up the space between us and kiss his tempting lips.

I draw a shaky breath. "We have to learn how to work together again. I miss my friend. And my bossy boss."

"I want that too," he replies with a long sigh. "And I'm not bossy."

"Yes, you are," I tease and throw him a smile.

A look of distress flashes over his face. Painful minutes pass, but I'm happy to lie here with him.

Eventually, he says, "I've loved you for as long as I can remember. I have nothing to hide from you anymore and I want you to know that it's never been *just* a stupid high-school crush or an infatuation. You are like no other woman I have ever met. You're stupidly smart, creative as hell, funny. You giggle at the silliest of jokes; you class everyone as your friend. You're accepting of everyone's quirks and you always make people feel important. You're all I've ever wanted, but everything I've never been allowed to have." The vulnerability drips from his words, making my heart and body ache for him.

Daily, Jacob displays big-dick energy. His presence can be felt from a mile away, but he's quiet and he never talks about his feelings; he's deeper than the abyss. However, tonight, he's so sincere, cracking open his heart and letting me see inside.

His thumb slowly brushes across the top of my hand. I could grow to like him doing that.

"I hate the weekends," he blurts.

Confused, I frown.

"It's the days I don't get to see you and if you leave Baxter and Bain, I might fucking die if I don't get to see your beautiful, kind face every day. I don't think my heart could survive not seeing you, Skye." A glimmer of sadness dances in his eyes as he keeps on talking. "I asked my father if I could move to a different role, away from Castleview. But honestly, I can't bear the thought of being away from you. I can't live without you—"

"Jay," I interrupt.

"Let me finish what I need to say." His eyes drop for a moment. "I've had a few girlfriends, you know I have, but none of them ever felt right and it always felt like I was cheating on you. That sounds so stupid when I say it out loud." Embarrassment reddens his cheeks, reminding me of that skinny, shy sixteen-year-old boy.

His eyes close. "The way I feel about you." A long sigh leaves his throat. "It hurts loving you. Knowing that you can't be mine when that's all I want. I want your morning smiles, to hear your laughter fill every space I am in, to hold you, douse myself in your magic. But I can't do any of that."

I'm too stunned to reply. My heart is about to burst for this man.

His deep voice vibrates in my veins when he says, "I don't know how to fall out of love with you. And if I'm honest, I don't want to."

I don't want him to either.

He looks up at me again.

"Owen is my *best* friend. He's always been there for me. Annoying as he is, he always stuck up for me at school, and he taught me how to do stunts on my BMX. He even taught me how to tie my shoelaces." He studies my face. "He's my boy."

"Your ride or die?" I keep my voice low.

"Yeah." He gives a soft nod. "Plus, he's troubled right now, and he won't speak to me or Lincoln about it, but I know he needs us."

"He won't speak to anyone, Jacob. You should know this by now."

He clears his throat. "He let something slip the other night when he was drunk. He said he was getting married."

Shocked to my core, I yell louder than I planned, "What?"

"I don't know anything other than that and the fact that her name is Evangeline."

"Evangeline Muircroft?" I exclaim, almost laughing at how predictable his mother is.

"Who's that?"

"One of his mother's friend's daughters. She's like ten years younger than him."

"Are you upset?" he questions quietly, as if he's nervous about my reply.

"Yes, but not in the way you think. I'm mad at his mother for making him marry her. Poor Owen." I'm so glad I'm out of all that. I was not suited to that role.

"Not about Owen marrying someone else?"

"Hell, no. Owen is just a friend," I reassure him.

"Like me?" he asks, and I can't decide if he's offering it as a reminder that we can never happen or a question to discover if I've forgiven him for everything he's put me through this week.

"You're a great friend, and you're also my boss." Disappointment flashes across his face, and his thumb stops tracing my skin. "But I think I might want more with you, Jacob."

"Do you mean that?"

I shuffle closer. The only parts of our bodies touching are

his hand in mine, but I can feel the heat emanating from him, lighting me up and filling me with a burning desire.

I nod. "I like being loved by you. And all those things you did for me. To make sure I was looked after. The gifts feel even more special now, knowing they came from you." I release my hand from his and rest it on his scruff-covered face. It's much softer than I thought it would be. "You are a very special guy and I would really like to explore *us*. It could be kind of wonderful."

His eyes, full of emotion, shine back at me, almost as if he can't believe what I am saying and he covers my hand with his. "I have to speak to Owen and tell him the truth," he says in a gentle whisper. "Lincoln thinks he'll punch me in the nuts."

That makes me giggle. "Lincoln knows?"

"And Violet. Lincoln guessed about a year ago, then he told Violet."

"I wish you had asked me out on a date first," I admit.

"Me too," he whispers.

"What if he doesn't take the news well?"

"I don't know." His honesty is refreshing, but he sounds disheartened.

"What if he makes you choose between him or me?"

Jacob flinches like he's been slapped. "I can't even think about that. I already lost you. I can't lose him too."

"You've not lost me, Jacob. I'm right here."

Jacob doesn't say a word, but dances his fingers over the side of my face, pushing a lock of my hair away.

"What if he gives you his blessing?" I ask.

"Then you'll understand the true meaning of what it's like to be loved by someone who loves you with every bone in his body," he says, his tone thick with possession.

"And what if I don't want to date you?" I tease.

"Then you'll have to watch me date other girls." He smirks, knowing he got me back.

Jealousy threads through my veins. "Like the girl from your office that night?"

He groans. "Her name is Verity. She's just a..."

"Saturday night booty call?" My eyebrows shoot up in curiosity.

"Kinda."

My tone drips with sarcasm. "Sounds like fun."

"She *was* a Saturday night thing. Past tense. I haven't hooked up with her or anyone since the night in the office with you, Skye, and I'm familiar with the jealousy thing. I know that feeling well." A frown darkens his face. "Not being able to touch you, to hold you, or to feel your lips on mine is slowly killing me."

"You need to speak to Owen. Soon." I won't let him jeopardize his friendship. I don't want to be the one that comes between them. "But will you stay with me tonight?"

He blinks owlishly. "I... can't..."

"Not like *that*, Jay. Just stay right where you are, fully clothed, and hold me. Or is that breaking the rules?" It may be all I ever get. "Give me just one night."

With ease and gentle dominance, and only the comforter separating us, he pulls me into his thick arms, tucking my head into his neck.

"You smell good," he mumbles, draping his arm around my waist. "Like coconut and vanilla."

"You feel good." I snuggle into his chest, relaxing in his bear hug.

"Now go to sleep, Butterfly. We have a big day tomorrow."

"We're traveling home. It's hardly exciting." I rest my hand on his pec and it flexes under my touch.

"Our flight isn't until tomorrow night. I have fun plans for us booked before then. Let me make it up to you for being an asshole?"

"Are we going to the Tate Modern?" I start to get excited.

"You'll see. Now sleep."

I bury myself against the solid frame of his athletic body, feeling his heart beating in time with mine.

"I think I found my new favorite place," I mumble, feeling tired.

"You've always been my favorite place." He pulls me in tighter, as if wanting to climb inside my body. "Thank you for accepting my apology and listening to me."

"Thank you for loving me."

"Night, Butterfly."

With that, I drift off in his loving arms and have the best night's sleep since arriving in London, where I dream of being wrapped in emerald silk, surrounded by ethereal butterflies, and showered in golden stars.

If this is what Jacob's love feels like, I think I want to stay here forever.

14

SKYE

Sadness engulfs me when I wake up alone. Deep down, I knew that as dawn broke, it would shatter our embrace. The way he held me tight all night, as if I was his life-preserver, swaddling me like a big soft blanket, was everything I never knew I always needed.

I could stay wrapped in his loving arms for eternity.

Jacob's turned my night into day, my push into pull, and my darkness into light.

With every visceral fiber of my being, all my body wants to do is seek him out.

Flinging back the bedcovers, I leap out of the giant hotel bed and welcome the day with a star-shaped stretch, feeling better than I have all week. Jacob and I have finally cleared the stale air between us. Moving into the lounge area, the faint sound of trickling water can be heard from the other side of the suite. My legs carry me toward the slightly ajar master bathroom door.

I can't stop myself peeking through the gap.

Cascading water streams down over Jacob's wide,

muscular body, making his skin glisten under the light. I take this moment to watch him as he lathers up and washes every inch of his perfect skin.

His back is facing the door and my curiosity gets the better of me. I push the door open further and, like a cat on the prowl, I walk stealthily through the blanket of steam.

I want to see his tattoo up close again. It's breathtaking.

As I reach the glass, I stop. My eyes take in every millimeter of artistry. I move closer still, trying to get a better look at the silhouette of a castle poking out of the sky-blue clouds. It looks like the castle at Castleview Cove. A sketchbook lies at the foot of the castle surrounded by snowdrops. Sitting smack bang in the middle of his shoulder blades are the words *Whatever, However, Forever* in elegant script lettering.

I lay my hand on the shower screen as if trying to touch it.

It looks like the hand lettering I've had on the pinboard in my office I did almost three years ago. It's one of the many practice pieces I've created over the years.

"Is that my writing?" I cry out in shock, my voice suddenly loud in the quiet space.

He whips around. "Holy shit, Skye," he shouts, throwing his hand to his chest.

I take a deep breath and point against the glass. "Is that my writing on your back?"

A subtle nod confirms it is.

"Jacob." My voice is thick with a mix of emotions.

I summon all the willpower I have not to join him in the shower and show him how much I appreciate him. But I can't. I have to stay here and respect his wishes to speak to Owen first.

"Who is that guy?" I point to the giant winged bird tattooed across the front of his chest.

"He's much wiser than me and helps guide me."

Damn, being good feels impossible right now.

His dark, soulful eyes burn my skin as he stares at me. Eventually, he lays his palm flat against mine on his side of the shower cubicle, our hands connected through the glass.

I step closer.

He stands, not moving.

My eyes drop down his body and for the first time I get a full-frontal view of every single hard inch of him and I have to swallow down a groan as I take him in.

His length hangs heavy between his thick thighs, and he's big, surprisingly so. No wonder he displays big-dick energy... he has a huge one to back it up.

An eight-pack stomach, scattered with black tattoos that weave into thicker, blacker body art across his collar, pecs, and shoulders; he's the sexiest man I have ever laid my eyes on... and he's completely unaware of his hotness.

I force my inner good girl back into her box and unleash my inner bad one. I want him.

Stepping back, I pull the hem of my pink camisole over my head, then free my long locks from my tight buns, allowing my hair to spill across my shoulders and exposed breasts.

It's the first time he's ever seen me naked, and I watch as his breath hitches as he takes me in.

An electric current fills the room.

I slip my matching sleep shorts down my hips, letting them pool around my feet.

Desire intensifies in his dark eyes, heating my skin with his gaze. With his hand still on the glass, his other one grabs his now hard cock and he begins to stroke himself.

If only I could touch him.

"You have a beautiful body, Skye."

"It's yours," I murmur as he fists himself faster, his biceps contracting with every jerk.

"Show me that pretty pussy." His words are almost desperate.

Bringing my hand to my mouth, I suck hard on my finger, coating it to make it wet.

He lets out a long groan and leans his forehead against the glass.

Sailing my hand down my body, I gently part my lips and touch my clit, causing a moan to leave my throat. "Feels so good," I gasp.

His eyes eat me up as he watches me circle my bundle of nerves over and over.

The head of his cock looks angry and about to blow as he continues to fuck himself with his hand.

I'm on the edge, about to explode myself.

A desperate sound from deep in his chest sends goose-bumps across my body and I can feel my impending orgasm weave down my spine, coasting its way to my center.

"Come for me, Butterfly. Fuck yourself with your fingers. Imagine it's my hand."

I do as I'm told and place my fingers on either side of my lips in a V shape, exposing myself fully, and rub myself harder. With my other hand, I push my finger deep into my hot, wet core and slide it in and out, chasing my release.

Our labored breaths kick up a notch as the water continues to rain down on him.

"I'm so desperate to touch you." The admission spilling from his mouth has me unraveling.

Jolts of desire take flight, my entire body needing the

release. Watching his tight fist stroke his cock sends me over the edge as I imagine him inside my pussy.

I clench my eyes shut until his commanding voice demands me to do the opposite. "Look at me when you come."

My eyes fly open and connect with his through the glass as we fuck ourselves to completion.

With feral groans, he roars his release.

His eyes never leave mine as he shoots his load all over his hand.

Gasping.

Panting.

Fogging up the glass.

I cry out as my own release hits me with full force. Back arching, I can't stop the best orgasm I've ever had tearing through my entire body.

Skin flushed, his body jerks a few more times and the wild tension that's been building between us eases a little as we descend.

Together.

Never in my wildest dreams could I have imagined doing that with him.

"Taste yourself." His eyes fall on my lips as I push my fingers into my mouth.

I've never done this before.

"Lick every drop," he demands, his chest still heaving. "I can't wait to lick that sweet pussy and taste you for myself."

I'm desperate for him to touch me, and then to touch and taste him, too.

I stand waiting to be told what to do, but he heads back under the water to clean himself up. Once he's washed his cock, he doesn't look at me as he scrubs his face and hair.

I take several steps back.

Is he regretting what we did?

"We didn't break any rules. You didn't touch me." I begin to panic.

"In my head, I was fucking touching you." He smirks, his face not showing an ounce of regret. *Oh, thank goodness.*

I turn to leave, but his words stop me. "Where do you think you're going? Get back and stand right where you were." He points to the other side of the glass then turns the shower off and quickly wraps a towel around his waist.

"So all this is mine?" He motions up and down my body with his pointer finger when I return to the spot I was just standing in.

"When the time is right, yes."

"And in the meantime?"

"Also yours. I don't want anyone else."

He steps out of the shower, and, with hunger in his eyes, he looks me up and down. "Do you know how beautiful you are?"

I shake my head.

"When I do get my hands on you, I won't be letting you leave my bedroom for a week. I'm gonna fuck you so hard and you're gonna love it. After I've fucked you the way we both need, I will make love to you like you deserve, and baby, I'm gonna make you fall in love with me as much as I love you."

I think I'm already there.

He steps closer to me and asks, "Do my tattoos make you wet for me?"

I like his cheeky side. A nervous giggle that's been stuck in my throat filters out, echoing off the bathroom walls. "Yeah."

"Good. I'll be walking about naked for the rest of the day."

"I don't think the people of London will like that."

"But you will." He winks.

Facts.

A question narrows his eyes. "If, and I hate to say his name after what we just did, but *if* Owen gives us his blessing, can you save yourself for me until then? I don't want another man's hands on you. Not ever." His muscled jaw tics when he finishes speaking and clenches together as if in pain.

"Will you do the same for me? No more Verity?"

"Consider it done."

"I don't want anyone else but you." My honest words spill from my lips easily.

"Fuck, you might actually be mine," he mumbles as if he can't believe any of this is happening... and he's not the only one.

"You need to speak with Owen as soon as we get back."

"I've already texted him asking to meet up."

I goofily smile at him. "It's gonna work out, right?"

"I fucking hope so, or we both die lonely deaths, and that delicious body that was made for mine will go untouched." He looks me up and down and rubs his towel-covered cock with the palm of his hand. "But you need to go and get ready. I have tickets for us for the Tate Modern. We are getting a private tour today, and afterward, a matinee showing of *Hamilton*."

"We are?" I can't contain my glee as my smile hurts my cheeks.

"Yes, now let me watch as you wiggle that beautiful ass across the room and go put on some of those sexy socks that make me hard for you."

I step back, grab my clothes off the tiled floor, and skip away. "Good morning, Jacob." I throw him a cheeky smile back over my shoulder before I slip from the room.

"It's better than good."

15

JACOB

"Thank you for an incredible day." Skye tosses her backpack onto the passenger seat of her baby-pink Nissan Figaro car.

I slide her pink suitcase into the small trunk of her unique car, then close it before moving around to the driver's side and opening the door for her.

"You're a real gentleman, you know that?" Skye teases, wiggling her hips my way and fluttering her big blue eyes.

"C'mon, get in. It's late and you need to get home."

If she doesn't, I might fling her over my shoulder and drag her to my bedroom, where I will keep her to myself for all eternity.

My sensibility almost snapped halfway through the day. The way she licked her strawberry ice cream seductively was enough to break even the strongest of men.

In between moments of caveman-level desire, I dreamed about walking hand in hand with her. It's all I've ever wanted.

Today felt like the beginning of something new, but it's a balance of emotions I'm struggling to juggle.

I'm not ashamed to admit I like that she's aware of what she means to me now, but I'm petrified we won't get a chance to explore what we possibly could be.

Sharing a bed with her last night, her flirting with me, the intimacy. It was my ultimate dream come true.

Then the shower this morning.

Fuck me, the shower this morning. That's an image I will never forget.

Her body. Man, has she got the most incredible pair of tits. They fit her slight frame perfectly. The perfect size for my hands, too. Her nice round ass and that little pussy of hers is waxed just the way I like it, bare with a sliver of a landing strip.

Fuck-ing yum-my.

I'm never getting any work done this week if it goes anything like it did today. She's constantly touched me, not inappropriately or anything. Just little gestures. Like when she laid her hand on my thigh as we watched *Hamilton*, squeezing it at the emotional scenes. The way she used my arm to balance herself as she threw her head back, laughing when I dropped my ice cream. She seems to like touching me.

I can't lie. I freakin' love it.

I've waited since I was sixteen for this and I'm now left wondering what would have happened if I'd said something sooner.

However, maybe we just had to wait for our moment.

But is it all too much too soon?

It scares me to think that I have loved her for so many years, but suddenly she's interested in me after only a few weeks. Could it really be *this* easy? Although it's anything but easy because we have an Owen-shaped block standing between us. But knowing she likes me too, that she wants me... it's enough. For now.

"C'mon, hurry up and get in the car. It's getting chilly," I instruct, pulling my attention back to Skye.

"I've driven the roads here since I got my license. Stop fussing." She comes to a halt on the other side of the driver's door.

This is the moment, if I was on a date with her, that I would lean down and kiss her. Reality is, we aren't and we can't.

"Text me as soon as you get in. It's late and a little frosty. Be careful on the bends."

"Okay." She bites her lip and then gets into her car. I close the door and she instantly rolls the window down, so I bend at the waist to meet her face to face.

As she turns the key, her little motor car sputters before humming contently.

"Please be safe," I say.

"Oh, do stop." She rolls her eyes.

"I worry about you."

"I know." A soft grin tilts her lips upward. "I like how you worry about me. It feels nice."

She steals my breath when she keeps talking. "It makes me feel warm and fuzzy inside." Her face turns serious. "If I feel like this now, imagine what it will feel like when we kiss." She stares at my lips as if picturing that in her mind.

"I can't wait to find out."

"I can't either." She shakes her head then clears her throat. "Tomorrow is Sunday."

"And?"

"You don't like Sundays."

I love that she remembered my admission.

"I have Sunday dinner with my mom and dad, but afterward, can I video call you?"

Excitement blooms in my chest. "I would like that. A lot."

"Seven o'clock?"

"Perfect."

After a moment, she sighs. "I gotta go."

Please stay.

"Speak tomorrow." I tap the window opening. "And remember to text me."

"Okay, big guy." Her tone is soft.

She pushes the car into drive, making her little car move slowly across the gravel; the crunches echo in the dark.

The red glow of her brakes shines bright, her car digging into the gravel as she comes to a complete halt.

Poking her head out of the window, she looks back at me, and with a beaming smile, she shouts, "Hey, do you know this one?"

My chest fills with laughter when the car speakers boom out "Butterfly" by Crazy Town. It's so fucking loud, it's just as well I live in the countryside with no one for miles around. She accelerates again, laughing and waving her hand out of the window.

Moving onto the narrow road, she disappears round the corner, off into the pitch dark, and I can still hear her for at least twenty seconds as she drives around the curves of the country roads and down into Castleview Cove.

Stuffing my hands in my jean pockets, I tilt my head back, eyeing the stars for reassurance, praying that it's all going to be okay because I might not survive otherwise.

Making my way back into my house, I pull my phone out of my back pocket.

Owen hasn't replied to me yet.

I grab a bottle of water from the fridge and head to my room to unpack, grateful Owen tidied up and stripped the guest bed before he left.

On silent, my phone vibrates on my nightstand.

Eager to see if Skye got home safely, I lower myself to sit on the edge of the bed. Grabbing my phone off the side, I smile to myself as I open her text.

SKYE

I am home. Not a car crash or mass murderer to be seen. Although my bedroom looks like a car crash. Kimmy has clearly been raiding my wardrobe and my underwear drawers are all in a muddle.

ME

Did she have a party this weekend?

SKYE

Not that I know of. I'll be having words with her tomorrow.

I take a sip of water from my bottle.

SKYE

Thank you for an unforgettable week.

She sends me a blue heart emoji, clouds, and a blue butterfly.

I quickly type out a reply.

ME

I'm sorry it wasn't the best start.

SKYE

But it ended on a high. Thank you for organizing everything, and Hamilton is now my favorite show. I'll remember it forever. Thank you for buying me my program.

ME

To add to your collection.

SKYE

How do you know so much about me?

ME

I watch.

SKYE

Stalker.

ME

Pervert?

SKYE

Perv away *winking face* What else do you know about me that no one else does?

ME

You want to visit Barcelona, New York again, and that place where the pigs swim.

SKYE

How do you know that?

ME

You saved your vision board in a client file by mistake.

SKYE

Did I? I'm sorry.

ME

Don't apologize. I put it back in your own folder on the server.

SKYE

Thanks. What else do you remember about my vision board?

ME

A house with a library.

SKYE

And?

ME

Buy a house for the library.

SKYE

What else?

ME

An axolotl. What the fuck is that thing, anyway?

SKYE

It's a Mexican salamander.

ME

It's fucking nasty is what it is.

SKYE

They have cute little faces.

ME

Looks like a badly circumcised ghost's dick.

SKYE

Well, I can't get one now, can I? That's all I'm going to imagine. What else do you remember?

ME

Castle.

SKYE

What was happening in the castle?

ME

A cool couple getting married. Looked amazing. Not a frilly white dress to be seen.

SKYE

What were they surrounded by?

Shit.

She worked it out.

ME

Snowdrops.

SKYE

Like the ones on your tattoo?

ME

You got me.

SKYE

Your tattoo is beautiful.

ME

So are you.

SKYE

And you are super handsome. You should be on a magazine cover. Ever thought about modeling?

ME

No way. I'm too rough around the edges.

SKYE

Stop it. The girls at work drool over you.

I've never noticed, but then I've only ever had eyes for one girl.

SKYE

Girls like the bad boy look.

ME

Are you one of those?

SKYE

Never used to be, but suddenly that's all I want.

ME

A bad boy?

SKYE

No.

SKYE

Not just any bad boy. Only you.

I smile.

ME

I can show you just how bad I can be.

SKYE

I hope you do *winking face*

I position myself against the pillows, getting comfortable. For the next ten minutes, we bounce messages back and forth.

SKYE

I need to go to sleep. I can barely keep my eyes open.

ME

Speak tomorrow. Miss you already.

A video drops into the chat and I hit play.

She's lying on her side, messy buns on top of her head,

makeup free; the shine from her screen lights up her elfin face.

Beaming down the camera, she whispers, "Night, Jay." She blows me a kiss and then says, "Dream of me."

My heart melts.

I'm so fucking head over heels for this girl.

Somebody pinch me.

16

SKYE

Waiting for the impending lecture and twenty questions, I scrunch my face up, worried what comes next.

"You split up? Forever?" my mom gasps.

Unable to look her in the eyes, I nod, count to ten, then pop one eye open.

I could feel the concern seeping out of my parents' bodies when I announced that Owen and I had, once and for all, broken up.

Oh, deep joy.

They were hoping for a big wedding. A grand event that townsfolk would speak of for years to come. Now that is never going to happen.

My mom will have to put her diamond-and-sapphire-encrusted tiara back in storage. She pulled it out around six months ago. It's the one she wore when she married my dad. It's vintage and has been passed down through four generations of women on my mother's side of the family.

"Oh, baby girl. It's okay." A secret look passes between her and my dad.

She lays her fork down on her plate, reaches across the dark wood dining table, and gives my hand a double pat. "Can we be honest?" she asks.

I bob my head.

"We just want you to be happy, and lots of times, when you were with Owen, you just weren't yourself, Skye. He's a nice boy." Tucking a blonde strand of hair behind her ear, she looks nervous. "But I want someone who will literally sweep you off of your feet."

"And look after my baby girl." My dad pats my other hand.

Emotion builds in my throat. "I want that for me, too," I croak, then take a sip of apple juice.

"Are you happy?" My mom picks up her fork and starts eating her roast beef again.

I swirl my apple juice around the glass, then smile. "Honestly? I am. Owen and I were no good for each other. I was never his priority." I lift my glass to my lips again and take a huge gulp. "I have a lot of good things happening. And... I need a drum roll." I look at them both.

Instantly, they both drop their silverware to their plates, making a clattering sound. In fake fanfare, they drum the tabletop in excitement. It's the thing we always did as a family when I was growing up when anything significant needed a big announcement.

I pause for dramatic effect.

"I'm getting promoted at work."

My dad cups his hands on either side of his mouth and whoops, causing my mom to join in and me to start giggling.

"That's my girl." My dad punches the air.

"So, you'll be working directly under Jacob?" I almost laugh when my dad asks me that question and he picks up his cutlery to finish the last of his meal.

I hope so. I want to get under him, on top of him. Just everything with him.

"Yes. I won't report to Robert anymore, and I will have to go away on business more often." I trace my hands over the wooden tabletop.

"You're keeping something from us." My mom smirks. She knows me so well.

A giggle leaves my throat. "I'm just excited," I lie. It's way too early to even mention anything remotely Jacob-related. My hopes for us are sky high, but I have a niggling feeling I'm being too optimistic. Owen may never be okay with me moving on with Jacob. I ignore the pain in my chest, not wanting to consider that.

"I might get my house sooner than I thought." I lift my shoulders to my ears, giddy at the prospect. "I'll get a pay rise, which means I will be able to save more money and have an even bigger deposit."

"About that." My dad puts his knife and fork together neatly on the plate like resting soldiers. "We want to help you." He pushes his glasses up his nose.

"No," I gasp.

"Yes," he says firmly, with a nod of his head. "We have been saving and we want to help."

"You can't do that." I wave my hands in front of me, brushing off his offer.

"Yes, we can, and we are. You are our only daughter, and we want to help." He looks at Mom and smiles.

"I might cry." I laugh and sniff at the same time to hold back my overwhelming gratitude.

Pushing herself away from the table, my mom starts clearing up our plates. "Happy tears, I trust."

My dad removes himself from the table, too. "Plus, we are

doing it for selfish reasons. You still have hundreds of books stacked in boxes in your old room. We want them out."

"I'm going to convert one of my rooms into a library. With a proper old-fashioned ladder and everything." I reach for my phone when it alerts me to an email. Checking the screen confirms my suspicions. It's from Jules, a super-fan it would appear, and someone who has been messaging me since I started my hand lettering video channel.

"I'm guessing I'll be helping you build the library?" My dad wanders into the kitchen.

"Oh, yeah, one hundred percent you will," I giggle.

I tap open the email, and read it quickly, then reply to her request to meet up for a coffee to discuss me giving a hand lettering lesson at the local art group she's started. She's been emailing repeatedly, and I'm hoping if I agree then it will stop her from emailing so much.

I close down my email and add our meeting on Tuesday at The Cove Coffee Shop into my diary.

No sooner have I sent it than a reply has landed in my inbox with a *Perfect, see you then*.

Great, another thing off the list is done for this week coming and I'm keeping my fingers crossed Jules likes my tutorial ideas.

"Pudding?" My mom pops her head around the kitchen door.

"I'm going to skip dessert. I want to head home and have an early night." I grab my things and make for the front door.

Leaving my childhood home, I look back over my shoulder at my mom and dad. They still look cute together. She's so petite compared to him. I'm sure she's shrinking as she gets older.

"Congrats again on the job, sweetie," my dad calls.

"Shh. It's our secret for now." I wink. "Love you two." I blow a kiss and begin the half-mile walk home.

I've never made it back so fast.

Because I have a phone date with Jacob.

I feel like a giddy teenager again.

"Hi." I lean back on my bed and bend my arm behind my head to prop myself up.

Jacob grins at me down the camera and I grin back and we both start laughing.

"Why am I so nervous? Are you nervous? I feel hot all over suddenly," I admit.

"You have no idea." He mirrors my position.

"Show me your bedroom," I say.

"I'll show you mine if you show me yours."

"Okay. You first."

He flips the camera.

Everything is bright. From the white gloss furniture with silver handles to the brave choices of white carpet and walls. There are multicolored abstract pieces of art lined up meticulously above the bed. It's chic and refined.

I let out a "*Wow*."

He flips the camera back to him. "You like?"

"I love." I nod my head. "You have impeccable taste."

"I've worked with designers long enough to know good from bad design."

"You're an excellent student. Gold star deserving," I tease.

"Now show me yours." He tucks his hand behind his head again.

"You've not to laugh. I'm in a rental, remember? So be kind."

"Just show me." He smirks.

I change the camera direction and slowly move left to right across my room.

"It's so white, too," he says, almost shocked.

"I like white. What were you expecting?"

"Color everywhere and loads of different styles flung together that you made work. But not white, clean lines or sharp edges. We have the same taste."

"We do." I pan the camera around again, stopping at my stretched-out legs.

"Nice socks."

"I know someone who likes them very much." I hitch my leg over my other knee and bounce it up and down.

"Oh, do you now?"

"I do." I pull my short, pleated skirt up my thigh.

"You're a menace."

"But one you love." I inwardly cringe at my use of the word "love."

"I do," he groans. "Turn the camera back round. I want to see your face." I hit the button to flip the video back to me. "Tell me about your day. Have you been to your mom and dad's?"

For the next half an hour, we fill each other in on our day. "I'm going to be an uncle again," he says proudly.

"Could you ever see yourself having children?"

"With the right person, yeah," he answers. "I know I want children."

I may have mentioned that when I was a little tipsy one night.

"You know me so well."

His cheeks flush.

I try reassuring him he's right. "Kids. Marriage. Sounds nice. I don't ever want a big, flashy wedding. Just a little one."

"In a castle."

I roll my eyes. "In a castle," I confirm. I'm such a geek and so predictable. "And I don't want to wear a dress."

"Figures. Nothing you do is standard."

White meringue dresses, giddy bridesmaids, and the pomp and circumstance are a real turn-off for me. I don't need a huge congregation of witnesses to watch me declare my undying love for someone.

It sounds horrid, and a lot of wasted money.

A smile curves my lips, a small chuckle escaping my throat.

"What are you laughing at?" He tilts his chin up.

I reply, "Owen's parents would never approve of my style had I married him. How would a white and sky-blue dip-dyed pantsuit go down?"

"Sounds perfect to me. You'd look beautiful in anything." His grin is playful. "What the fuck is happening between us?"

"I don't know, but I could get used to this."

"But what if?"

"Shh," I stop him. "Speak to him." I don't want to say Owen's name out loud.

His expression grows serious now. "I can't reach him. He's not replied to my request to meet up."

"Keep trying."

My screen goes black. "Oh, you've disappeared."

"Sorry, Linc is calling me."

"Answer it."

"I'll call you back."

"It's fine. I'll see you tomorrow at work."

"That feels too long," he groans. "If only things were different."

My thoughts filter back to the day we met. "Everything happens for a reason, Jay."

"You're the reason I get up every day."

"And you're the reason I've started to feel like true love exists." I've never felt this way before. "I don't know if it's too quick or too soon. But I feel it."

"Hold on to that feeling. I want to show you how true that is."

He's such a sweetheart. "Night, Jay."

"Sweet dreams, Butterfly."

He hangs up our call and I roll onto my back. My heart feels like it's drifting along like a cloud on the wind.

A knock on my door halts my thoughts. Sitting upright, I move my feet to the floor and pull myself to my feet. "Come in."

Kimmy turns the door handle and sticks her head around the door. "Hey, gorgeous." The warmth of her smile forces me to smile back.

"Hey. Sorry I didn't see you today. I got back late last night," I say, reaching up to unravel my tight space buns.

"Did I disturb you?" The amusement in her voice is evident as she points to the pink vibrator on the bed I had plans to use later while thinking about Jacob.

"Shit." I push it off the bed and it lands with a thump on the floor.

"You get it, girlfriend, don't be ashamed." She plonks herself down on the edge of the mattress, making it bounce. Leaning back, she crosses her enviable legs. Kimmy wears the shortest of skirts to show them off. She is worse than me.

"Did you have a nice time in London with Mr. Grumpy Pants?" Kimmy pulls a loose thread from the hem of her skirt.

"He's not that bad," I snort. If truth be told, he is with everyone else, just not me.

"You said it yourself the other week."

That was before he told me he was in love with me.

It's no wonder he's so ill-tempered with everyone. He's been harboring all these frustrated emotions he has for me. For years.

She leans her other hand back against the bed, pushing her chest out. The buttons on her pale lemon shirt strain under the pressure of her large boobs. Kimmy sure does like tight-fitted clothing. Every cell of her oozes sexy confidence.

"It was fun. He took me to the theater to see *Hamilton*." I feel giddy at the memory.

"Oh, really?" Her eyes narrow as if she's thinking.

"And he booked a private tour for us at the Tate Modern. It was awesome."

"Uh-huh." She keeps staring at me.

I thread my hands into my now loosened hair to massage my sore scalp. My buns have been tied too tightly again today. *When will I ever learn?*

"What?" I stare back at her.

"Nothing. Nothing at all." She shakes her head back and forth with her mouth downturned. She looks like she knows something.

"It was fun. London was a success. We won a number of new contracts. All in all, it was awesome. Oh, and we stayed in the penthouse. There was some sort of mix-up with the rooms."

"I'm sure there was," Kimmy states dryly.

"We had a hot tub."

She goes silent. "Did something happen when you were away?"

"No," I respond all too quickly.

"Sure?" A hawk-like expression in her eyes, she pushes me again. "Because that man has always looked at you as if he's fucking starving and wants to devour you."

"He does not." My mouth goes dryer than the Sahara.

"You're in denial."

"And you're deluded." I bat away her suspicions.

She flops back on the bed and looks around my immaculate space. "Whatever," she mumbles. "Your room is super tidy."

"Yeah, well, you left it in a mess so I went to town cleaning my room when I got back from mom and dad's. What the hell were you doing in here this weekend? It was like a hurricane had been through it." Getting ready for bed, I grab my makeup remover and begin cleaning my face.

"I haven't been here since Thursday; I've been staying at Luca's place."

"What? When I came back last night, every one of my drawers was open and rummaged through and my photo of me, Mom and Dad was missing." I point to the empty space on my nightstand where my picture frame used to sit then wipe the cotton wool across my skin to remove my skin cleanser.

Holding her hands up in mock surrender, she says, "I swear, it was not me."

Has someone else been in my room? That disturbing thought causes a wave of shivers to run down my spine.

"Are you cold?"

"No, I just got an odd sensation. Ignore me."

"You left in such a hurry when you left for London, are you sure it wasn't you? It was all very last-minute."

Hell, maybe it was me.

I'm usually a neat freak and would never leave my bedroom in such a mess. However, I've been oddly distracted recently.

Jacob is screwing with my equilibrium.

If it wasn't Kimmy, it must have been me, after all.

But where is my photo?

I'll look for that tomorrow. It's possibly fallen down the back of my nightstand and I'm too tired to start pulling everything out now.

I park my backside on the edge of the bed and roll my long socks down my legs to remove them. Kimmy springs back up to a seated position.

"What the hell?" She grabs my leg and places my ankle gently on top of her knee to get a better look at what I did this afternoon. "Wow. It's beautiful." Her infectious grin is contagious.

"Show me properly." She urges me to take the protective film off.

When I finally remove it, I smile as I speak. "You like?"

"I lurrrrve it." She rolls the *R*.

I hope he lurrrrves it, too.

17

JACOB

Stuck in meetings all day, only managing to speak to Skye once via email, I'm glad to be kicking back, having drinks at Lincoln and Violet's house tonight.

I sent Skye a quick text earlier to let her know I will call her when I get home. It's still unread, which is most unlike her.

Flicking through the television menu, I scroll aimlessly, not paying an ounce of attention.

"Did you speak to Owen today?" Lincoln swaggers into his living room, passing me a beer. I shake my head. "You need to do that ASAP." He raises his eyebrows in an *or get punched in the nuts* look.

"I know."

He pulls the remote out of my hand. "You're on Violet's profile. Look at all the romantic comedy she gets recommended." He uses the controller to point at the screen.

"You love that shit."

He grins. "I really fucking do." He turns the television off and flops down onto his sofa. "Man, what a day."

"Busy?"

"Paperwork and police."

"Police?"

"Yeah." He leans forward, placing his beer on the table, and rests his elbows on his bowed legs. "A woman died on the dance floor on Saturday night."

"No shit?" I splutter out.

"Yes shit. Utterly shit," he sighs. "Some fucking wedding that turned out to be for the bride. It was her great-aunt."

"She died at a wedding?" I exclaim.

"Awful. That poor bride will be traumatized forever. Happy wedding anniversary, oh, and while we're at it, I'm sorry for your loss."

"Fuck. That's horrible. How did she die?"

"She had a massive heart attack while she was dancing."

"And the family witnessed it all?"

"Yeah. They watched on as her son gave CPR. But she was already gone."

"What was she dancing to?" I don't even know why the fuck I'm asking that.

"Shania Twain's 'Man! I Feel Like a Woman!'"

Trying to stifle how funny I find that, I snort. "Fuck, I'm sorry." I cover my face in shame. "I didn't mean to laugh."

"What a way to go." Lincoln tucks his lips into his mouth. He thinks it's funny too.

He raises his beer bottle, gesturing for me to lift mine. We clink them together and he says, "To Shania."

I repeat, "To Shania." I take a swig of the ice-cold liquid.

Laughter from the front door alerts us to Violet's arrival home.

I know who that other giggle belongs to.

Skye.

"Hello, you two." Violet bounces into the living room.

"How was pole-dancing class?" Lincoln asks as Violet smacks a kiss on his cheek.

Skye steps into the living room and my heart almost stops. Silver hair piled high, she's wearing a pale pink crop top and matching yoga leggings, leaving nothing to my imagination.

Although, I no longer have to imagine anymore. I've seen her, every inch of her, naked.

"Pole-dancing classes are shit. I'm terrible." Violet rolls her eyes. "And Skye landed on her head tonight. Funny as hell, though."

Skye looks across at me shyly.

Well, this is new. How do we behave around our friends now? After what we did together? In secret.

Concerned, I ask Skye, "Did you hurt yourself?"

She reaches up to touch her head. "Yeah. I have a bump."

"Do you have an ice pack?" I ask Lincoln.

Lincoln shakes his head, mumbling, "You've got it so fucking bad." He pushes himself to his feet.

"Please don't fuss, I'm okay. Honestly." She rests her hand on Lincoln's forearm when he passes.

"Alcohol will help." He exits and heads to the kitchen to get the girls a drink.

"Just a little one. Prosecco, if you have it." Skye bounces her shoulders up to her ears. "I'm working tomorrow." She walks around and slides gracefully onto the seat next to me.

"Aren't we all? You can get a taxi home," Violet suggests as she chases after Lincoln.

Shoulder to shoulder, an awkward silence dances between us.

Keeping my voice low, I say, "I sent you a text."

"I was just heading into dance classes when you sent it. I haven't had a chance to reply," she whispers back.

Turning her body round to face me, she says, "Hi." I love her soft voice.

"Hey, Butterfly." I lift my hand to her cheek, but I stop myself and rest it back on my lap.

"I missed you today." She looks at me, then looks away. "And thank you for my new stylus pen. You didn't need to get me one." She fiddles with her shoelaces on her sneaker like she's nervous.

"You are more than welcome. You're right, I didn't have to, but I wanted to."

I had bought a new one and left it on her office desk.

Changing position to face her, I swivel around in my seat. "This is so hard," I confess. "What I wouldn't give to bite the curve of your neck." I move my mouth to the shell of your ear, then blow softly against her neck.

"That feels nice," she says breathlessly, tilting her head to the side.

"You like that?"

"I do." She almost moans.

So close now, but not touching, I let out a long gasp of hot breath on the spot she wants me to, causing her to shudder.

"Oh, yes, I love that." She sounds contented.

"I'll remember that for the future."

"If only we could now."

"Soon." I'm praying it's soon. I'm praying for all the yesterdays I missed and the tomorrows I want to be a part of. "Soon, Butterfly." I can't make any promises, but I want to. "Then I will do so many sinful things to this beautiful body of yours," I whisper into her ear.

"I can't wait another minute."

"You'll have to."

She pulls in a breath. "I just... just so much... I want..."

"To touch?"

She wrinkles her nose. "Yeah." She lets out a frustrated sigh.

Where the fuck is Owen?

A tendril of hair escapes her updo and she pushes it behind her ear. "You don't have to call me tonight anymore. You've seen me now."

"I'd like to see more of you," I admit.

"I need to record a tutorial for my video channel, you naughty boy. You're a bad distraction."

"You're a fucking nice distraction." She catches me staring at the hard outline of her nipples.

"Behave."

The faint sound of Violet and Lincoln messing about in the kitchen drifts into the room.

I change the subject because I might just push her against the sofa and devour her if we keep up this level of teasing. "Tell me about your video channel. Do you take your clothes off? 'Cause if you do, I might just go a wee bit crazy." I put her off the scent that I already watch her channel and know every fucking thing about it.

For the next couple of minutes, she tells me everything there is to know. "And the best thing ever happened. I am going to be speaking at a local arts group." She grabs her phone to show me their website and social media presence and chatters away excitedly. "I'm meeting the group leader tomorrow for coffee to discuss my tutorial for them."

Thank Christ she's meeting them in a public place.

"Her name is Jules, and she's very excited to meet me."

Congratulations, Mr. Baxter, it's a girl!

Thank fuck for that.

She rests her elbow on the back of the sofa and looks at me with mischief in her eyes. "I have something to show you later."

"Oh, do you now?"

She bunny-twitches her nose. "Yeah."

"Here we go. Prosecco." Violet appears with her dog, Pom-pom, hot on her heels. "Oh, sorry, I'm not disturbing anything, am I?"

"Nope. We were discussing a project timeframe. Boring stuff," she lies. "Hey, boy, come sit on my knee." She picks up the tiny dog and rests him on her lap.

For the next hour we chat shit about everything and nothing and then we get onto the subject of our childhood in Castleview Cove.

"I love Castleview. Not at first, but it didn't take me long to fall in love with our little town." Skye rubs her hands down her thighs. "I was so nervous when I started my first day at school. Jacob made it better, though."

"Did you hang about with the guys at school, Skye?" Violet snuggles into Lincoln's shoulder.

"Yeah, from the first day. Jacob invited me for lunch." She lifts one shoulder to her ear. "And that was our friendship sealed."

"I bet you three boys all fought over her." Violet eyes me, smiling against her champagne flute.

"Nope. Owen and Skye started dating about six months after she arrived here." Lincoln stops, his brows pinching together. "Am I right?"

Skye nods in agreement.

"I bet you are kicking yourself now, Lincoln. Skye is quite a catch." Violet is fucking playing with me.

"We've kissed," Skye laughs.

"No, we haven't." Lincoln rubs his hand across the dark scruff on his jaw. "Have we?"

"Lewis Mitchel's party. A few months after I moved here. We played truth or dare."

Deep in thought, Lincoln looks up to the left.

"Your dare was to kiss me," Skye informs him.

Fuck, fuck, fuck.

As if remembering, his whole face lights up, then he smiles. "Yeah, no, eh, that wasn't me that kissed you."

Shut up, Lincoln.

"Yes, it was, silly," Skye giggles. "I was given a blindfold, made to go into the hall closet and wait in the dark for you, and then you came in and kissed me. With tongues and everything." She plays with her fingers. "My first kiss."

I subtly draw a line across my neck, trying to get him to stop saying the words I think he's going to say.

"It was most definitely not me."

Bastard.

"Huh?" Her mouth twists in confusion.

"It was Jay." He points at me.

She whips around to look at me. "You were my first kiss?" she almost yells.

I force a smile, annoyed at myself that I never told her. "You were my first kiss, too," I confess.

"No way," she exclaims, her lips parting in shock.

"Sounds like a memorable first kiss." Violet smirks, hiding behind her glass again.

Tomorrow, I'm going to put an advert out looking for new friends. Violet and Lincoln are a pair of schemers.

"Jacob kind of had a thing for you in high school. So, I let him take my place." Lincoln takes another long mouthful of his beer.

"Will you shut the hell up, Lincoln?" I'm suddenly aware of how hot I am all over.

Skye pushes for more information. "So, you kissed me before Owen did?"

"I did," I say so low I'm surprised she heard me.

"And that would have overruled your silly no exes agreement?"

Lincoln jumps in. "Technically, no. You weren't dating Owen or Jay. It was just a game."

"It was more than *a game and a kiss*." Her voice is laced with annoyance as she shoots up to her feet and stomps out of the room.

I place my beer on the coffee table to go after her. "Nice one, douche canoe."

"I thought she would find it funny." He pinches the bridge of his nose. "I'm sorry. I totally misjudged that."

"Oh, Lincoln." Violet slaps him playfully across the back of his head.

As I step out of the living room into the hall, Lincoln's front door swings wide open.

Oh, fuck off, Owen. Not now.

"Hey, man." He slams the thick wooden door closed behind him. "Thought I would just fly in to see you before I head out to Barcelona on business for a couple of weeks. I'm off to that stupid digital factories expo we go to every year."

"Skye's here," I blurt.

And she's just found out I kissed her before you did.

"Good. I need to speak to her."

"And I need to speak to you. I've been trying to contact you for days."

"Can it wait until I'm back? I'm only staying for one drink and then heading home to pack. I'm on the red-eye flight." He pushes his fingers through his blond floppy hair. "Sorry, Jay. I've been so busy with one thing and another."

"Sure," I say, defeated. *What will another few weeks matter? I've been waiting my whole life for her.*

Maybe it's an omen and someone in the heavens doesn't want Skye and me to be together.

"Hey, buddy," Lincoln shouts through the living-room doorway.

Owen throws him a wave. "Hey, guys."

I must admit, he's looking better than he did when he was at my house. Shaven, haircut, and his clothes are freshly pressed again.

His mother has probably seen to it that he gets back on the straight and narrow. Because *whatever will the Muircrofts think of him?*

Owen spots Skye hunched over the kitchen island. He points in her direction.

"I'm just heading to the bathroom," I lie and hop onto the first step of the stairs. I don't want to hear what he has to say to her.

18

SKYE

"I don't want to talk to you, Owen." I'm already in a weird mood after Lincoln's admissions and seeing him reminds me how pissed off I am that I wasted fourteen years doing a relationship jig with Owen when I could, sorry, *should*, have been with Jacob all along. I think I would have been happier with him. My ever after.

"So you keep saying."

I finally lift my head to look at him. "You look well."

"Because I looked like shit before?"

"I already know you're getting married, if that's what you want to talk to me about."

"Where the hell did you hear that? It's not public knowledge." Realization falls over his face. "Jay and Linc?"

I nod.

"It's complicated," he tells me like that's enough of an explanation.

"Everything is complicated at the moment, it would seem."

"How? What's up with you?"

"Nothing," I mumble. "Anyway, if that's what you wanted to talk to me about, I don't care."

He walks over to me, lifts my hand off the kitchen island, and turns me to face him. "We haven't spoken properly for over a month. You won't speak to me or return my calls. I know I've been so wrapped up in myself, but I need to know you're doing okay." He slides both his hands down my arms and threads his fingers with mine.

The familiarity of our relationship is easy to find in his touch, but it's not a relationship I want anymore. Owen and I are only friends and have been for a really long time.

I screw my face up. "Why the hell would you start caring now?" I try pulling my hands away, but he refuses to let go.

"I always cared for you, baby." He gives me his puppy-dog eyes.

"Don't touch me. And don't call me baby."

He looks hurt. "What's going on with you?"

"We wasted years together. When I could have been with someone who would burn down an entire city for me. Or pick me up from the garage when they are meant to, or have a tattoo branded into their skin that's dedicated to me." Shit, I shouldn't have said that, but I'm mad. At him. Us. Me.

Stroking his chin, he watches me carefully. "I'm sorry that I never made you feel special."

I don't want to fight with him, and I hate confrontation. Harmony is more my jam. Conflict, not so much. Although this is probably the reason we dragged on for as long as we did. I was too much of a wimp to confront him.

"You make me sound like a prize prick and you know we shared some great times too. Don't you remember?"

I actually can't.

"The party at my parents' house when we drank champagne in the bath."

Only because his mother was pissing him off and he was hiding from her.

"One weekend I took you to the Grand National Ladies Day."

It rained all day, and he spent most of his time talking to clients. I did win a hundred pounds on one of the horse races though.

"We were good together. You've just forgotten."

He's delusional.

"And we were good sexually, too. You can't deny that, Skye."

"I suppose so."

"Give me a chance to remind you. Spend the night with me? For old times' sake." He cups my face with his familiar hand, the ones that have been all over my body. The only man I have ever let touch me intimately before.

The sound of the front door slamming shakes the house.

I stand, looking up into his wide, expectant eyes.

"I've met someone," I tell him.

"What?" He grits his teeth.

"I've moved on." He's in no position to be mad. "Maybe you should go home to Evangeline. Isn't she waiting there for you? Made you a three-course meal? Wearing the perfect string of pearls for you and fertile, willing, and able to spawn and expand your Brodie empire?"

"What the fuck, Skye?" His hand slips off my skin.

"You know I'm right and please, I mean it, don't ever touch me again." I don't know where my inner confidence has come from. I should have had the backbone to speak my mind when I was with him.

I leave him standing there.

Walking back into the living room not expecting to find Violet, I'm surprised when she's sitting snuggled up with Lincoln and Pom-pom.

"Did you not go out for a walk with the dog? I thought I heard someone go out?"

"Jacob left." Lincoln pauses. "He overheard you and Owen talking." He lowers his voice, looking awkward.

"Oh, bumheads. I have to go." I pick up my backpack from the entryway and shout bye.

"He's walking," Lincoln calls.

"Where the hell is she going? And where's Jay?" Owen asks Lincoln and Violet.

Pulling the door closed, my sneakers crunch underfoot as I kick up the gravel with my swift motion.

And then I sprint down Cherry Gardens Lane to the man who makes my heart race. The man I feel so deeply in my soul is made perfectly for me; the man I don't ever think I can live without.

19

JACOB

"Jacob." A voice calls my name from behind me.

I stop in my tracks and whip around to discover Skye running faster than a whippet, down the darkened street.

She smiles wider than the Golden Gate Bridge. Thumbs hooked into her backpack straps, she waggles her free fingers to wave to me. She's so fucking cute. Her usual neat buns are now a complete mess as she bounces toward me.

"Oh my God, you walk so fast," she pants, her hot breath creating billows of clouds into the chilly night.

"Where's your jacket?" I ask.

"I don't have one. I got a lift with Violet."

I pull my arms out of my black leather jacket and lay it over her shoulders like a cloak.

"Thank you." She grabs the collar and pulls it around her neck before she bends at the waist and grabs her knees. "My lungs are burning. I can't run," she says through struggling breaths.

"What are you doing running in the dark?" I push my

hands into my pockets to keep them warm, pulling my shoulders up to my neck.

"To get you, silly."

"I thought you'd be spending *one last night for old times' sake* with Owen?" I feel sick to my stomach at the thought of his hands on Skye. Jealousy is a familiar but unattractive trait of mine when it comes to her.

"You are such a doofus." She stands up straight again. "Urgh, my heart is beating so fast. You should feel it."

I step back.

She's a temptress. It'd be really easy for me to place my hand between her boobs.

But I don't.

"If you had stayed around, you would have heard me telling Owen where to shove it and also..." She takes another deep breath, puffing and panting, as she tries to get her words out. "I told him that I'd met someone."

In utter disbelief, I open my mouth to say something, but no words come out.

"He's a doofus too. But you're a gorgeous doofus, and you're my doofus." Then she throws me a megawatt smile. One that melts me to my core.

"You haven't changed a bit, you know that? You still look like the girl who sat beside me in high school."

"Because I still behave like a child?" she jests.

"No, because you've barely aged."

She taps her foot against mine playfully. "So you were my first kiss?"

"Yeah." Baring my teeth, I cringe. "About that."

"I shouldn't have gotten upset when Lincoln told me. It was a beautiful first kiss."

"It was?" I ask in disbelief. For me, it was an incredible first kiss. A kiss of all kisses. One I have never forgotten.

"The best. Are you sure you'd never kissed anyone else before me? You French-kissed me like an expert."

"First kiss," I confirm. "Also, my first boob squeeze."

She snorts. "Why didn't you tell me afterward and then ask me out?"

"Because Owen beat me to it two days later."

"Even though you told him you'd kissed me?"

"Yeah."

"Jay," she whispers and her eyes go soft with emotion.

"Don't feel sorry for me. I only have myself to blame. I'm not that same guy anymore."

"You're really not." Her eyes linger on my tattooed arms. She licks her lips. "You have huge muscles now. How often do you go to the gym?"

"Almost every day. Do you like my arms?"

"I love your arms. Your tattoos are so sexy and the whole bulging bicep thing is..." She fans her face with her hand. "So hot."

I wink. "Keep imagining what my body will feel like pressed against you."

She whimpers. "Stop, Jay, or I might drag you into the bushes and let you show me."

"If only."

"If only," she repeats.

I have to change the subject because there is no way I can give in to temptation now. "Owen is away for a few weeks, then I'll speak to him."

"Okay. I wish it was sooner." She sighs, looking around, and shivers. "I don't like the dark," she whispers.

"C'mon." I summon her to move. "Let's quick-march into town and grab a cab."

"Good idea."

"Give me your backpack and I'll carry it."

"Just like old times, when you used to walk me home from school? I have fond memories of you walking with me."

"Good times."

"There are always better times to come." She bumps her shoulder against mine as we begin the walk into town.

20

SKYE

"Do you want to come in for a coffee?" I look into the back seats of the taxi where Jacob is sitting.

Doubt lines furrow his brows. "Um."

"It's just coffee." I wink. "Promise."

"What about the tutorial you need to record?" His hands squeeze the knees of his widened legs.

I flippantly wave my hand. "It can wait until tomorrow, and besides, I have something to show you."

He rubs his hand over his buzz cut a couple of times.

"Just a coffee, Jacob," I reassure him.

Before I know it, we are sitting on my bed together, with our hands around our hot mugs of sweetened steaming coffee.

I brought Jacob up to my bedroom because I'm not sure when Kimmy is due home from work, and I wanted some privacy in case she does come home early.

"Is it weird that I can't stop looking at you?" I ask.

He rolls his head to the side. "Nah." Mischief twinkles in his eyes as if to say, *I've been doing the same to you for years.*

He made himself at home as soon as he walked through the door. Scanning my bookshelves, just like he used to do in my childhood room. Pulling a few out to read the blurbs on the back.

He even picked up my still working iPod I got for my sixteenth birthday, scrolling through the list of songs, nodding in approval at my music taste.

It feels nice; him being here feels natural. Like he belongs.

"So, what did you have to show me?" he asks.

Placing my coffee on the nightstand, I pull off my sneaker, then remove my ankle sock.

Out of curiosity, he leans forward to see what I'm doing. I stand tall and lift my foot to rest it on the edge of the mattress.

I ease off the protective film around my ankle to reveal my surprise.

He dips his head to get a better look. "You got a tattoo?" he gasps, his voice barely a whisper but full of admiration.

"Yeah, yesterday."

He studies it carefully. "It's really cool. Wow! Who did you go to?"

"Vance at The Bodyworks in the city."

"That's who I go to." He looks up. "He's the best."

Well, there's a coincidence. I didn't know Jacob goes there.

"He squeezed me in." I grin. "Do you know what it is?"

"A bird."

"You are so literal." I try hard not to roll my eyes. "It's a special type of bird."

"A blue one."

I snort. "Yup, a blue one. But it's called a blue jay."

He looks back at my new three-inch watercolor body art.

"A blue jay?" He bites the side of his mouth.

"Yeah. Blue for me. But jay is for you, and can you see what color his eyes are?"

"Green," he says, oh so quietly.

"The same emerald-green as yours."

He gulps so loudly it echoes around the room. "You got a blue jay with green eyes tattooed on your ankle for me?" His eyes never leave my skin as he points to his black-tee-shirt-covered chest.

"Yeah. Do you like it?"

"I think I want to fucking marry you right now. That is so fucking sexy."

His words do things to my heart, making it feel like a field of butterflies is dancing in it, and I don't think he's realized the enormity of his words.

"It's still a bit red. He said it would settle in a few days. I have some antibacterial ointment to put on. I must remember to do that before I go to bed."

"Go get it and I'll put it on for you," he says, unable to stop looking at me.

He follows me to the bathroom, and I grab the cream while he washes his hands in the sink.

When we return to the room, he sits down on the bed and tells me to lie back on the pillows and rest my ankle on his broad thigh.

He pops open the tube and squeezes out an inch of ointment along the pad of his thick forefinger.

"I'm serious about us," I say dreamily.

He covers the soothing balm across my newly inked skin with such tenderness.

I sigh with contentment.

He lifts my ankle and kisses the outer perimeter of my

tattoo. Peering at me, his lips lift away from my skin. "Feel better?"

"Much."

He bends my knee toward my chest and lays my foot flat against the mattress. From the foot of the bed, he crawls toward me.

I spread my legs wide to welcome him.

His eyes never leave mine as he hovers over me, never touching me once.

Looking up into his lust-filled eyes, my heart hammers in anticipation.

"I want to show you how grateful I am."

I can't speak.

"Take off your leggings," he commands, and I'm powerless to resist.

He sits back on his heels and watches me as I whip them off, being careful not to nudge my new tattoo.

I spread my legs wider so he can get a better look.

"You're wet for me already, aren't you? Your panties are soaked." He licks his lips. "Now, take off the panties."

I push them off my hips and nod because I don't seem to be able to form words anymore.

"Now spread yourself wide again, Butterfly. Your pussy is fucking beautiful." His words cause a heavy ache of need between my legs. "Do you have a vibrating friend?"

"Yes." I blush before scrambling around in the drawer of my nightstand and pull it out.

Smiling, he quickly takes it out of my hand and spits on it.

Holy fucking shit, I didn't expect him to do that.

He passes it back to me, and with his voice dripping with desire, he instructs me what to do next. "Now touch yourself."

I take it from him and glide it down my pussy lips before I talk myself out of it. Having only ever been with one man, this is all so new, scary as hell, but so exciting.

"Don't power it on yet." He rubs his hand over his now semi-erect length through his jeans. "Let me see that lovely little clit of yours."

I continue to rub myself back and forth with the toy, using my fingertips to gently open myself up for him.

He tries to contain his gasp by biting his bottom lip with his teeth. "Rub your clit with the toy, then turn it on."

Circling my clit once, then twice, desperate to come, I click on the power button.

His groan rumbles deep in his chest.

A whimper escapes my throat when the vibration of the toy hits my swollen bud.

"How does it feel, Butterfly?" he rasps.

"So good, Jay. So, so good. I wish it was you touching me." I arch my back off the bed.

"How bad do you need to come?"

"So bad, Jay. I want you. So, so bad," I stutter.

"Imagine it's me. Imagine it's my fingers pressed against you. Now fuck yourself." His velvety voice, low and raspy now, vibrates through my body, adding to the sensations that are overwhelming me.

I tease the tip at my entrance before inserting the wand, sliding it deep so the little bunny ears touch my clit. My body clenches around the vibrator as the burn of it spreading me slowly transforms into pleasure.

"God, Skye, you look so beautiful. I wish it was me inside you right now. What I wouldn't give to feel how tight and wet you are for me."

His words push me to the edge. My body begins to tingle as the telltale feeling of my orgasm building takes hold.

I move the toy in and out of my body faster.

"Aw, fuck, yeah, just like that, Butterfly."

"I won't last," I pant.

"Then come for me." His face disappears between my legs and there's a sudden burst of warm air on my clit unlike anything I've ever felt.

I look down and watch him as he blows again and again, the unfamiliar sensation working me into a frenzy.

I push the toy further into my body and hold it deep to rub against my G-spot. Between the vibrations and him blowing on my clit, a white-hot climax rips through me, causing my back to arch off the bed again as I dig my heels into the mattress for leverage. My heart pounds in my chest and I see stars that feel like burning flames of scorching heat.

"That's my good fucking girl."

I silently wish he would run his tongue up my inner thigh to give me a taste of what it will be like when he finally touches me between my legs.

Every inch of my body feels alive with energy, as if his commands and instructions have reached each and every nerve ending in my body.

"Such a good girl." His praise sends a wave of pleasure across my body.

Through hooded eyes, he continues to watch me come down from my high, my breath slowing to its normal pace.

I wince when I remove the vibrator as it tries to pull more pleasure from my body.

Jacob watches with fascination. "You are soaked." He bites his lip.

Tapping the power off, I don't get a chance to lower it to

the bed because he takes it from my fingertips and sucks the toy into his mouth, moaning loudly as he does.

Removing it from between his lips, he rests it on the bed. "You taste fucking amazing. Sweet like honey."

Between my legs, still fully exposed to him, he hovers back over me again. Looking down, he grins. "Thank you for the tattoo."

"Thank you for the orgasm."

His mouth twists up to one side in amusement. "No one has ever thanked me for making them come before."

I wrinkle my nose. I don't want to think about him with anyone else.

Detecting how uncomfortable that makes me feel, he says, "I'm so fucking hard for you. I'm going to have to go home and jerk off in the shower."

"I wish I could do that for you," I whisper teasingly through soft words.

"Me too," he groans, rubbing his hand over his hard length again. "You're all I can think about." Carnal ferocity burns in his eyes.

"You seem like a dream. One blink, and *poof*, you might just disappear, and we won't get our happy ending," I admit.

"Neither of us is going anywhere. Whatever difficulties we face, we'll face them together."

"But what if I get kidnapped by a horrible prince who wants to do unspeakable things to me and lock me in his castle?" I go all out on my *The Princess Bride* themed question.

"Have you seen the size of my sword?"

I laugh at his silliness. "You'd rescue me?"

"I would fucking die for you."

"Don't die for me; we need the happy-ever-after part."

"Okay." He rolls his eyes. "Until then, *my* happy ending is waiting for me, in my shower, at home. With Palm and her five friends." He lifts his hand from the mattress and wiggles his fingers.

He lightens the moment and all my concerns about us subside.

At least until tomorrow.

21

SKYE

Drumming my fingers against the wooden tabletop, I sit in the coffee shop, waiting patiently for Jules to appear.

Inhaling the scent of comforting coffee reminds me of coming here with my mom when I was younger. With fall now firmly taking hold, the dark nights are drawing in. As if someone flicked a switch, it's dark by six o'clock.

I shiver, imagining the impending snow that's on its way in a few months.

"Hey." A male voice appears at my table.

I find myself looking up at a portly-looking gentleman. Wild curly brown hair, with eyes to match. He looks nervous as he stands, staring at me.

"Hi," I reply, hoping this stranger leaves me alone.

"I'm Jules. From the local art group."

I snap my head back to look at him.

Oh, what a fool I've been; I thought Jules was a girl, not a man.

I'm too stunned to say anything as he takes a seat on the opposite side of the table. "And you must be Skye?" He pushes his hand out for me to shake. "I recognize you from your video channel."

I stare at him.

"Annddd you look like you're not expecting me." His face falls.

I wiggle in my seat uncomfortably. "Sorry. I was—well—" I stutter.

"Expecting a woman?" He smiles. "I get that a lot."

"Yeah." I shake my head. "Gosh, sorry, forgive my terrible manners. Let's start again." I hold my hand out for him to take this time. "Pleased to finally meet you, Jules. I'm Skye." Getting over my initial shock, I try to be polite.

"Pleased to meet you too, Skye." His hand feels clammy.

"What would you like to drink?" I start to push my chair back, but Jules stops me, informing me he'll get his own.

While he waits in the queue, I sit scrolling through my emails to see if there was any indication whatsoever that Jules was a man.

But there's nothing.

I pull up my video channel and check some of the comments from his username—Crazy4Blue.

You look so pretty today.

I am obsessed with your work.

I am your biggest fan!

I naturally assumed Jules was a woman. Then I invited him for coffee.

What a fool you are, Skye.

My only saving grace is that we are in a public place and he seems okay. Nervous. But okay.

Placing my phone back on the table, I try to shake the feeling of unease gnawing at me.

"I got you a bun," Jules says as he reappears and lifts the plated sweet treat off the tray and passes me it, then places his hot tea and cake down.

"I am starving." I lick my lips. "Thank you so much."

He waddles over to the service area, disposes of the tray, and sits himself back down at our table.

"So..." I wait a couple of seconds, not really knowing what to say.

I tug my skirt down, suddenly aware I'm sitting opposite a strange man. "So you would like me to talk at your creative arts group? Can you tell me more about it?" I start.

Jules dives straight into enthusiastic mode when he explains more.

He seems nice enough, although, on closer inspection, he could do with scrubbing under his filthy fingernails. Clearly, he's been painting today. His crumpled shirt is missing a couple of buttons, too.

Jules is a little eccentric, to say the least, with his clashing-colored clothing, paisley patterned bow tie, and unbrushed nest of hair.

He looks like a typical fine artist, choosing to buy tubes of paint over clothes. I know what one of them looks like; I spent enough time with them at art college.

Alerting me to a notification, my smart watch vibrates on my wrist.

JACOB

Who's the dude?

Subtly twisting my head to the side, there he is, five tables over, watching me like a hungry lion waiting to pounce on his prey.

I lift my phone from the table, nodding and smiling at Jules as he continues to chatter away.

He pauses for a moment, watching me as I look at my phone. "I'm just going to check my schedule to see when I'm available for the group," I lie, pulling up my text message app instead.

ME

It's Jules.

He takes no time to reply. Three texts fly in back to back.

JACOB

I thought he was a she????!!!!! WTF, Skye?

JACOB

Do you feel safe?

I almost burst out laughing at his texting meltdown.

ME

Calm down, big guy. He's okay.

JACOB

And he's Crazy4Blue?

ME

How do you know that?

The reply dots bounce on my screen.

JACOB

I knew you had a channel. I've been watching you since you started.

ME

See, I told you... Stalker!

JACOB

Pervert... remember?! *winking face*

Announcing the arrival of another customer, the doorbell of the coffee shop dings. A beautiful white-blonde-haired woman steps through the door, bringing with her an unwelcomed bracing gust of wind as she snicks the door closed again.

I follow her path, and my tummy swirls with a sudden pang of jealousy when Jacob rises to greet her.

Bleurgh. That must be Verity. Seeing them together again, I'm reminded just how similar her hair color is to mine. I try not to think back to that Saturday in the office because the thought of Jacob inside her makes me want to vomit.

Unable to watch the two of them, I go back to pretending to check my schedule.

"What date works for you then?" Jules, who I'd completely forgotten about, pipes up.

I shake my head. "Sorry. Yeah, so. What about next Wednesday? Would that work?"

"Perfect." He firmly taps the tabletop as if sealing the deal.

I make a quick note on my phone and excuse myself. "I'll be right back."

Strutting across the coffee shop, quicker than normal, I try hard not to look Jacob's way, but I fail, discovering the two of them laughing like old friends... or familiar lovers.

My hand finds my stomach. *I feel sick.*

Sick with envy.

I quickly enter the bathroom, pee, then leave the bathroom stall.

Not wanting to exit the restrooms and have to see them again, I take my time to wash my hands.

The door swings open, and Jacob's broad frame fills the doorway.

Oh great.

"Hey," I mumble. Not looking at him, I walk over to the hand towels and grab a couple to dry my hands.

"Hi." He eats up the space between us and is by my side in a heartbeat. "I'm here to break up with her. Well, not break up 'cause we aren't together," he explains. "You know what I mean. Call it a day. Even though we haven't been together for weeks, but to stop our Saturday night..."

"Fucking sessions," I finish his sentence.

"Hookups."

I don't know why I am mad or jealous. We aren't even dating.

"Look at me," he demands.

Head bowed, I look up to meet his concerned gaze.

"Skye, I made you a promise. I am ending things with Verity. Next stop is talking to Owen as soon as he's back from Barcelona."

I lean against the vanity unit and let out a long breath. "I don't think I'm coping very well with how quickly things are moving between us, but so slow all at the same time." I stare down at the floor. "And I know it would be so easy to fall in love with you," I almost whisper. "I'm already feeling things for you that I never felt for Owen." I scrunch my nose.

He places a knuckle under my chin to tilt it up.

"Easy to fall in love with, huh?"

"I mean it." It's the truth. "I don't like Verity," I blurt, not meaning to. "I'm jealous of the fact that she's been with you in ways I can only dream of," I sigh.

He runs the back of his knuckles along my jaw. "She means nothing to me because I am so fucking in love with you, Skye McNairn, and I would never do anything to fuck up this chance I have with you. Finally, I feel like this could be it. Us. Together. I met her here because I knew you'd be here. I saw your calendar. I have nothing to hide and I wanted to show you that with every inch of my heart, I am all yours. You're all I want. All I see." He spreads his arms wide as if to say, *take me*. "The things we've done together. I haven't even touched you yet, but it's better than any sex I have ever had with anyone. You are *it* for me."

His words register in my brain. "Where have you been all of my life?"

"Waiting for you."

"I want to kiss you."

"I am *not* having our first kiss in a bathroom."

"Our second," I remind him, making him smile.

"I've waited all this time. I can wait a little longer. I would wait a lifetime for you, Skye. I know the perfect time is coming."

"How do you know?" My eyes search his for answers.

"I feel it, way down deep in my soul. I just know."

I grab his tie, pulling him closer to me. His head bows slightly and for a moment, I think he's going to kiss me, but he doesn't.

"You're sweet when you want to be."

"Don't tell anyone. I have a reputation to uphold."

Lips inches away from each other, I can feel his breath against my skin as we smile together.

Suddenly, a customer flies through the bathroom door, laughing her head off. Immediately, Jacob steps back, his tie slipping from my fingers, breaking our connection.

"Oh, sorry." She makes her way into one of the bathroom stalls.

Through the opened wedge of the door, I see Jules, standing on the other side of the corridor. For a moment, he scowls and his entire face changes as if he is mad. He clenches his jaw tight, making his cheek twitch, then, as if with the flick of a switch, he throws me a smile that almost looks forced. Then he disappears back down the corridor to our seats.

"I need to go. Verity is still out there waiting for me."

"I'm sorry for being a buffoon," I murmur.

"I like you being jealous. It tells me you care." He straightens his tie. "And you are not a buffoon. You're a beautiful butterfly. Text me when you get home, yeah?"

I nod in agreement.

I point to the door, urging him to leave before me.

He winks knowingly and slips out.

Waiting a few minutes, I head back into the coffee shop to find Jules sitting, waiting patiently for me.

I plonk myself down on the chair and try to avoid staring at Jacob anymore. "Sorry, I bumped into my boss. He wanted to talk about a project."

"No worries. You haven't eaten your bun." He points to it.

"How could I forget about that?" I dig into it, finishing every crumb, while Jules continues to distract me with his endless chitchat.

I lick my fingertips. "That was yummy. Just what I needed."

"Finish the last of your coffee and I'll walk you to your car," Jules suggests as he finishes his cup of tea.

Jules and I finish up and make our way to the exit.

I glance to my left and Jacob gives me a quick wink.

My watch vibrates again.

Text me when you get home, please. xoxo

I reply with a thumbs up emoji.

As soon as the cold air hits me, I suddenly feel a little woozy.

"Woah." I sway on my feet.

"Are you okay?" Jules looks at me, his sweaty forehead wrinkled with concern.

"Yeah." I rub my temples. "Must be going from hot then into the cold."

"Let's find your car. The sooner you're home, the better."

"It must have been the bun. I feel sick." I stagger, almost tripping. "Oh God, I don't feel so good." My voice sounds strange as if I'm listening to it from outside of my body.

"Here, pass me your backpack." Jules holds his hand out to take it from me.

Walking another thirty steps or so, my stomach lurches.

I've never taken drugs, but I'm sure this must be what it feels like. My body feels like it's made out of rubber.

"You can't drive like that, Skye. C'mon, I'll take you home."

"I feel so silly. You don't have to do that. My boss is back there." Stumbling, I try turning around, but Jules ushers me up the unlit alleyway past the coffee shop.

"I'll take you home," he says more firmly.

"I can't see straight," I cry in horror as the edges of my vision blur.

A hand lands on my arm to help steady me. From my side, I hear Jules' distorted voice. "I've got you. My car is just here."

Jules loops his arms around me to keep me upright because I can barely put one foot in front of the other.

"Here we are."

I squint my eyes, trying to see the car, but all I can see are the faint outlines of random objects. Nothing makes sense.

I want to scream for Jacob, but my mouth refuses to form his name. In fact, I can't say a word.

The click of a door is the next thing I hear, and then I feel myself being bundled into what must be Jules' car.

"Let's strap you in the back seat to keep you safe. We don't want anything happening to you now, do we? No, we do not," he chuckles. His voice sends a strange cold shiver in my soul.

The last thing I remember is Jules' faint words. "You're safe with me now, my beautiful Skye..."

Jacob, help me.

22

JACOB

I glance up from my tablet screen and look around the boardroom table, searching for Skye.

She's not here yet, which is totally out of character.

She didn't text me last night when she got home like she promised she would either.

I figured she was too busy doing her weekly video tutorial for her channel. When she gets focused on something, the whole office could go on fire, and she wouldn't notice.

She didn't reply to my text this morning either.

Not wanting to come across as a paranoid boyfriend, because we're not quite there yet, I didn't want to call. But I have to admit, I'm beyond worried now.

"Where's Skye?" I ask.

Every member of my team shakes their head and looks around the room.

"Did she take a sick day? Anyone know?" I ask no one in particular.

As if a rusty nail is scraping along the pit of my stomach, a gnawing sensation takes hold.

I pull my phone out of my pocket, locate her number, and call it.

Going straight to voicemail, I leave her a message before I hang up.

"Shona, please check with human resources to see if she's called in sick today."

My assistant pushes her chair back and heads out to check Skye's status.

"We'll wait for Shona to come back," I inform the room.

While I'm waiting, I text Violet asking if she's heard from Skye.

She messages me straight back with a no.

Fuck.

Shona steps into the room with a downturned mouth. "She hasn't called in."

"Meeting postponed. We aren't doing this without her."

As everyone filters out of the boardroom, I ask Shona, "Do you know where Skye's roommate, Kimmy, is working now? Is she still at The Vault?" Kimmy changes job every two months. I can never keep up with where she works.

"Still at The Vault," she confirms.

"Can you get me her number?"

"On it." She lifts her phone off the table and within two minutes, I'm calling Kimmy.

On my feet now, I pace back and forth across the room.

Kimmy picks up. "Hello." Her groggy voice greets me.

"Hi, it's Jacob Baxter."

"Urgh, morning."

"Sorry to bother you, but we haven't heard from Skye today. Is she sick?"

"I don't think so. I was on the late shift last night and the house was dark when I came in." She yawns down the phone. "Let me go check. What time is it?" she mumbles to herself.

"It's quarter past nine." Skye is usually the first one in here and the last one to leave.

A few shuffles and the opening of a door drifts down the earpiece of my phone.

"Her bed looks untouched." With a hitch in her voice, Kimmy sounds concerned. "Let me check downstairs."

Looking out the office window across the wild sea of the cove, I clench my fist.

Where are you, Butterfly?

I hear Kimmy running down the stairs. She's silent for a few moments and I assume she's searching the house.

"She's not here."

"Is her car outside?" My stomach begins tying itself in knots.

There's a pause. "No."

"Have you not heard from her at all?" My pulse is now racing.

"No. But I've been working late most nights. It's normal for me not to see her. Did you try calling her?"

I grit my teeth together. "Of course I tried calling her, Kimmy, or I wouldn't be calling you."

"Geez, take a chill pill."

I try a calmer approach. "I've called her. It goes to voice-mail. She didn't text me last night to tell me she was home safe after leaving the coffee shop. She hasn't called in sick and she didn't book a day off for today. So, where the fuck is she?" Unable to hold in my anguish, my voice raises as I speak. "This isn't like her, Kimmy."

"Oh..." She has a sudden thought. "We have the Find My Phone app. We have that on our phones to keep tabs on each other. She will have stayed at Owen's or something, Jacob. Be cool."

Her words are like a knife to my heart, even though I know she wouldn't do that to me.

"Owen is in Barcelona. Check that app. Now," I yell as I pinch the bridge of my nose.

"Okay, okay. Calm your shit."

Feeling hot, blood racing through my body at a million miles an hour, I tug off my tie and undo the top three buttons of my shirt.

"Not found," she whispers. "Last location..." she reads from the app, "...the alleyway past the coffee shop."

"What?" I cry. "So she never made it home?"

"Were you with her at the coffee shop?"

"Yes... No... I was with someone else, and Skye had a meeting with this guy she made friends with. He runs some fucking arts group or some shit. She met him through her video chan—" I stop speaking and fall into my chair. "Oh, my fucking God."

"What is it, Jacob?"

"She's with him." I fling my hand to my pounding heart as I feel like I'm having a heart attack. "The guy from the coffee shop. The guy from her video channel. The guy who said he was a fucking girl!" I stand to my feet and kick a boardroom chair across the room. Hitting the wall with force, it makes a loud clattering noise and leaves a huge dent.

Shona screams, and my father comes running into the boardroom.

Of all the days for him to come into the office, he chooses today.

"Jacob," my father shouts at me forcefully. "What the hell do you think you are playing at?" he bellows.

I hold up my hand to say sorry. With my phone firmly held against my ear, I say, "Kimmy. Hang up the phone and call Skye's parents. Call them, ask if they've seen her and I'm going to call the police."

"Jacob?" Kimmy whispers.

I close my eyes and tilt my head back. "Yeah?"

"What if something happened to her?"

Then I will die in pain, with a broken heart, knowing I was fucking feet away from being able to help her.

"I'm sure she's fine. It's just a precaution," I say unconvincingly. "Give her mom and dad my number, please."

"Okay." And she hangs up.

"Jacob?" My father walks round the table in my direction. "What's going on?" Concern is written all over his face.

I cover my mouth with my hand, not believing the words I'm about to say. "I think Skye's missing."

"Phone the police." My dad lays both his hands on top of my shoulders. "Now."

23

JACOB

I'm sitting with my head in my hands on Skye's parents' sofa, answering questions the police detective keeps throwing at me.

The same questions she's asked me three times now.

I'm trying not to lose my patience, but it's hanging on by a thread.

"And that was the last time you saw her?" she asks again.

"Yes," I sigh frustratedly. "She left with a man named Jules. Although I don't even know if that's his name. He lied about his gender. How can we be sure of anything now?"

"Thank you for the clarification, Mr. Baxter." The sharp-nosed detective closes her notepad and looks at the uncertainty around the room.

I keep talking. I want her to know how serious this is and what I found out myself. "I looked up the creative arts group she said he was the founder of. It doesn't exist. I've checked Skye's video channel too, and all of his comments have disappeared. His username was Crazy4Blue."

That fucking name.

It all makes sense now, as everything starts slipping into place; he's crazy for her. I feel wretched.

"So are you saying he's just disappeared, Mr. Baxter?"

Like Skye. Vanished.

I keep sharing what I know. "Yes. Skye showed me the website for the art group the other night. There was even a social media presence. It's been taken down. The whole lot, just gone. He asked a lot of questions. What makeup did she wear? Where did she buy her clothes from? She, I mean, he, always said Skye had pretty eyes and told her how beautiful she was."

How did I miss this?

I look up, avoiding Skye's mom's anguished face. I can't handle it. She's been crying since I arrived.

She called me immediately after I called the police and I rushed to their family home.

Having spent hours in this house as a teenager, wanting to spend lots of time with Skye, I no longer want to be here.

Not like this, when my girl is missing, and no one knows where the hell she is.

My mood's about to go thermonuclear if they don't stop their line of questioning and start searching for her.

"Please find my baby," Mr. McNairn begs the police detective, his voice laced with pain while holding his wife tight.

Skye looks just like her mother; it's almost too painful to look at her.

Oh God, this is awful. Worse than awful. There are no words to describe the atmosphere of dread in the room. It's thick with unanswered questions. Desperation and fear all rolled into one weigh heavy on our shoulders.

"It's all my fault." I can't help saying what's playing on my mind.

"What makes you say that, Mr. Baxter?"

"Stop calling me that. I've told you, it's Jacob," I spit back, pushing my fingertips into my throbbing temples. "I'm sorry. I'm just worried. Should you not be out there looking for her?" I point to the street out the window.

The detective subtly nods, ignoring my question. "Jacob," she stalls, "what makes you say it's your fault?"

"I bought that tablet for her, the one she used to set up and create her video channel. That's how he found her. That's how he's been contacting her. Without that channel, she wouldn't be missing. It's all my fault," I admit guiltily, my voice full of anguished pain and apology.

What have I done?

"I was there last night when she met him. I should have made her wait for me. I would have taken her home myself. He said he was a girl!" I bellow, unable to hold it in any longer. "She told me it was a girl she was talking to online. I should have gone with her to meet her. I mean, him. Is it him? Does he have her?"

Skye's mom, Rhona, wails. "Oh no, my poor girl." She covers her mouth, trying to hold in her fear.

I'm making everything worse.

"I'm sorry. I shouldn't have said that."

A uniformed police officer ambles into the living room. "We found Skye's car. It's parked on Morris Way."

That's three streets over from the coffee shop. That's not the information I was hoping for. She's been gone all night. Without a trace.

Detective Becket clasps her notebook tight against her lap. "Unfortunately, Mr. and Mrs. McNairn, there is no evidence of anything suspicious. She met with someone she knew and had been talking to via email for a number of weeks. And left with him. There is no evidence of her being taken against her will. Jacob, here, saw her leaving with him. This man, Jules, and Skye, were chatting as they left together."

"No." I shake my head furiously. This can't be right.

She continues spewing words I don't agree with. "She may have stayed at his house for the night. Was she unsettled in any way? Not happy in her work, perhaps?"

Now, I'm fucking furious. "Most definitely not. This is so out of character for her, and she was about to be promoted. She was ecstatic about it. She's the happiest person I know." I take another deep breath before I really lose my shit with the detective. "She was going to text me when she got home. She promised she would and didn't." I grit out my words.

"Is that normal for your employee to text you their where-abouts, Mr. Baxter?" The detective sounds patronizing.

Detective *Fuckface* is walking a thin line. "Of course it is. We work late, often, and sometimes meetings run over. It's my duty to check their safety."

She eyes me suspiciously. "We need to wait another twenty-four hours, but as a favor and because we've found her car, we will check the town's CCTV."

Skye's mother gasps, "No, that's not good enough."

"Castleview Cove is a very safe place. No one has ever gone missing from here." The detective's careless words piss me off.

"How long will it take to check through the footage?" I ask with force.

"It will be tomorrow before anyone can look at it, then they need to write the report, maybe another day for that," the police officer replies.

I shoot to my feet, pulling my phone out of my pocket. "Days? That's too long," I rage.

Fuck this. I'm hiring a private investigator.

Storming into the hallway, I call my dad.

He answers straightaway. "Any news?"

"No. I need your help." My words are frantic now. "What is that friend of yours called, the PI that helped find the school-girl that went missing in the city? The one that was all over the news? Do you have his contact details?"

"I do, but Jay, you need to let the police do their job."

I fling my free arm to the heavens above. "No, I don't, Dad. They won't do anything for twenty-four hours and it's going to take two days—that's forty-eight hours—to check through the CCTV and write a report. They aren't taking what we are saying seriously. We need someone on it *now* and I'm willing to pay... anything. I'll never forgive myself if something has happened to her." I cover my mouth to hold back the bile I feel rising in my throat. "What if we don't find her?" Feeling empty, hope seeps from my body, the weight of my words stabbing through my heart.

My gaze lands on a photograph of Skye. I pick up the picture frame and take every inch of her in. Looking back over her shoulder, it looks like this was caught in an innocently candid moment. Full-on wide smile, her crystal-blue eyes shine down the camera.

"We have to find her, Dad," I whisper.

For a moment he goes quiet, then he finally says, "His name is Walter Forrester. Ex-Special Forces. Tell him you're my son. I'm sending you his contact details now."

"Thank you." I feel slightly relieved that he might be able to help us.

My father lowers his voice. "Can I ask you something, Jay?"

"Anything."

"Are you and Skye—"

I don't let him finish. "I'm in love with her."

"I'll pay for Walter. Tell him to do whatever it takes."

My eyes blur with tears. "Thank you."

"Go find your girl and keep me informed. I want to know everything." He hangs up.

I open his contact details and dial Walter immediately.

When he takes my call, I move into the kitchen to fill him in. I don't leave out any of the details. From the suspected bedroom break-in, Jules' social media comments, the lies about his gender, the coffee shop meeting, his website disappearing, and the local arts group. Without hesitation, he agrees to meet me in an hour at the exact coffee shop where Skye was last seen.

When I hang up, exhausted from going through it all again, I leave the kitchen just as Detective Becket steps into the hallway. Her hawk-like eyes narrow as she says, "Just a heads-up, *if...*"

If... is she fucking messing with me? There is no doubt about it. Skye is missing. I'm so fucking glad I decided to get a PI involved.

Detective Fuckface continues, "If we do have to escalate the missing persons' report, we may need to check all of Skye's digital devices. Including her work computer and emails."

"Call me and I will have the IT department give you full access."

The detective looks back over her shoulder and then back at me again. Lowering her tone, she says, "Is there anything I should be made aware of Mr. Baxter—forgive me—Jacob?"

Unsure about what she means, I ask, "Like?"

"For instance. The relationship between you and Skye? Is it strictly business? Or..."

"We went to school together. She's my best friend's ex. She's worked with me for years. She's like family to me." I'm not telling this woman, who is too calm, and who shows no tenderness in her eyes, fuck all. Yet.

"If she shows up, please call me." She passes me her business card.

Taking it from her, I push it into the back pocket of my dress trousers.

"So, what now?"

"Now we wait…"

Skye's mom bustles through the door. Whipping past us, suddenly brimming with determination, she says, "I'm not sitting here waiting for you to find her. I'm putting a search party together myself." Her whole demeanor has changed since I left the living room.

She runs up the stairs, shouting as she goes. "Jacob, use that Facebook thingy to put a request out for help. I want everyone looking for her. I want her face all over social media and I want to do a press conference."

Atta girl. Here we fucking go.

Still shouting instructions at us from up the stairs, Skye's mom bellows, "Ring the local television networks. The nationals too and the newspapers. Call them all. I want posters and tee shirts. I want everything." She zooms back down the stairs dressed in warm clothes. "We are getting our girl back."

24

JACOB

It's only eleven in the morning and I feel like I have been up for hours.

It feels like she's been missing for days.

A year.

A whole fucking lifetime.

My blood pressure has reached peak levels. My pulse hasn't stopped racing and I've gone into fight or flight. In fact, I am in pure fight mode.

And I won't stop until we get her home.

After making phone call after phone call to get everything we need for the search party, I've arrived ahead of schedule to meet Walter, the infamous PI.

Being back in the coffee shop feels awful. Just being in the last place she was safe strangles the air from my lungs. The police informed us at the house there was no point sweeping for fingerprints, since all the tables had been sanitized before they closed last night.

While I'm waiting, I make the phone call I've been dreading.

It rings for ages and goes to voicemail. I try again. He still doesn't pick up, so I leave a message.

Elbow on the table, I push my fingers into my eye sockets, wondering what the hell I'm supposed to say.

The beeps finish and I begin my message.

"Owen, it's me. Jacob. I need you to call me as soon as possible. It's about Skye. Your dad said he tried contacting you, too. Can you please call me?" I suppress my inner frustration. "It's urgent." With a heavy heart, I hang up.

"Jacob Baxter?"

A deep raspy voice startles the mental breakdown I'm currently having. Or maybe it's a heart attack. I feel horrific.

Where is she?

I take Walter's welcoming hand and shake it.

He sits down on the wooden chair opposite me, making it creak under the pressure of his weight.

I'm big.

He's a giant.

A hairy motherfucker too.

Shoulder-length hair, a full bushy beard, and dark-as-coal eyes.

Walter places a laptop on the table and starts tapping away on his keyboard. "We are only staying here for a couple of minutes, then we will go to my car. Just be patient with me, Jacob."

I don't know what the hell he's doing. But his enormous size and bear-like hands tell me not to question or mess with him.

My phone is blowing up. Never-ending swooshes and dings alert me to dozens of notifications, but I don't bother looking. Skye's mom said she would call as soon as she heard anything. That's the only call I'm interested in, and this meeting with Walter is more important.

He pulls a bottle of water out of his backpack, hands it to me. "Drink."

I look at him, confused.

"You've probably not eaten or drunk anything since you made your discovery this morning, am I right?"

Christ, he's good. I down the bottle of water. *I'm so thirsty.*

I wonder if Skye has drunk anything since she was here yesterday, and a wave of sadness hits me like a tsunami. My body and mind are being pushed in so many different directions, I don't know how I should be feeling.

I have never felt this level of devastation before.

It's fucking awful.

Where is my beautiful Skye?

Is she safe?

Is she alive?

Walter coughs, pulling me from my thoughts. "Okay. We can go." He pushes the chair back, making it screech across the tiled floor.

I follow him back to his blacked-out Range Rover Sport, and I hop in when he tells me to.

Once seated, he opens his laptop again and points at the screen. "Is this Skye?"

Fucking hell. It is.

Did he just hack into the security system at the coffee shop?

My beautiful girl looks so innocently unaware of what's about to happen. How could any of us have known?

I stare at the screen, watching her smile every now and again. The smile I want to be part of every day. The smile I have yet to see today.

I let out a sound I've never heard myself make before as I clutch my chest.

Is this what heart failure feels like?

A sinking feeling turns my stomach as I watch her interaction with Jules, or whoever the fuck he is, knowing what comes next; she goes missing.

When she heads to the bathroom, two minutes later, I follow her into the women's restrooms.

We both watch intently as Jules follows in the same direction. He hovers in the hallway outside, pretending to read the noticeboard, but every few seconds he eyes the bathroom door.

Walter changes the camera angle so we can get a better look.

A girl appears in the corridor, head back, laughing at whatever her friend, who slips off into the gents' bathroom, says to her. She pushes the women's restroom door open. Standing inside is Skye with her hand wrapped around my tie and we're so close we look like we're kissing.

The security camera shows Jules' whole stance change as his body becomes rigid. He turns on his heels faster than a bolt of lightning.

Storming back to his seat, he snarls, his lips moving as he chants inaudible words through a tight jaw. "Go back to the other camera," I say, pointing at the tiles of footage on the screen.

We watch as Jules throws himself back into his chair; fist clenched, he clicks his neck.

Walter zooms in on Jules and we watch as he pulls something out from his jacket pocket, leans over, and with what looks like a small white pill placed between his chubby fingers, he drops it into Skye's coffee cup.

"He drugged her?" My heart splits open.

Walter stays quiet, watching everything while the footage keeps playing.

Jules picks up his phone, furiously scrolling, waiting for Skye to come back.

"Can you zoom in on just his phone screen?" I ask.

Walter taps a few buttons making the camera angle change again, where we witness him deleting his social media account.

"You've got yourself an obsessive stalker. Did you see his whole mood change when he saw you two together? You triggered him."

The horror of Walter's words whips through me in a flash. *If he hadn't seen us in the bathroom, would Skye be here, safe with me?*

"I think I might be sick."

"Not in my truck, please," Walter says calmly. I swallow down the fear and guilt currently trying to break free from my body as I watch the camera zoom in on Jules' face. At the click of a button, Walter runs it through a piece of software that automatically begins zooming through data at lightning speed. He then hits play on a different video. This time, it's from the street outside. The one we're currently parked on.

Barely keeping one foot in front of the other, Skye is being held up by Jules. Further down the street, he ushers her up the alleyway. The one we are sitting at the end of.

I look up out of the front car window. The CCTV is right above us.

Walter is smart as fuck and shit-hot with tech. I didn't think hacking into the town's security footage would be so easy.

I can barely look at the screen when Jules lifts her lifeless body into the back of his car.

"He's a stupid motherfucker," Walter mumbles.

"Why? I would say the opposite. He's organized and seems to know what he's doing."

Without lifting his head, Walter points at the CCTV pole in front of us and then back at the screen, as if I've missed something obvious. "His number plate is right there. He's an amateur and I can tell you now, this was unplanned. He's considered it, planning it in the background for some time in the future, but he had no intention of taking her last night. He saw you with her, got jealous, panicked, and he didn't want you to have her. He wanted her all to himself. He saw an opportunity and took it. All signs point to him never having done this before. That's a good sign."

"But he had drugs with him."

"Practice run. Bringing a few things with him would make him feel prepared. He wanted to feel powerful, but he had no intention of using them. Knowing he *could* was enough. Seeing her with you made him escalate. But he wasn't ready, and that's making him sloppy."

He looks me dead in the eye. "We're going to get your girl back."

"What, now?" I ask, not feeling as confident as Walter appears to be.

"Now I rally my team together. I'll meet them at the office as soon as I leave here. We trace every step he made. There are CCTV cameras everywhere from here, right into the city, and all along the highways. My team is extremely experienced. We've got you covered, Jacob. I will make sure I do everything to get her back."

"Quicker than the police?"

"You should have called me first. The whole context and circumstance of Skye's disappearance tell us that she is the victim of a crime. Fucking twenty-four hours, my ass. I'll find her. You have my word."

All the hope that left my body earlier floods my skin. A huge wave of emotion hits me, making my eyes go blurry.

I shake my head to dry up my damp eyes, wiping my nose with the back of my shirt sleeve.

"Sorry," I mumble.

"Don't be." He squeezes my shoulder. Hard. Then he pulls his hands away and slams his laptop shut. "Now, we get to work. I'm running his photo through advanced facial recognition software as we speak. I'll pick that up when I get to the office. My right-hand man, Tim, is coordinating with the team. *When*, not *if*, but when, we locate this guy, we'll move in at night. It's the only way. Don't tell her parents I'm looking. Let them keep searching for her. When he sees them on the television, he will think he's winning. He'll probably get off on the attention. All his focus will be on the press and social media. He won't expect what's coming." His grin takes an evil twist. "Me."

I like this guy.

"How long?"

"You need to give me forty-eight hours. If I don't have her back to you by then, I'll give your father back his money." He pushes his hands through his unruly hair.

Fuck me. That's some serious confidence right there.

"We're already further along than the police. I would hope to have her back to you sooner."

Momentarily basking in his confidence, I believe him.

"We're done. Keep your phone on, Jacob."

My head bowed, I utter the words I never thought I would. "Will she be alive?"

"The first seventy-two hours are critical. He's left a lot of breadcrumbs for us to follow, and you've given me lots of information, plus we have the CCTV footage. We know what he looks like and his car registration number. We'll be able to pinpoint his exact location by tracing his website IP address. It doesn't matter if he deleted it or his account he posted on her channel from; we'll find it. I hire the best cyber hackers and engineers from all over the world. We've got this."

That didn't answer my question.

"Wait for my call. Eat something. It's going to be a long night, maybe two." He nods to the car door, giving me my cue to leave.

Not knowing when I'll speak to him or if I will get my girl back safely, my fingers clamp around the door handle and I push the door open, stepping back out into the street.

Walking to my car, I take a moment to gather myself. I'm desperate to go to the town hall where the search parties are meeting up, but when I slide into the driver's seat, I tip my head back and let out a long exhale. I need to contain the combined rage and sadness bubbling away in my gut.

I pull out my phone and try calling Owen again.

No reply.

Where the hell are you, *Owen?*

25

___

JACOB

It's been thirty-six hours since we realized she was missing.

She's been missing for much longer. With every hour that passes and every beat of my heart, I give up hope. It's becoming more impossible to stay positive.

I'm desperately trying to feed from Skye's mom's never-ending positivity; however, it's flowing away like the fine grains of sand in an hourglass.

Every inch of me wants to believe we will find her, and yet a second night without her has crept in, with no sign of her and no call from Walter.

Search parties have been out since yesterday lunchtime and all day today, calling her name, scouring the fields and hills all around, as well as the beaches and surrounding villages. Not a street has been missed.

Nobody has found anything. It's as if she's vanished into thin air.

I stopped at my house for five minutes to change into warmer clothing and since then I've been out searching, relentlessly, alongside everyone, and by myself.

Friends, old and new, high-school pals, work colleagues, family members and their friends all pulled together. If I thought we were a tight community before, then we're even tighter now.

We agreed to end the search parties at six o'clock in the evening; it's too dark to keep looking as night falls. Today we mainly focused on the nooks and crannies of Castleview Cove's cobbled streets. My feet are aching. However, I would walk across a blazing hot desert with no shoes on, just to catch a glimpse of her again.

For the first time today, I'm sitting down, my joints aching, heart broken, and consumed with so much hatred for myself that I couldn't save her from that creepy-ass fucker.

Having just read a *still no sign* text update from Kimmy, who's been patiently waiting at their house since yesterday morning, with a heavy heart I place my phone on the table in front of me. I'm better off staying here at the community hall. I don't want to go home. It's pointless; there is no way I will be able to sleep, anyway. My mind is reeling, going through so many different scenarios of what I could have done.

No matter how many times I've been over it, I know I am the one to blame for this because without that tablet and pen she would never have learned how to hand letter or started her video channel.

I feel sick to my stomach again. It's all because of me.

I ended up throwing up in an alleyway earlier when my anger turned to disgust. My thoughts visited a place I don't want to return to. *What does he want with her, what is he doing to her, is he touching her?*

I can't think about that again. It doesn't change anything; I can't exactly turn the clock back now, can I?

Everything feels impossible.

Pressing my fingertips into the back of my neck to relieve the permanent tension in my shoulders, I then give a small wave of appreciation to the last of the volunteers.

As they leave the hall, with fighting spirit, they all reassure Rhona and Seth that we'll find her.

Violet plonks herself down beside me and starts babbling, "She'll come home. She's okay. I know she is. She's fine. I can feel it, can you? I can. She has to come home, right? Who will I go to my dance class with? Who will laugh with me when I fall over? She's been my one true friend since I arrived here. I love her like a sister and she's so kind..." Drawing breath, she says so quietly, "We have to find her."

My shoulders bounce up and down with the emotion I've been holding on to. Sobs escape my throat, fat tears soaking my black sweatshirt.

Leaning forward, my hands cupped around the top of my head to hide my sadness, I watch as my tears make a small puddle on the wooden floor. Like a river, they keep flowing and I can't stop them.

Pulling me in tight to their chest, broad arms wrap around the top of my shoulders. "Let it all out, buddy."

Lincoln.

Using him as support, my body falls into his, pain passing through my heart as tears flow one after the other. No words are needed as Lincoln holds me firmly, letting me weep.

Pulling the sleeves of my jumper down, I push the palms of my hands into my eyes to soak up the tears and move away from Lincoln. Head bowed, I flip the hood of my jumper up over my head to hide my embarrassment.

Violet kneels at my feet and passes me a handkerchief, her kind hands cupping both of my knees. "We're here for you, Jay. We'll find her."

"Yeah." I don't know if I believe that anymore.

I use the tissue to blow my stuffy nose and exhale a deep breath. Crying hasn't made me feel any better. I feel hot and my face feels swollen.

Skye's mom pulls a chair by my side. A strained sigh leaves her throat as she falls into her seat.

Only the five of us left now, me, Linc, Violet, and Skye's parents. I look around the empty hall.

It was bustling earlier, and the noise distracted me from our predicament.

The contrast of the silence of the hall is almost deafening to me now.

Lincoln and Violet pulled a twenty-strong team of staff together from their five-star hotel resort, having enough food delivered to feed an army. It's just as well because hundreds of people showed up. It felt like a military operation.

My mom and dad left about an hour ago, along with my brother and sister.

The whole community came together for her.

She's loved beyond measure.

Wherever she is, I hope she feels it.

An endless stream of news channels, reporters, and media from across the country have been out filming and interviewing local town folk and the search for Skye has taken on a life of its own with well wishes pouring in from around the world.

Lincoln holds his hand out for Violet, summoning her to give me some space.

"Still no word from Owen?" he asks.

I shake my head. "Nope. I gave up calling him. He's never around when you need him, and he sure as hell doesn't give a crap about the girl he spent the last fourteen years with or he'd be here."

"I'll try him again when I get home." Lincoln lets out a long, drawn-out yawn.

Every one of us is shattered. We all need our beds, but none of us have been able to sleep.

Rhona holds her stomach. "I haven't eaten all day. I don't think I could hold anything down if I tried."

"Same." I reach out and give her hand a quick squeeze. She and Seth have been incredible, knowing what to say, and when to say it. They've organized every search party with military precision, their teacher planning skills playing a strong role. Add that to the fact that the entire community loves and respects the local headmaster and his teacher wife, and you've got yourself a clan of non-bloodline family.

I check my phone again for the billionth time, my battery now on red and at ten percent life. I need to find a charger.

"You're a good man, Jacob." Rhona's surprising words turn my head in her direction. "Look at what you did for her. You have helped us so much."

I eye the missing person posters piled high on the table across the room. I can't look at the photo of her. It's too painful. I still can't believe we are doing this; it all seems so surreal.

"I wish I could do more." My body is heavy with defeat, my hope dwindling. "I feel like I've let you down."

"Jacob," she says firmly.

I gaze up tentatively and she smiles at me. "None of us could have known."

"You're so strong."

"I'm not," she sputters. "I'm bluffing. I'm putting one foot in front of the other because I can't give up hope. It's the only thing keeping me going. Plus, the police are on board now. Stupid rules," she mutters, then turns her seat to face me. "You must stop blaming yourself for this. You could blame me or social media, or anything. Skye missing is nobody's fault, except for this Jules, who we know nothing about, and I'm trying desperately not to think about him." She waves her hand in the air as if batting the wretched thoughts away. "As a community, we are all going to work together to get her back, and when she does come back, whatever she's been put through, she will need us. She will need you." She raises her eyebrows. "I figure you two are..." She doesn't say the last few words.

"I love your daughter, Rhona," I say without hesitation. Those words have been buried in my heart for so long that I want to tell the world, and that includes Owen.

Why hasn't he called me back?

With a gentle smile and warm eyes, Rhona says, "You've always loved her. Do you think I don't see it? I've known you since you were sixteen years old. You spent more time in my house than your own." She points at Lincoln. "And you." She looks back at me. "I silently prayed you two would get together. You are perfect for each other and you've turned into such a lovely man."

Too much emotion hits me all at once. Drawing my hands into tight fists, I push them into my eyes. Clenching my jaw together, I groan and shake my head. I don't want to cry again.

It's been the worst two days of my life.

"Although you still drive too fast through the town in that silly sports car of yours, Jacob." Rhona lightens the mood with her smart-ass words, her comment making us all laugh.

It's only been two days, but I forgot what laughter sounds like.

Fuck, what a day.

"We all need to go home and try to get some sleep." In full teacher mode, she gives us all a stern look.

Sleeping is the last thing I want to do.

Knowing how we all feel, she says, "You're all staying right here, aren't you?" Rhona removes her jacket, hanging it over the back of her chair.

Violet offers to make everyone a cup of tea while Seth organizes a bite to eat for everyone.

We're not going anywhere.

26

SKYE

It's daylight outside again. Although I have no idea what time of day it is.

Tap, tap, tap, tap, tap, tap, tap.

The constant sound vibrates through the sickly yellow and pink floral walls over and over.

It sounds like someone hammering, and it's the exact same pounding noise I've listened to for what feels like hours.

They beat in perfect synchronicity with my dying heart.

I don't know how long I've been chained to this bed or what time it is. The only thing that's kept me sane since I woke up again is that I am still dressed in the clothes I was in when I left the coffee shop.

Never one to go to church, not since I was a little girl anyway, I silently pray for someone to find me.

A million and one thoughts have gone through my mind since I woke up from yet another black hole of unexplained slumber. Although this time I knew he'd drugged me, my stiff and sore neck is confirmation of where he punctured me again.

With only the faint hint of the moon to light the room, confirming what I already saw earlier, it highlights the outline of crisscrossed metal bars across the window, their shadows falling heavily onto the sickly pink carpet.

Is anyone looking for me? Why haven't they come?

The hammering sound stops and the clatter of something heavy from somewhere in the depths of the house, or cabin or warehouse, whatever I am in, makes me jump.

Heavy footsteps appear next.

The door clicks open and Jules bursts into the room.

My breathing instantly picks up, my chest rising and falling in stuttered gasps.

He flicks on the light, forgetting to close the door behind him, and he stalks across the room and with every step, panic threatens to strangle me, my heart hammering fast against my ribcage.

Straddling me with his portly form, he runs his pointer finger down my cheek.

I squeeze my eyes shut and breathe short and fast breaths through my nose.

"We're going to have so much fun together."

Panic crawls up my throat, and I shake my head furiously back and forth as I prepare for the worst, but nothing follows.

It's then I hear a deep, raspy voice I haven't heard before. "Don't move a fucking muscle, you slimy-ass fucker."

Turning my head back to center, I pop my eyes open, but my tears blind my sight and I can't see anything clearly.

A black shape in the form of a man stands to the side with what looks like the outline of a gun pressed to Jules' head. I fall apart at the sight of the huge, masked man dressed from head to toe in black combat gear and a bullet-proof vest, with another three identically dressed men to the side of him. Each one of them is pointing a gun in Jules' direction.

"Slowly move off the girl, Jules," the masked man instructs with a steady voice.

But he doesn't listen.

His hands fly down to my neck and I tense up, expecting his hands to grip my neck, but they never land because quicker than the blink of an eye, one of the masked men throws a punch to the side of his throat, making Jules' eyes roll back into his head.

The masked man, who's bigger than a tank, lifts his heavy body off me like he's a featherweight and throws him to the floor.

A quick wrestling match ensues, but Jules is no competition for the tactical swat team.

Mr. Raspy Voice bows down, takes off his mask, and a gentle smile fills his face.

"You're okay, Skye. You are safe now. Jacob sent us."

I begin to sob with relief.

He saved me.

27

JACOB

Bursting through the swing doors of the emergency room, our legs can't carry us fast enough to the reception area. Thankfully, we weren't greeted by a barrage of media and news reporters. They clearly haven't caught wind of the update on Skye's status yet.

For that, I am grateful.

Out of breath, Skye's mom pants, "My name is Rhona McNairn. I believe my daughter was brought here."

The receptionist looks at us with wide eyes.

She knows.

Rhona's eyes roam the busy waiting room. Chewing her mouth, she nervously drums her fingers against the wooden reception desk.

"The doctor wants to speak to you." The receptionist picks up the phone, dials a number, informing whoever answers that we are here.

Hands linked behind my head, I'm wearing down the floor beneath my feet as I pace, when the doctor strides up the corridor.

Unspoken words between the doctor and receptionist, she nods with the raise of her brow over at us.

"Mr. and Mrs. McNairn? I'm Doctor Cunningham. Let's go somewhere private." He ushers them away.

"Jacob." Rhona stops walking. "Come with us." She beckons me with her hand.

Seth's eyes soften as I move swiftly, eager to see my girl.

The doctor opens a private waiting room off to the side of the reception, where we all take a seat and wait for the impending update of Skye's well-being.

"Is she okay? Can we see her?" Seth says quickly.

"Is she awake?" Rhona shoots out.

I want to know everything too, but I'm too anxious. I made the fatal mistake of searching online *what happens when someone gets abducted.*

Big mistake. Huge.

"Do I have your permission to share everything with Jacob here?" The doctor looks at me.

"Yes, he's Skye's boyfriend." We're far from that, but I love Rhona's belief in us and I love how that sounds.

Seth takes his wife's hand in his.

"Skye is much better than we expected. She's dehydrated and on a saline drip. Her physical injuries are minimal and somewhat superficial. She has bruises from the shackles she was restrained with, both around her wrists and ankles."

Shackles. Fuck.

Needing to move, I get up to pace the room while the doctor continues to share her injuries.

"Both her cheeks are very swollen and some bruising has begun to form under her eyes from where we think she's been struck. She has no other physical injuries that we can see. She hasn't really said much." He pauses. "However, she did give her permission for us to carry out a sexual assault test."

"What?" I stop pacing.

"We did it as a precaution. Skye was very heavily drugged for a lot of the time and she wanted us to check. Our initial examination shows no signs of forced sexual assault. The tests will tell us for certain. It really is a precaution. But it can take up to a month for the results."

I fall into the chair behind me.

Rhona covers her mouth with her hand to hide her shock while Seth pulls her into his chest.

I wish Lincoln was here for support. I could do with him right now as my heart shatters into a million fragments.

"Can we see her?" Seth's face is full of anxious hope.

"Yes. But only two at a time."

"I'll wait here. It's fine. Go get your daughter." I try putting on a reassuring smile.

"You can go in after us, Jacob," Seth reassures me. "Thank you for everything you've done for us. I will repay your father for the PI."

"I won't have it. Your happiness and her safety are the only things that matter. Go see your girl."

Then I'm left in the room all alone.

I text Walter to ask if he can speed up the results of Skye's sexual assault tests.

Instantly texting me back with a yes and that we can get the results within three days settles some of my anxiety. We just need a signature from Skye to release her test to the private laboratory, and Walter will do the rest.

Ten minutes later the door opens and in walks Miss Marple her *fucking* self.

"Detective Becket." I'm more abrupt than I should be.

"I've spoken with Mr. and Mrs. McNairn and informed them we have a Mr. Jules Howard in custody. Skye's parents wanted you to know, too."

"I already know everything."

Unable to look me in the eye, she says, "Look, Mr. Baxter—"

"It's Jacob, and I don't need you to tell me how you found her, because you didn't. I've already been sent a full report from the private investigator. The one *I* hired because you didn't do your job," I say, trying to remain calm.

Walter sent me a full report, along with body-cam footage for evidence. I never want to watch it.

I read the report on the way to the hospital, while Lincoln drove us here. None of us were in a fit state to get in behind the wheel.

Walter's team of expert marksmen located Jules, only ten miles away from here in some creepy-ass cabin in the woods just outside Bayview.

Jules Howard, who also calls himself Silas, suffers from dissociative identity disorder and has been in and out of psychiatric facilities since he was a child.

Walter presumed that Jules stopped taking his medication, and no one had noticed his symptoms worsening.

The walls of his house were decorated with pictures of Skye. He'd been watching her for months.

The sooner he's behind bars or back in the confines of a psychiatric facility, the better.

Sensing I don't want to speak to her, Detective Becket turns around to walk out the door, but she stops. Looking back at me over her shoulder, she says, "I just wanted to thank you, Jacob, for all you did and for helping to capture him. I'm sorry if you feel like we failed you. However, I was following protocol."

I scoff.

Once she leaves, I sit back in the uncomfortable chair, close my eyes and rest my head against the wall. I'm so tired.

28

JACOB

The next thing I know, I'm being shaken awake by Seth.

The sunlight spills through the window in the small room, alerting me to the fact it's morning.

"I'm sorry. I must have fallen asleep."

"We left you to rest. You needed it."

I rub my hands down my face to wake myself up.

"She wants to see you," Seth says.

My body feels like pure static energy as we walk along the corridor. I want to run to her, not walk.

My phone is now completely empty of battery, so I push it into my pocket.

As soon as I get the opportunity, I need to find a phone charger and check if Owen has called me back. I'm praying he has. I don't want to miss out on any more time with Skye.

Coming to a standstill, Seth pushes his hand out to open the door of the private room.

Buzzed to be finally getting to be with my girl, I feel like I'm a racehorse waiting to bolt out of the starting gate.

Before he twists the handle, he looks over his shoulder at me and says, "She's had a little time to process what happened to her. She's showered. She seems fine, but I know she's putting on a brave face." Worry etches across his forehead.

My heart pangs with pain for her. I wish I could take all her memories away from the last few days.

Seth glides the door open, and I'm greeted by an extraordinary sight.

The whole room is flooded in the sunshine radiating through the windows and sitting in the puddle of blazing light is my extraordinary girl.

"Jacob," she gasps as tears free-fall down her face.

Unable to wait, I run to her and launch myself into her open arms, squeezing her, holding her tight against me, not believing she is here.

"Skye," is all I can get out as my chest fills with emotion that I can't even begin to explain.

I almost lost her.

"You rescued me," she whispers, as she squeezes me tighter.

Nuzzling deeper into her neck, my hand at the back of her head, holding her firmly against me, I never want to let her go. I'm not waiting anymore; I want everything with her.

The time for us is now.

I don't know how long we stay like this, but eventually, I pull out of our embrace and just look at her.

She's here.

"You saved me," she says again, resting her hands on my face, staring at me in complete disbelief. "You've no idea how close he was to... I can't even begin to think about what would have happened to me if Walter hadn't come in at that exact moment. Without you... I... I... you saved me." Her voice cracks under the weight of her emotions.

I can't bear to think about it but try humor to lighten the situation. "I didn't save you, silly. I paid someone. Well, my father did. He knows how important you are to me. To all of us." I look behind us, but Seth and Rhona have left us to be alone.

"He was like a man mountain version of James Bond." Tears pool in her eyes.

"He was exactly like that. Walter's a badass."

"And you're my knight in shining armor."

"And you'll always be my Butterfly." I kiss her on the nose.

"How will I ever repay you?"

Marry me.

"You'll have to put in some serious overtime at work." I make a joke instead of blurting out what's on the tip of my tongue.

She chuckles lightly.

"I'm joking. I want you to take as much time off as you need."

"I don't want to," she argues.

"You are banned from work until further notice."

Her shoulders fall. "Okay," she reluctantly agrees.

Taking in her bruised face, I ask, "Does it hurt?"

She cups her cheek. "It did at the time." She flinches as if remembering. "I don't care." She shakes her head as if breaking free from her memories. "I'm home, and safe. With my family, and you."

Our eyes lock. "I didn't think I'd see you again," she exclaims, her blue gems turning glassy. Sucking in a deep breath, as if to steady her voice, she stares down at the bed sheets as if reliving her ordeal.

She doesn't need to say a word. I don't need to hear what she went through or how horrible the experience was for her. It's written across her face and I can read every second of pain she had to go through. I feel it as if it is my own and I hate that I can't take it away from her or help her forget. I might have helped rescue her, but I can never turn back the clock and stop it from happening and I have to live with that for a lifetime.

In that moment, I silently pledge to protect her for as long as my heart beats in my chest.

"I thought I'd lost you." I cup her face.

"But you didn't."

"I thought I'd lost you before we got our chance." I still can't believe she's here and I'm touching her.

"But you didn't."

"You're here." I rest my forehead against hers, basking in our reunion.

Skye lets out a soft sigh as she gazes at my lips. "Now would be the perfect time to kiss you, but there are too many people around."

"I haven't brushed my teeth since yesterday morning, so maybe now is not the time for a kiss."

"You're a filthy pig," she joshes with me, which I take as a good sign.

"An ogre," I argue.

"With tattoos and muscles."

"Exactly. I'm the underdog."

"He always wins the girl."

"I hope so."

"I know so," she murmurs as she bites down on her bottom lip, making her look adorable, despite the damage that psycho did to her face.

Holding her hand now, I lace our fingers together.

"More bruises," she says when I rub the small vein on the top of her hand. "It's where the IV was. Whatever was in that, it's made me feel so much better."

"How are you feeling? You can be honest with me, Skye."

"They've said I need to see a therapist."

"I would agree."

"I don't want to talk about any of it." She looks out of the window.

"Maybe not now, but soon. You might be fine one day and then *boom*, it might hit you. It would be better to have some coping mechanisms and tools in place before that happens."

She goes quiet for a moment. "You're right and so smart." Then she mumbles something under her breath.

"Sorry, I didn't catch that."

Punching her clenched fist into the pale blue hospital blanket, she says, "I said, I feel stupid."

"Why?"

"For speaking to him online, sharing things with him. I thought he was a *girl*. That, right there, was a huge red flag. I'm angry at myself for being so stupid. What was I thinking?" She rubs her forehead.

I can't help noticing the bracelet bruises around her wrists. Thank fuck they will disappear. The last thing she needs is a permanent reminder of her ordeal.

"Hey, you think you're stupid? I let you leave with him. I will live with that regret forever. However, I will do my damnedest to make it up to you. Every. Single. Day."

"You didn't let me leave with him. I left willingly." She covers her whole face with her two hands.

I peel her hands away from her face. The face I want to stare at for all time. "Look at me."

My hands in hers, being more serious than I ever have before, I say, "We can blame a lot of things, but please know you had no control over his thoughts or his behavior." I reach out to trace the scratch on her cheek with my thumb. "I'm just so fucking happy you're safe."

I kiss her forehead again to remind myself she's real. I'm touching her. I can feel her. She's here and I'm never letting her go.

"I did the rape kit test." Her voice is low when she says the words that make my blood boil. She should never have had to go through that. "I don't think anything happened to me. I mean, I would feel it, wouldn't I?" Her brows furrow as unspoken fear fills her face. I lace my fingers with hers and try to pour strength and support into her so she knows she's not going through this alone.

"Whatever happened to you, we will get through it together, with your mom and dad, your friends, and whatever medical support you need. We'll be with you every step of the way, and we'll do everything in our power to make him pay."

"He's not getting away with what he did to me. I'll make sure nobody else ever has to go through what I have."

"You're just like your mom. She's an awesome little firecracker. Much bossier than me."

"She is." She smirks, nodding her head in agreement. Then she blurts out what's on her mind. "What if he's touched me where he shouldn't have?" She dry heaves. Pulling her hand out of mine, she slaps it over her mouth. The bed sheets get thrown back as she jumps out of the bed and bursts through the bathroom door to vomit. Fast on my feet, I jump over the bed into the bathroom to help her. Not like her to have her hair down, I pull it into a high ponytail, and rub her back while she empties the contents of her stomach into the toilet bowl.

I want to kill that motherfucker with my bare hands for making her feel like this.

"Oh gawd, I'm so sorry," she coughs and splutters.

I pass her a tissue to wipe her mouth.

"You don't have to apologize."

"Thank you." Shoulders hunched, she moves onto her bottom and rests her back against the bathroom wall.

"I don't want to feel like this." When she breaks down, I'm on the floor beside her, scooping her into my lap and enveloping her in my arms at the speed of a heartbeat.

Holding her firmly to my chest, I cradle her in my arms, just holding her as sadness and devastation engulf her.

I repeat comforting words over and over again. As I swaddle her, she buries herself deeper and deeper into my chest, until eventually her little sobs and whimpers subside.

Using her pale blue hospital gown to wipe her nose, she tilts her head back, leans it against my bicep, and looks straight into my eyes. "What would I do without you?"

"You'd have no one to talk to about the books you're reading at lunchtime, and you'd be having to use a substandard backpack that was just plain ugly and so *not* Parisian chic." I put on a fake high voice toward the end and roll my eyes mockingly, which makes her laugh.

"The police have my backpack as evidence."

"I can buy you a new one. Now, let's get you back into bed."

We both move off the floor, her face now red and swollen from crying.

When I tuck her back into bed, she hooks her leg outside of the blanket and she says, "I always get hot feet. I like them outside of the covers."

"Good to know." I wink, then kiss the top of her head again to comfort her. I like kissing her; it feels nice.

"Would you like something to dri—" I don't get a chance to finish my sentence as an out-of-breath, flustered Owen bursts through the door like a tornado.

"Oh my God, Skye. I'm so sorry, baby." He runs to her.

I step away from the side of the bed.

"I'm here for you now. You're safe. I've got you," he says, puffing and panting, threading his arms around her, but she doesn't hug him back.

Over his shoulder, Skye side-eyes me with a frown. "I'm fine, Owen." She pats him twice as if he was a friend and then leans back away from him.

Moving out of their hug, he inspects her. "Look at your face. You're not fine."

"Owen. I really am fine," she insists, swiping his hands off her face. "But please don't touch me. I'm just a little tender in places."

Keeping him in the dark, she's not willing to share with him how emotionally fragile she is or the fact that she just broke down in the bathroom with me. And she certainly doesn't want him touching her like I've been doing.

"I tried calling you over and over again, Owen. Where have you been?" I snap at him.

He finally looks over at me. "I told you I was going to Barcelona. I was busy, the exhibition was huge, and I was entertaining clients I met over there."

That's code for boozing it up and partying, no doubt.

"Too busy to listen to your voice messages?"

"I'm here now, am I not?"

Too little too late, Owen.

Owen defends himself. "If I'd known, I would have been here in a flash."

"If you'd listened to your voice messages, you would have been here sooner."

"I was working."

"So you've said." I fake-smile at him.

Skye's gaze bounces back and forth between the two of us.

He turns his attention back to Skye. "I heard on the news that they got the guy who took you and that you met him online? When you told me you'd met someone, was that him?"

Not wanting to answer, she shakes her head.

Nope, Owen, that guy she's met is me. Yup, I feel like a bastard.

"You work in digital media, Skye. You should have known. Don't talk to strangers online, don't give them your details, and never meet up." He keeps pushing.

"Owen." My voice rises in a warning. "Don't do this now. Skye isn't ready to talk about it."

Looking between us, he raises his hands in submission and reluctantly agrees to stop.

A soft chatter behind the door emerges before it opens and in walk a much more relaxed-looking Rhona and Seth.

Owen rises from the edge of the bed.

A caring smile lines Rhona's lips as she checks her daughter over. *Are you okay?* she mouths.

Skye yawns. "I'm just a little tired."

"C'mon then, boys, let's leave her alone." Seth instructs us to leave.

Owen takes Skye's hand and gives it a squeeze. "I'll be back."

I want to scoop Skye into my arms, tell her I love her and that *I'll* be back, but I can't.

As Owen and I begin to leave the room, Owen says, "You have a tattoo?" He points at Skye's ankle, bending to get a better look.

For a moment, she and I exchange a look. I'm not sure what she's thinking, but I know she doesn't want him to see the watercolor bird symbolizing her and me when she tucks her foot back inside the bedcovers.

"It's cool," Owen comments.

Giving Skye a quick wave, I push my hands into my pockets and, with a heavy heart, exit the room.

"I'll text you when I get my phone back," Skye calls after us.

"Okay," Owen replies.

I think that was meant for me.

The two of us, who usually have so much to talk about, walk back along the hall in silence. I'm likely to lose it with him if anything stupid falls out of his mouth.

"Jacob," a voice calls from the end of the long corridor.

I stop in my tracks when Seth jogs toward us.

"I just wanted to thank you, personally, for everything." He flings his arms around me in a giant hug of appreciation. "We wouldn't have got her back without your help."

As quick as the hug started, it finishes: prompt and to the point. Eyes full of emotion, Seth steps away from me.

"Owen." He nods in a parting gesture, and he walks back in the direction of Skye's private room.

Owen stares at me. "What did you do?"

"I hired a PI."

"Shit. How much was that?"

At half a million, the money was never an issue. "Doesn't matter how much it was. She's back and safe." He follows me when I take a step in the direction of the side exit but doesn't say anything else until we're outside. There are too many news teams and reporters hanging about outside the main entrance, all desperate to speak to Skye and her parents.

"Thanks for doing that." He runs his hands through his blond hair.

"Well, someone had to do something," I say through gritted teeth. I'm irked by his aloof manner.

"My father will pay your family back."

"No need."

"Skye is my responsibility."

My head jolts back. "Oh really? Since when?"

"Since always."

"You are fucking kidding me, right?" My blood boils in my veins. "Do you even know what Skye's favorite movie is?" My voice is full of irritation.

He frowns. "What kind of question is that?"

"What is it?" I stand and wait for an answer.

"*Spider-Man*." He holds his hands out to the sides as if to say, *what a stupid question.*

My voice on the rise, I correct him. "It's *The Princess Bride*. And what about her favorite book?"

"*Lord of the Rings*?" He looks confused.

"It's the same fucking answer. *The Princess Bride*." I'm on a roll now. "Tell me, the night you were supposed to pick her up, to take her to the garage to get her car. The night you left her standing waiting for you in the rain, in the dark, where were you exactly?" I hold my pointer finger up. "In fact, don't answer that. I'm not fucking interested."

I whip around and stomp across the parking lot. If I don't move away from him, I'm going to say something I regret.

"Jay," he calls out; on fast feet he runs after me.

I don't stop walking. "Jay," he calls again, grabbing my shoulder to stop me moving.

He runs into my path, preventing me from getting to my car that Lincoln dropped off for me.

"What's up, man?" he asks.

"What's up? Christ, Owen. You have never cared about that girl. She's always been your afterthought. She was abducted by a severely mentally disturbed man. She's been drugged, had to have a rape test kit... do you know what's involved in one of them? And all you said was *nice tattoo*, and she should have known better because she works in digital media. You should have just told her it's all her fault instead, because that's what you implied." I run my hands down my face. "Fuck." I'm mad now. "You're an inconsiderate prick some-times. Do you know that?"

"I do care for her."

"How? Explain to me *how* exactly? Is it the fact that you have had me buy her every Christmas, birthday, and Valen-tine's Day present or is it the way you took her to a Revolution concert when she doesn't even like that band?"

"Yes, she does."

"No, she doesn't. She thinks they're too shouty." I should stop now before I say something I regret and I want to speak to him properly. Face to face, man to man.

Not like this.

"Jay," he scoffs as he holds his hands up to stop me saying anything else. "You are clearly having a meltdown due to lack of sleep. I know you. When you haven't had enough sleep or food you are one grumpy asshole. So, go home and sleep it off. Whatever the fuck this is." He wiggles his finger down my body. He's so fucking casual and blasé about everything.

"Whatever." I stomp to my car. Over my shoulder, I shout,

"I need to talk to you about something but now is not that time. Call me to arrange it."

I pull my car door open with such force, I'm surprised I don't pull it off its hinges.

Zooming out of the parking lot, I head back to my empty home, too far away from Skye, but not far enough away from Owen.

29

JACOB

Having not had a decent night's sleep for days, I shower then fall into my big comfortable bed like dead weight.

I stuck my phone on the charger as soon as I stepped in the door and dozens of notifications appeared on my screen at once. I'll read them all properly tomorrow; for now, though, I need to sleep. Owen was correct. I am a grumpy bastard without sleep or food, and I made the right decision to walk away from him when I did, or I would never have found the correct words to describe how I feel about Skye.

Almost asleep, a soft ding makes me open my eyes. I grab my phone off the nightstand to see who it is, and I'm instantly awake.

SKYE

I'm getting out of the hospital tomorrow
smiling face

ME

How did you get your phone?

SKYE

The police returned my backpack with my phone, tablet and laptop in it. They pulled all the information off my devices needed for their investigation. Walter provided everything though, so I don't know why they needed to do it again.

ME

Walter is super tech smart and his team is insanely talented.

SKYE

Hackers?

ME

Don't know and don't care how they did it. I only care they got you back.

SKYE

Super smart.

ME

They are. Can I come see you when you get out?

SKYE

I'm staying at Mom and Dad's for a couple of days. Mom's decided no visitors, so I can rest and recover.

ME

Okay.

Disappointment at not getting to see her for a few days is something I'm used to.

ME

Have you been able to sleep?

SKYE

A little. I'm tired, but my mind won't switch off.

ME

I'm in bed now. I know it's only midday, but I haven't slept properly since you went missing.

SKYE

Mom said you slept sitting up in the waiting room.

ME

I did. My neck and shoulders are killing me. Want to have a snuggle together?

SKYE

How do we do that?

I take a photo of myself lying on my side and send it to her.

ME

Take a photo of yourself and send it to me.

SKYE

But I look terrible.

ME

You do not. Now send me one.

Thirty seconds later, one appears in our conversation. She looks tired, but every inch of her is beautiful. Bruises and all.

ME

Now open the photo of me, full size, lie on your side, prop up your phone, if you can, and before you close your eyes, I'll be the last thing you see before you fall asleep.

SKYE

I'm not doing that.

ME

No?

SKYE

No. I'm going to look at your photo before I close my eyes and hold my phone to my heart.

ME

Butterfly, you are killing me with the cuteness.

SKYE

And you are killing me with the sweetness. Night, Jay. Or good afternoon.

ME

Night, Butterfly.

SKYE

Dream of me.

ME

Always.

30

JACOB

We've been texting back and forth for the last three days while Skye's been staying at her parents' place.

My father instructed me to take some time off as I've been working so hard recently and haven't had a holiday since the beginning of the year. Add that to the stress of Skye going missing and I'm exhausted. It's as if the tension I was holding in was released when she was found and streams of stress hormones flowed into my body, making everything feel impossible. My dad noticed and demanded I step back and try to take some time for myself before I broke. He was right. My body was screaming out for me to rest and I've slept more over the last few days than I ever have before.

So, after spending a couple of hours on the phone with clients explaining their projects will be handed over to a new account manager, I completely wound down and have spent the past three days doing a combination of some lightweight workouts at the gym and sorting out my spare room that still has at least thirty boxes waiting to be unpacked.

Having been in the house a year already, I never bothered unpacking what I didn't require.

Now I have a little time on my hands to read again, I thought I'd fill the bookshelves I bought months ago for the spare room and finally display my coveted books.

Almost nightfall, my takeaway pizza box lies on the navy carpeted floor of my guest bedroom.

To get my body in good shape, I've been watching everything I've eaten over the last year, but tonight I was done with being good. I needed comfort food and calories. Loads of calories, and a beer or two.

Surrounded by flattened boxes, boxes still to be unpacked, piles of books I am going to donate to the local library, and some of the wall-to-wall bookshelves finally filled, I neck the last of my beer from the bottle.

I texted Owen earlier to ask if he could meet me today, but he replied with:

OWEN

> I'm afraid not, amigo, my father has me stuck in meetings all day. Hope you're feeling better now that you've been fed and watered. Tomorrow afternoon at mine?

Relieved I'm finally getting to speak to him, I sent a message back agreeing. Although I may not feel relieved when he hears what I have to say. I'm preparing myself for the worst. Although, part of me no longer cares what he thinks anymore. I love her and want to be with her.

Note to self: find my jock strap and protector cap I wear for soccer.

I'm reviewing the back of one of the books I'm considering re-reading when the doorbell chimes.

Checking my wristwatch, I realize it's nine. Christ, I've been sorting through my books since midday, and I only texted Skye about four times today. This afternoon, the police were visiting her with an update on the case. I must see how that went.

My bare feet slap against the marbled flooring as I jog along the glass corridor to answer my front door.

It's barely open an inch, and I almost fall over when Skye forces her way into my house and pushes me backward. With determination in her eyes, she flies through the door at breakneck speed, making the door bang off the wall behind it with such force, it bounces back again and slams shut, allowing me just a glimpse of her father's car driving off before it closed.

"What the—" I don't get the chance to finish my sentence when she pushes me against the entrance wall and crashes her lips to mine.

Not a soft kiss, like how I imagined our first kiss to be. This kiss is full of passionate force and want.

"I'm not waiting anymore," she pants, as she pulls her jacket off her shoulders, letting it drop to the floor.

"Sk—" She pushes her tongue into my mouth, and I can't stop my tongue twisting around hers.

Her soft lips force mine wide open as she continues to invade my mouth. "My tests came back." Breathing hard, she gives me her news. "Negative. Everything was negative. He didn't..." She trails off.

My legs almost go from under me, but she holds my head firmly in place as she devours me with her lips.

"I want you." Her hand moves down my tee-shirt-covered chest.

I pop my eyes open and move my mouth to the side. "Wait,

wait, wait." I try to catch my breath. She kisses my jaw, then my neck.

Holy shit, this is all I've ever wanted and suddenly I'm stopping her.

Standing up on her tiptoes, she whispers in my ear. "You're going to stop the doubt, Jay. Right here in this hall. Shred everything right now because you're going to take me into that bedroom of yours and show me what it's like to be loved by you. Just like you told me."

I groan as my inner conscience messes with my primal instincts.

Fuck, I so want to do this, but... "I'm meeting Owen tomorrow."

She licks, then bites the shell of my ear. "I don't care. I need you now."

"Skye." I raise my voice to get her attention. She stops, allowing me to look at her. "Is this what you want? Are you sure?"

"I want it all with you, Jacob." The spark that was missing from her three days ago in the hospital is back now, making her crystal blues sparkle. "The awful things that happened to me this week, if anything, they've shown me that life is too damn short. I don't want to live with regrets, the 'what ifs', and 'if I'd never'. We've wasted enough time." She bites her bottom lip. "You saved me."

"I can't live without you." My voice breaks with longing.

"Show me how true that is." She fists my tee shirt and pulls me to her. Ghosting my lips, she says, "Now show me what I've been missing."

Throwing caution to the wind, I can't help but agree with her; life is too short to live with regrets. We need this.

I'm risking my friendship with Owen, which is already

hanging in the balance, anyway. He should have realized how close Skye and I were working together every day. How much she means to me, even just as a friend. He only seems interested in himself and his life. I care for him, but he's properly pissed me off of late.

There are no two ways about it. I need her.

I fucking want her.

And I won't lose out on another moment with her. I could have lost her forever, but she's here and she wants me too and I won't say no to her. Not again.

With open mouths, our tongues curl around one another in desperate need to feel that connection that's been smoldering between us for weeks. To taste, explore and finally find the true half of each other.

I slide my hands under her short skirt and grip her perfect bare ass as I lift her into the air. No instruction needed; she wraps her legs around my waist as I carry her to my bedroom.

As if in a dream, I don't know who I am at this moment as I continue to tongue-fuck the love of my life... my fucking best friend's ex.

I push Owen from my mind. God, I want her.

I have wanted her for so long.

"You're gonna be trouble," I mumble against her lips between our desperate kisses.

My cock now rock-hard, my heart racing, I can't think straight or remember how we got here.

Soft hands rub the back of my head and beard as if she's memorizing every inch of me, dousing me in her intoxicating scent.

Reaching the foot of my bed, knowing she's probably still fragile from her ordeal, I lower her gently onto the mattress.

She looks up at me with bright eyes. Confidence oozes out of her, eager to seal us together, forever, finally.

As she moves up the bed, she lifts her legs, then widens them for me in an invitation, treating me to a sliver of white lace between her legs.

I lift the hem of my light gray tee shirt, pulling it up and over my head, then move to the zipper on my black jeans to unzip and remove them too.

Watching every move I make, her eyes wander over my body.

I rub my cock through my boxers and groan. It's aching.

Aching for her as precum leaks from my tip.

She giggles at my choice of underwear. "I like your Batman boxers." She stares at the giant logo across my crotch.

"Your hero." I wink.

"Your dick or you?"

"Both."

She laughs again as she undresses, arching her back off the bed to allow her to pull her fitted white tee shirt up over her head, at the same time shucking her chunky shoes off, making them land on the floor with a *thud*. Unclipping her lace bra, she unthreads her arms from the straps and throws that away too.

She curls her finger, beckoning me; her bold eyes full of heat rake my body.

We've seen each naked before, but this, this is different.

Having her laid out on my bed, waiting for me, wanting me, it's next level.

On my hands and knees, I crawl to her and wedge myself between her legs until we are face to face.

"Are we really doing this?" I ask.

"Yes, we are."

31

SKYE

So much has changed. I've changed, but I *cannot* and *will not* sit back and let the world go by as I watch on.

I sat at my parents' house for three days; I couldn't wait a minute more to see him.

He has texted every day, almost every hour. Checking in on me, asking me how I am. But all it did was make me want to see him more. To wrap myself around him, for him to hold me.

Fed up with people turning up at my mom and dad's place, with flowers and gifts, and food—God, so much food—I needed to get out of the house. It felt stifling. Like I'd become the next exhibit at the petting zoo.

I don't want to be treated any differently, but Mom explained how everyone wanted to help in some way.

I get it. I really do. And while I am grateful for the enormous kindness and generosity the entire community has shown me, right now, I don't want the constant reminders of what happened to me because it could have been worse; much, much worse.

Thankfully, it wasn't, and I'm here and alive and I'm not prepared to *not* live my life because of him.

When the sexual assault test came back negative, I made my decision. I can't play the victim. I won't allow it. I have so much to be grateful for.

I'm alive.

I'll be damned if I let him impact the rest of my life or prevent me from living my best life or from having adventures.

The good news kept on coming when the police informed me this afternoon that Jules was admitted to a psychiatric hospital under the Mental Health Act until further notice.

As soon as the police left, I made the decision that I would educate people. Show them what to look out for, the red flags —the ones I didn't pay attention to.

I was put through this ordeal for a reason, and if this is what I was put on this earth to do—to educate others and help—then that's what I will do. Even if it means I only save one person, I will have still saved one person.

But no one, nope, not even a seriously unwell man with an unhealthy obsession for me, will stop me.

I'm grabbing life by the balls and I'm making sure I get my happy ever after and that's how I talked my dad into reluctantly driving me here as I wasn't quite ready to drive myself here in the dark.

So here I am, with my arms laced around Jacob's neck. He's what I need, the one I crave, the one that breathes air into my lungs, and the one that saved me because he loves me.

I've fallen for him. Fallen hard. I'm so deeply in love with him I'm drowning and I'm not sure I ever want to come up for air.

It caught me unawares... threw me off balance, but he's what I need and he's been standing in front of me all along in plain sight and I'm not letting some childhood promise to his best friend stand in our way for a second longer.

I'm looking up at him as he hovers over me; he cups my face with his hands and asks me, "Are we really doing this?"

I smile back at him as my heart fills with love for this beautiful human being. "Yes, we are," I reassure him, hooking my fingers into the waistband of his boxers.

He helps me remove them fully, then he throws them away and I look down to get a proper look at him.

"You have a beautiful cock. I can't wait to taste you."

"Those are words I could only have ever dreamed about before." He looks nervous as he bites his lip.

"You're not dreaming anymore."

For the first time ever, our bodies touch one another. Chest to chest, lips on lips, he presses himself firmly against me.

My body comes alive, quivering in anticipation, every nerve ending tuned in to his movements as he glides his hands all over me.

We slowly explore each other, learning every small detail, with our hands, tongues, and lips.

We've been waiting for this moment. Desperate to be together.

Finally, we're here and it couldn't be more perfect.

My heartbeat shoots through the roof when his firm and expert mouth moves from my jaw to my neck, licking the exact spot I told him I loved just a few days ago, causing me to shudder; goosebumps dance across my skin.

It feels like months have passed since we were sitting on Violet and Lincoln's sofa, but it's not. It's only been a week.

The rush of lust and static electricity runs between us as he drifts his fingertips down my neck, then my chest, until he reaches my hardened nipple. He pulls a gasp from my throat when he pinches it between his deft fingers.

Moving down my stomach, over my skirt, he skims his hand over my outer thigh. I hold my breath for a second when he moves his touch up the inside of my thigh, then back down again. He does this over and over, teasing me, tickling me until I can't take it anymore.

Desire sizzles, pleasure burning my skin as emotion floods into my heart.

"I want you, Jay." I grab his hand and lead him under my skirt, guiding him where I want him to touch me.

"I want to be everything you need." His hard length digs into my leg as he mumbles against my lips.

"You already are." I press his fingers to my center, making my back arch off the bed. He slips my panties to the side and I gasp when he touches my pussy for the first time.

I let go of his hand and reach out to cup his balls.

He stops kissing me, his open mouth against mine as his eyes roll back into his head.

"Stroke me," he gasps, sliding his finger down my pussy lips. Flames lick around our self-control, as the fire between us burns hotter by the second.

Using my thumb to rub the precum over his tip, I fist my hand around him and begin to stroke him soft then tight, soft, and then tight.

"Aw fuck," he mutters against my lips, as he bucks his hips, fucking my hand. "Are you wet for me?" He doesn't wait for my answer as he pushes his thick finger deep into my body, curling it inside of me as he slides it in and out, as if beckoning me to come; my lungs struggle to find air.

His dark eyes intensify, making my heart zoom.

"So wet for you, Jay." Synchronized, we both moan together. "I want you inside of me. I need to feel you."

I stop stroking him to find the buckle of my wrap skirt. Undoing it quickly, I pull one side apart, then the other, as if giving myself to him, pulling it out from underneath me.

"You should wear this skirt all the time," he says, still sliding his finger back and forth.

Naked now aside from my panties and socks, I lean to the side to pull them off but he stops me.

"Leave the socks on," he commands, his voice deep and laced with sin.

I'm distracted by his command when he pushes another finger inside of me and I cry out from the feeling of him stretching me.

"Getting you ready for me, Butterfly." His thumb rubs my clit, making me instantly feel the need to come.

"Oh, God," I cry out. "I'm gonna—" I can't form my words as he hovers over me with a look of sheer passion in his dark eyes. Thrusting his fingers deep, up to his knuckle, he curls them inside of me, touching a spot so deep inside that I can't remember my own name. He presses his thumb against my swollen bud again and I explode around his fingers, bucking myself into them as I chase my orgasm.

I don't want it to end as stars burst like dazzling glitter behind my eyes. The feeling of happiness and joy dances across my skin.

I reach for his hand that's inside of me, to hold him still and to allow me to hold on to this incredible feeling a little longer.

"I think you needed that," he whispers in my ear.

"What do you expect after weeks of all this foreplay we've

been doing together? You've been edging me for what feels like forever."

He chuckles against my skin, kissing my neck gently, then he licks it, causing a wave of pleasurable shivers down my back.

I let go of his hand and as he removes his fingers from my body, he looks me dead in the eye when he sucks them into his mouth.

He closes his eyes as if it's the best thing he's ever tasted.

I could watch him for hours. He's so hot and his body is insanely sexy.

Like his tattoos that bleed across his skin, I want him to cover me with his body. I want to lose myself in him. Forever.

He slips my panties off one leg, then the other, before he sucks my nipple into his mouth, pinching then rolling the other between his fingertips.

I've never been much of a fan of nipple play in the past, that is, until now.

It's as if all of my senses have switched on like he's my lighthouse... he's my home. His body speaks to me in ways I can't describe, but everything feels... perfect.

He flattens his tongue over my nipple and sucks it into his mouth, giving it a gentle tug between his teeth, causing me to squirm.

"You have the perfect body, Skye. I think it likes me."

It loves you.

"Your body responds to everything I do." He flicks his tongue fast over my nipple and a feeling deep in my pussy makes me feel like I could come again.

Loving the sensation, I moan, pushing my chest into his face.

"I'm going to make you feel so good, Butterfly." With the need to find his own release, he leisurely fists his cock.

I reach for him, guiding him to me. "I have a contraceptive implant."

He frowns, and then it dawns on him. "Really? Bare? With you? I've never..."

I nod, smiling up at him, telling him it's what I want.

Adrenaline rushes through my veins, knowing what comes next as we get to the point we've both been desperate for.

He moves his knees closer to me and I widen my legs to welcome him.

He bows his head, hesitating then hisses, "Fuck."

"What's the matter?" I place my pointer finger under his chin and lift it, so he can look at me.

His frown lines deepen as he admits, "I'm gonna fucking blow in like three seconds of being inside of you, Skye. I... I... I just..."

"Shh." I place my finger to his lips to hush him and tilt my hips. I then grab his ass, guiding the tip of his cock inside of me. "I don't care. That means we get to do it more than once."

His eyes fix on me as he pushes in a little before pulling out slowly. Moving again, he pushes in a little further and he holds there, staring at me, as if not believing that we are crossing into this forbidden territory.

He slides back and forth, taking his time. All the while, his thumb moves back and forth across my temple.

I'm done with waiting, so I grab his ass again, hard, and pull him into me, making us both cry out in pleasure.

"Fucking hell, Skye." He looks at me as if to say, *what are you doing to me?* "Christ, I feel like a goddamn virgin again."

I smile up at him. "I want you." I lace my fingers around his neck, pulling him down to me, and kiss him with undeniable passion and love. The love I feel for him is like nothing I have ever felt before. It runs in my veins, through my sanity, and makes me feel giddy all of the time.

"Fuck me," I mumble against his lips.

"I never thought I would say this, but you telling me to fuck you is so hot. Especially since you never swear."

"This good girl is going bad," I giggle. This urges him to finally move and when he does, he gasps and moans as he glides in and out.

"You feel so fucking good, Butterfly." He rests his open mouth against mine, not kissing, barely touching, as our hot breaths dust each other's skin.

I wrap my legs around his waist, digging my heels into his ass, urging him to go deeper.

His hand runs down and up my leg as we rock together, finding our rhythm. His pelvis rubs my clit over and over as he goes a little deeper with every thrust.

I cry his name a few times as he picks up pace, burying himself deep within me; he widens his knees to give him more power behind his movements.

My mouth leaves his lips as his thrusts make my back arch off the bed, and I feel every part of him inside of me, the head of his cock teasing my G-spot.

"You are mine," he growls before he sucks my nipple into his mouth and bites down.

"Oh, do that again." I push my chest into his mouth for him to repeat his action.

"Come for me, Butterfly. Wet my cock with your tight pussy." His filthy words are my undoing, causing the beginning of my orgasm to weave its way through my body.

He bites down, then flicks my nipple with his tongue, and

the orgasm that's been building suddenly explodes, causing me to cry out his name, claiming him as mine.

My whole body lights up like the fourth of July, my legs shaking, the sensations ripping through me like an avalanche.

His grunts and thrusts become feral as he fucks me through my orgasm, pounding me into the bed. I want more. I want all of him and I don't want him to ever stop. It feels like we've been doing this forever together.

Skin on skin, he fucks me harder, my hands exploring his hard body, memorizing every part of him, praying he can feel my love for him pouring through my touch, as he slides into my heart, flooding my soul in the best way possible.

"I want to go on top," I gasp.

Without hesitation, he loops his gigantic arm around my waist and flips us over. Never losing the connection, I sit upright. Moving my pelvis back and forth, I grind my clit against his pelvic bone.

The low light across the room makes him look darker, his pecs flexing, his tattoos almost dancing like shadows across his body.

I run my hands down his chest. "You're so sexy, Jay." Butterflies dance in my lower stomach, knowing he's all mine.

He reaches up and pulls the elasticated hair band out of my long silver locks.

I shake my hair to fluff it out.

Looking up at me with hooded eyes, he smirks. "You should see yourself. Sexy as fuck. Your hair." He thrusts. "Your fucking beautiful body." Another thrust. "Your nipples are fucking delicious." Another thrust. "And these fucking socks." He pings the elastic hem of my thigh-high socks. "They will be my undoing. You'll be the death of me, you sexy little minx. Aw fuck. I'm gonna—" He squeezes his eyes shut.

"Look at me." I move my hand behind me and squeeze his balls, making his eyes fly open.

I squeeze them tighter, clenching the inner walls of my pussy, as I reach down to play with my clit.

And I rock, fuck me, do I rock my hips to give him the ride of his life. Because while a slow gentle love-making session would have been nice, it would be exactly that, nice, and that's not what I wanted. This is everything I want and more, and he needed this to finally bond us, to show him I'm not shy or quiet. I know what I want. Him. I want to show him the real me, the one I have always wanted to feel like. To feel free, loved, and adored. To be myself and let myself go.

He moves my hand out of the way to take over, pinching my clit. He rubs it then pinches it again, repeating the same motion over and over. Molten desire floods my core as I come again, taking him with me, as I tighten my grip on his testicles.

"Aw Jesus Christ, what the fuck—aw, Skye. What are you doing to me?" Words that make no sense spill out of his mouth as he shoots his load inside of me, filling me with his cum.

I arch my neck back, my eyes rolling into the back of my head as I shudder and clench all around his cock. The feeling of my release burns between my thighs and low in my spine.

He pants, his chest heaving. He slowly sits up, looping his arms around me. "That was the best fuck of my life."

Too tired to speak, I rest my head on his shoulder, letting him hold me.

"Hey, are you okay?" He lightly strokes my back.

"You made me orgasm three times. I'm tired," I mumble against his skin.

He laughs out loud, making his chest rumble. "You ain't seen nothing yet."

I nuzzle into his neck and sigh. "Can you show me tomorrow?" I say sleepily on a yawn.

"C'mon, my little sleepy Butterfly." He lies back and rolls us onto our sides then slowly slides out of me, and I miss the feeling of him inside me already.

The weight of his stare makes me pop one eye open.

"Hi." His smile is wider than the Grand Canyon.

"Someone is looking pretty smug with themselves." I hook my leg higher up his waist. His hand instantly grabs my ass, and he gives it a squeeze.

Staring at each other for a while, he finally breaks the silence. "I love you," he whispers, sending a thrill of energy up my spine.

I go to speak, but he places a finger over my lips. "Don't." He shakes his head. "Not yet."

He kisses me softly, setting my heart on fire. "I'll go get a washcloth to clean you up." Turning over, he jumps off the bed, and he's back before I know it, cleaning me between my legs.

"No one has ever done that before." I suddenly feel self-conscious.

He clenches his eyes closed with a half-smile, half-cringing. "I didn't want to know that."

Shit. I've only ever been with Owen. "I'm sorry."

"It's fine." He urges me to get under the bed sheets. "C'mon, Butterfly, shuffle under."

I struggle because I can't be bothered moving. I'm so tired, my body feeling like a dead weight, I can barely lift my head off the pillow. I do an awkward worm type movement, making Jacob laugh until I snuggle deep inside the covers.

"Your bed smells nice," I mumble.

"Does it?"

"Yeah, it smells like you." I inhale his scent again. It instantly makes me feel calm.

Jacob slips in next to me and I wiggle in closer to his bare chest when he threads his arm under my head, snuggling me into him like this is the most natural thing in the world and we've been doing it for decades.

Resting my hand on his chest, he lays his hand over mine. Almost asleep, my heavy limb is lifted off his chest and is held up in midair. I open my tired eyes and watch him as he examines the bruises around my wrists, running his thumb over my deep blue and purple marks.

"Are they sore?"

"No." I pull my hand out of his and tuck it under the covers to hide my injuries. At least those will fade; others will last longer and be embedded in my memory forever.

"You know I'm here for you come rain or shine. You can talk to me about anything."

"I know." I turn onto my back, moving his arm from behind my head, and stare at the ceiling.

Jacob turns onto his side to look at me; he props his head on his hand. "Tell me what you're thinking?"

I dive under the covers to remove my long socks. "Well, for a start, these have to come off, because I get really hot feet at night."

"Righhhttt. And…"

I throw them onto the floor and turn to face him again, tucking my hands under my cheek. They aren't so sore anymore and even though I was hit hard, the skin on my face is healing quickly, with fewer blood spots around my ear now, too. It's less red than it was and the scratch has almost gone. It was mostly superficial but still hurt like a bitch, and I still look like I've been slapped across the face, worse on one side than the other.

"I hate what he did to me and how he made me feel," I whisper.

"How did he make you feel?"

"Stupid."

"You're the smartest woman I know."

"Not smart enough to see the signs or not meet him or share things with him in private emails." I don't know how many times I've voiced this to my mom already.

"He's a predator. That's what they do."

"He's a maniac."

"That too."

"He made the room he kept me in look like a replica of my bedroom." I pull a little thread from the pillowcase. "He bought clothes from the same shop I go to. He even bought the same makeup I wear. He said he did it to make me happy, but all I felt was scared. I was petrified."

Jacob gives me space to think.

"I can't go back to the room I rent. I'm having Kimmy pack all my things for me but leaving all the furniture. I don't want it and I'm going to move in with Mom and Dad until I get a new place. A place of my own."

"You could move in with me." Jacob lays his hand over mine to stop me playing with the thread.

I look deep into his eyes. "Although we know each other really well, we don't know each other romantically and I've never lived with a boyfriend before..."

"Skye, I know you better than anyone else. I know what time you have breakfast and what time you reapply your lipstick in the afternoons. Where you buy your coffee from. I know you better than I know myself."

"I think you do." My heart pounds in my chest as it whooshes with emotion. He's so sweet, and he doesn't know how beautiful he is.

"I fucking love you with every breath in my body, every blood cell within me. I care for you and I want to love and protect you for the rest of my life."

"I know, big guy." I pat his hard chest mockingly, trying to wave off his sweet words that might make me cry again. I am done with crying. "I quite like you too though. Just in case you're wondering."

"Was that before or after the sex?"

"Before," I snort. "The sex was, well... average."

He turns onto his back and mutters, "Some people are difficult to please."

Then we both burst out laughing.

Jacob isn't usually the playful type, but I feel like I've unlocked a new level with him these last few weeks and then another after what we just did in his bed.

Sex with Jacob Baxter is another level I wasn't prepared for.

They do say sex with your soul mate can be life-altering.

I think perhaps I found mine in him.

"I have to tell you some things," I whisper.

He turns to face me again, mirroring my position, and rests his hands under his cheek too. I reach out and run my hand down his soft scruff. I'm most likely to have a beard rash on my chin tomorrow. It already feels raw.

"Share away." He looks concerned.

I clear my throat, preparing myself for the first and not the last time I say these words. "You can't ever call me doll face, baby doll, or dolly. Ever. When I testify against Jules in court, I will no doubt have to repeat these words that sound creepy to me now."

"Okay." He nods in understanding.

"You're not to treat me any differently. I will not let that evil psychopath ruin my life."

"Understood."

"I don't want any special privileges at work."

He frowns as if disagreeing with me.

"I mean it," I say firmly.

He doesn't agree or disagree.

"I want to speak to a therapist. I think I should speak to someone outside of Castleview Cove. Someone in Edinburgh maybe."

"I'll take you."

I knew he'd say that.

"I want to tell you everything, but I'm not quite ready."

"That's okay."

"Two more things. I think I would like to, maybe, eventually, share my story. Not sell it to the papers or anything but do talks, digital media awareness training in schools and universities, perhaps. I'm living proof that you can work in the digital media industry and still fall subject to its dark side."

"My father will be one hundred and ten percent on board with that. We'll support you and give you time off work to do it."

"Thank you."

"Anything else?" he asks, pulling me to him. I hook my leg up over his hips again, loving the way he feels against my skin. His solid frame is addictive and I could spend forever being wrapped around him like this.

Our lips brush together. "I'm in love with you, Jacob Baxter."

32

JACOB

My lips freeze as she says words that fill me to the brim with gratitude and excitement. I am beyond grateful for this beautiful woman and so excited for what our future holds together.

"Say that again."

"I said I love you, Jacob Baxter." She smiles. "I think I've loved you since the day we met. I've loved you as a friend since we were sixteen years old, and now I feel like you've planted roots in my heart and you've never dug your way out. All the things you did for me, without me ever knowing, the gifts and the days out, the lifts to and from work when I needed them. You've cared for me in such a special way; I feel you everywhere. I know you're the one. I mean, you hired a PI to find me." She shakes her head in disbelief. "If it wasn't for you, I may not be here. Mom and Dad told me everything, especially the twenty-four-hour waiting game the police wanted to play. Twenty-four hours is a long time to be missing before they start looking for you. I could have been in a different country by then." Her lips ghost mine. "But you... you knew what needed to happen. You knew it was out of character for me and you did what you needed to do to save the one you loved."

"Love, present tense."

Her smile grows wide. "Love. I love being loved by you, Jacob."

"And I love being loved by you." My mouth is on hers within milliseconds as her hands cup my face.

I gently roll her onto her back, and she spreads her thighs for me, letting me in.

The tension my body has been feeling for days rolls away, evaporating into the heated air.

I rub my hard cock up and down her wet-for-me pussy lips, my tip weeping for her, eager to slide home.

She whimpers when I push myself into her already wet core.

Blood rushes to the head of my cock, making me harder as I drive myself into her with long, languid thrusts.

I don't want to rush this; I want to remember this moment, imprinting it in my memory for eternity.

Our kiss turns passionate as we taste and lick one another, going deeper as she sucks my tongue into her mouth, making my cock thicken.

Undulating my hips in slow waves, I drive myself deeper, tilting her hips to hit the perfect spot to get her there quicker.

Her whimpers become louder, her chest heaving.

Leaning back, I smile down at her, loving every hot fucking minute between us, completely in awe of her and that this is us. Finally.

She pushes her hips into mine.

"Oh, that feels so nice," she squeals. Fucking squeals.

Knowing exactly how she responds to my touch already, I

lift her hips further and lean back to rub against the front of her inner walls.

I rest back on my haunches.

"Oh, Jay," she gasps when I push in further, applying pressure to her lower belly with the palm of my hand.

I stroke her clit with my other hand, stretching her hood back slightly to pinch, then rub it, stroking it over and over.

"Why does that feel so good?" She grabs my ass, driving me into her harder.

Her hair fanned over the bedcovers, her brow lined with a frown, she looks beautiful. I can't take my eyes off her.

"Relax," I coax her.

Her brow lines disappear with my gentle words.

If I fucking get this right, then my heart may give out.

I stroke her clit faster now and push down on her tummy a little more.

"I feel like I need to pee," she gasps.

"Just go with the feeling, Skye. Let it happen."

She starts crying out and moaning longer, as I go faster with every thrust and stroke of her clit.

"Let everything go. Relax."

She squeals again, then she lets out the most extraordinary long deep moan as she squirts all over my stomach, over and over again.

I pull myself out of her, slapping and rubbing her clit as she calls out my name, her orgasm almost endless.

Her body goes completely rigid, fisting the covers into her hands, digging her heels into the mattress.

"Fuck yeah, Butterfly, come all over my cock." I rub her arousal over my dick, then slam myself back into her pussy. Hard. Fucking her a couple more times before I explode inside of her.

Her warm walls continue to flutter around my sensitive cock as she experiences a super-intense orgasm.

Her moans begin to trail off, her body relaxing as if allowing the pleasure to radiate through her entire body.

My cock pulses inside of her as I spill every last drop.

"What just happened?" she says between pants, threading her fingers through her hair.

"That was the hottest thing I have ever fucking seen." I'm pretty sure I have hearts in my eyes.

"That's never happened before. That felt incredible. Like overwhelming and super intense. So strong."

"Soul *fucking* mates."

Getting the joke, she giggles. I could get high off that sound.

"It's a bit embarrassing though, no... yes?"

I grin wider than a Cheshire cat. "No fucking way. You're a wet dream come true. So sexy."

"I think angels sang." Eyes dazed, she looks like she's about to fall asleep, which I prevented her from doing earlier.

"So, we're in heaven now?"

"If we are, can we do that again? Maybe tomorrow though, I'm so tired." Her little pink pouty mouth yawns wide.

"Shower first." Still seated deep inside her, because my dick appears to like her a lot, wanting to stay permanently hard for her, I pull her up and carry her to the shower.

I pull her up and carry her to the shower, and she loops her arms around my neck, then asks, "Is it always hard?"

I bounce her up and down on my dick a few times. "I think that answered your question."

"Again?" She looks shocked.

"If you can handle it." I turn the shower on and stand us under the instant hot water.

"Fuck me slow against the wall, then fuck me to sleep, Jay."

"You know I'd give you anything you wish for."

She smiles against my lips when I push her against the tiled wall. "I love you," she breathes.

"I love you, whatever, however, forever."

33

JACOB

"What the actual fuck is this?" A familiar voice wakes me up from my deep slumber.

My eyes pop open; my heart takes flight at the speed of light, making me spring out of the bed, naked. *Shit.*

Owen.

He's standing at the foot of my bed, pointing at a still-sleeping Skye, her tattooed leg hooked outside of the bedcovers; she's wrapped around the comforter. She looks fucking edible.

Fuck.

"I can explain." I hold my hands up, bending at the same time to reach for my jeans.

"Explain?" Boiling with fury, his face turns red. "I think it's pretty fucking clear."

Quicker than a heartbeat, I step into my jeans, pull them over my hips, tuck my cock in and zip them up.

"So you two are fucking?" His nostrils flare as he grinds his teeth together.

Skye grumbles, pulling the covers up over her head. "Why is the television on?"

Owen ignores her. "Is this what you've been so fucking desperate to speak to me about? To tell me you've been sleeping with my girlfriend?" He shoots me a sour look.

"She's your ex. Has been for months," I correct him. "You're getting married, remember?"

A small gasp and mumble of "*Oh no*" from under the covers escapes as Skye finally wakes up.

"You are unbelievable, Jacob." He pulls his hair in distress. "I can't deal with this."

He turns on his heels, storming out of the room.

"Don't go, Owen. Let me explain," I shout after him, pulling the covers down from Skye's face. "Get up, get dressed, now." My eyes widen, begging her to do as I ask.

"How did he get in?" she whispers.

"He has a key. Text Lincoln for me. Tell him to come here. Right now."

"Oh my God, Jay. This is not good." She leaps out of the bed as I run out the doorway.

"Owen." I jog down the corridor into my living space and find him staring out of the windows at the evergreen fields around my house.

"How long?" He doesn't turn around.

"Last night was the first time we..." I need air. I can't breathe.

"Is that why you hired that fucking PI? Like some sort of superhero? How long?"

My voice raises. "I just told you, last night was the..."

"You're a fucking liar, Jay." He turns around, angry energy bouncing off him. I can feel it from across the room as I move toward him, closing the space between us.

"I'm not. I didn't touch, kiss, or sleep with her until last night." I gather all the strength I have, straightening myself up to full height.

"And before then? Have you been messing about with her behind my back?" he yells in my face.

"It's not like that." I show no signs of backing down, as I refuse to deny how I feel about Skye.

"Explain what the fuck it's like, then?" His face is tormented with confusion.

Skye runs into the room, looking panicked, dressed in my tee shirt from yesterday. "Owen, stop this." She piles her hair on top of her head, making my top creep up her thighs.

If she lifts her arms any higher, she'll flash her pussy at him.

Aw hell, he's already seen it. Fuck, I feel sick.

"Stop? I haven't even started." He scoffs. "I fucking know you, Jay. You've had several girlfriends, but none of them ever live up to your standards and then you move on. But you like to fuck all night to keep them happy." He sneers.

I clench my jaw tight. "Is that how you see me?" I thread my hands on top of my head and pace back and forth. "Fuck, Owen, if you'd paid enough attention, then you'd know why none of them lived up to what I wanted."

"What, did none of them give good head or like it rough enough?"

Skye gasps at his crass remark.

"How fucking dare you, Owen." I throw him a brutal stare. "You are so far off the mark."

"How far?" he laughs mockingly.

"Try Skye fucking high off the mark." I point at her. "That's how far."

He looks confused.

"I'm in love with Skye and have been for years." My loud words echo across the open space.

His head shoots back as if struck by lightning, brows dipping low. "What?"

"You fucking asked her out in high school, knowing that I liked her."

"No, I fucking didn't."

"Yes, you did!" I roar. "Trust me, I know you and how you work. You think you know me, but you know fuck all about me or Skye. You never cared about her. Everything you did, organized, or went to, there always had to be something in it for you. You never, *ever* put her first. But I did. Always."

"You're fucking delusional."

I'll be damned if he thinks I am. "Who took her home from prom when she ripped her dress?" I storm across the room in his direction.

"Me?" He looks at me like I'm an idiot.

"Mehhh." I make the noise of a buzzer. "Wrong. It was me." I dig my finger into my chest. "Who helped Skye fill out her art college application? Who went with her to her first driving lesson because she was nervous? Who went to her college interview with her? Who organized your five-year anniversary meal at that fancy restaurant in London she always wanted to go to that appeared on that television cooking show? And who else knows that when she's happy she sings to herself? Did you ever pay attention to anything or even care about her?"

"Can you hear yourself? You sound like an obsessive stalker. He's talking shit, Skye, tell him." He points from her to me.

She shakes her head. "He's not wrong, Owen." Her voice is gentle. "He's right about everything."

"That's not right." He waggles his finger at me, dismissing me, almost accusing me of being a liar. "I care. Don't I?"

"You have a funny way of showing it." Skye hugs her arms around herself.

Owen takes a moment to himself as he looks out of the windows again.

I step closer to him, no longer caring if he fucking punches me or not. I will fight to the death for her. "Owen, I would never do anything to hurt you." He keeps looking ahead. "I am in love with her. I hid my feelings for so long. Then I told Skye when we were in London. Something happened between us at the office a few weeks before that. But I swear on my life, I never touched her." I leave out the part where I made her touch herself. "What started as a spark turned into something bigger. I've tried to speak to you so many times, but you kept ignoring my calls, and that's what I was coming to your house about today, to tell you how much Skye and I want to be together, then last night..."

"I turned up here and told Jacob I love him." Skye steps by my side, exuding confidence like I have never seen before, and if Owen wasn't standing there right now, I would kiss her.

"Right." He turns and throws us both a fake smile. "Well, I hope you'll be happy together." He storms past us, heading for the door.

"Owen, p-please don't be like that," Skye stammers at his cynicism of us.

Owen spins back around. "Like what? What exactly should I be like? You've just told me you've been in love with the girl I have spent half my life with. Told me that for four-teen years you've harbored all of these feelings for her, but you never acted on it? I don't believe a word of it."

I've never been a liar. I can't believe he would think I was lying right now. Screams of frustration bubble in my chest. "Hey, the reason I didn't was because of our pact. Remember the one we made, no kissing ex-girlfriends or sisters? That's why."

He lets out a maniacal laugh. "Fucking hell, you didn't think we were serious, did you?"

Lincoln runs through the door out of breath. "Oh, thank Christ, you're both still alive." Fighting for air, he clutches his chest.

"You knew?" Wide-eyed, Owen asks Lincoln.

"Sort of. Not really. But it's really fucking obvious. Have you seen the way he looks at her and follows her around like a lovesick puppy?"

Someone kill me.

Lincoln keeps talking, not giving Owen a chance to respond. "I heard you talking. I kept my end of the bargain on our pact."

"What? That stupid pact we made when we were thirteen?" Owen's brow wrinkles.

"Fourteen," I correct him.

"Well, I broke that two weeks after we made it, when I kissed your sister out on the porch at your house." He looks at me smugly. "Bonus points for the boob squeeze."

"What?" Lincoln and I both shout at the same time.

Asshole.

"Angela Blackwood too." Owen looks at Lincoln.

"She was my first girlfriend." His mouth falls open in shock.

I look directly at Owen. "You're a prick."

"It takes one to know one." He points at me. "And you're wrong about me. I did care for you, Skye, maybe not how Jacob does, but I did. I always bought you nice things."

"I don't need things, but what makes it worse is that Jay bought me those things. You still haven't given him the money for the tablet and stylus pen," Skye fires back, getting her point across.

"Fuck sakes, can a guy not catch a break?" He pushes his fingertips into his closed eyes. "Is this gang-up-on-Owen day? Did I not take you to the nice parties my mother threw and buy you nice dresses?" He looks at Skye for an answer.

"You gave me the money to buy something new, but Jay always went with me to the shops to make sure I looked the part. Then your mother would parade other women in my face because she thought they were more suitable for you. And usually, you would spend it flirting, eye-fucking those suitable women, and Jay and I would end up dancing and drinking the night away. He was always the one who took me home. He cares about me, Owen. He always has."

He pulls out a chair around my dining table and falls into it. Head in his hands, he mumbles, "What the fuck is wrong with me? How have I not seen this?" He runs his hands through his hair as if distressed. "Is your favorite movie *The Princess Bride*?" He looks at Skye, waiting for an answer.

Skye smiles. "Yeah. I didn't think you knew that."

"I didn't. Jay told me the other day." He blinks with bafflement.

"Do you know how long Jacob has been in love with me for?" She walks over to Owen and sits next to him.

Mouth downturned, he shakes his head.

"Have you seen Jacob's tattoo on his back?" She takes his hand.

He frowns again.

I want the world to swallow me up.

"Those words he has written, *whatever, however, forever*, it's his code for *I love you*. Jay and I... we love each other. He's loved me for, well, since high school, well, forever. He said those words to me on the first day we met when we spoke about code words for *I love you*. Those are his. For me. But he's never acted on his feelings. Not once. Not ever. I promise you."

Standing in just my jeans, my whole body feels hot. My cheeks heat under Lincoln's grinning stare.

Yup, anyone, just fucking kill me, right about... now.

I don't want to talk about my feelings in front of my two huge, burly friends. While Lincoln could talk about his feelings all day, I am fine just keeping them to myself. Thank you very much.

"Is that what that fucking means? You got that tattoo like last year." He sits back in his chair. "Oh my God." Realization falls over his face. "And the book, the clouds and the blue sky, the snowdrops and the castle? You did that for her?"

The room goes quiet.

"Jesus Christ, you really do love her. You're a fucking hopeless romantic."

He stares at me with a mixed look of confusion and admiration. "I wanted to punch you earlier and now I can't do that." Owen bites his bottom lip. "I should maybe thank you for loving my girl the way she deserves to be loved."

I don't know what the hell to say to that.

"I'm not your girl anymore and maybe you could start by apologizing to me." Skye pats the back of his hand. Her strength knows no bounds today. She's having her say and making sure we sort this.

"What for?"

"Blaming me for encouraging the seriously unwell man that abducted me?"

"I need a lesson in sensitivity." He rubs his forehead. "Am I really that bad?"

Lincoln squeezes his shoulder. "You live in a different world, filled with yes-people who would literally lick your feet if you asked them to. We keep you grounded."

Tense lines of worry tighten more. "I'm sorry, Skye. If I ever did anything or said anything to hurt you. That was never my intention. My life is a fucking mess. I can't do anything right," he groans.

Our poor friend is suffering in ways we can't imagine; if he would just speak to us, maybe we could help, or at least listen.

Knowing I'm safe from being punched—although I would have let him; I'd do anything for her—I sit down at the table beside Skye. Instinctively, she rests her hand on my thigh and gives it a gentle squeeze.

"You can tell us about it," I offer.

For the first time since he arrived, he smiles at me, genuinely. "Nah. I've done enough talking and sharing today." Although I can feel the pain in his voice.

He considers what he says next. "This is like, whoa, *a lot*. So you two, huh?"

Skye smiles, lifting her shoulders to her ears. "Yeah." She looks so fucking happy, happier than she ever was with Owen. "We were going to tell you. I promise."

We all fall quiet again. In meetings, I'm great with words. Right now, I'm speechless. This is not how I saw this panning out.

Owen can't stop looking at us seated together. "You look good together. I see that whole opposites attract thing now. The tatted bad boy and the sweet, innocent blonde. Although she's more like Harley Quinn if you piss her off."

Skye chuckles. "I don't have a baseball bat."

I'll buy her one if it means she dresses up for me in a Harley Quinn costume. She'd look hot as fuck in those little red and blue shiny hotpants and pigtails.

I'll maybe suggest that later.

Owen pushes his chair back. "Fuck." He looks at us both again. "This is going to take some getting used to, and it's too early for this shit. I need a drink."

"Please don't do that, Owen." Skye urges him not to fall back down the hole he's been in.

"Maybe later." He pulls his phone out of his pocket. "Shit, I gotta go. See you around, bab—Skye."

"I would hug you goodbye, but I don't have any underwear on," she says, innocently.

I pull my hand down my face. Owen's right, this is going to take some getting used to. "Fucking hell," I mumble.

I hear Lincoln chuckle as he heads to the front door. "Good chat, boys. I'm still pissed off at you for kissing Angela Blackwood." He throws shade over his shoulder at Owen as he leaves.

"And my sister," I pipe up.

He points at Skye, who is walking back to the bedroom, waving goodbye. "Don't. Even. Go. There."

"Deal."

He shoves his hands into his pockets. "You love her?"

"With my whole fucking heart."

"I'm sorry if you feel like I took her from you." Pain etches across his face. "I didn't know you had such strong feelings for her."

"You knew," I remind him and emphasize my point. "All those years ago, I told you and then you went ahead and asked her out anyway. You knew that I liked her, Owen."

"I'm so fucking sorry, man."

"You treated Skye like shit."

His forehead wrinkles. "I was a shitty boyfriend."

"You were."

"And an even shittier friend. I'm really fucking sorry, Jay."

"What's done is done. Bygones." I can't let what has happened linger any longer. She's mine now. Excitement bubbles in my chest at that thought.

"How can I ever make it up to you?" He looks at me like I have all the answers.

"You don't have to. Skye and I are together now. That's all I have ever wanted." Honesty rolls off my tongue.

He waits a beats before he says, "Promise me one thing."

"Anything."

"Don't break her heart like I did."

I don't think you did.

"And hold on to her. Love her better than I ever could have. She's—"

"I know." He doesn't need to tell me how incredible she is. I already know. "Look, this is not how you were supposed to find out. I wanted to tell you face to face."

Before I can comprehend what's happening, he pulls me into a fierce hug and slaps me fondly on the back. "You're a good man, Jacob. I didn't mean the things I said about you."

"I forgive you, but you have to forgive me, too. I should have told you years ago."

We let go of each other.

"It's done now, Jay, and hey, I have a new fiancée to look after now. Maybe I'll do a better job with her?"

"Or maybe you need to find your own woman who actually loves you for you, that you love so fucking fiercely you may even want to buy your own Christmas presents for her, and not someone your mother tells you to marry."

He considers that for a moment. "Touché. Good one. How would I do that?"

"Stand up for yourself. Tell your parents where to shove it. Sell your house. Disown them? You've been unhappy for years, Owen."

"Yeah. That sounds like financial suicide." He pulls another fake smile. I know him so well, I can tell. "I'm off. Oh, I will leave my key." He pulls it from his pocket. "I don't ever want to walk in on, well, you know." Then he turns to leave.

Smirking, I nod. Yeah, I never want that to happen either.

He stops walking, then swivels back round to face me. "I never would have punched you. You're my boy. You know that, right?"

I nod my head.

He keeps going. "She's been through enough trauma. I would never, *ever*, have been violent in front of her, or hurt you. That wouldn't be fair to her."

Christ, maybe he does have a heart after all.

With a wink, Owen leaves.

"Thanks for not punching me," I call after him.

"I'm too pretty for jail," he shouts back. "So is Lincoln. You'd fit right in, though." We both full-belly-laugh as he shuts the door.

With excitement brewing in my belly, I run... fucking run, to my girl.

We're gonna be just fine.

34

JACOB

"Mine." I kiss Skye's tattooed ankle, trying to ignore the bruises, just below it, from the chains she'd been restrained in.

"Mine." Moving up her body, I kiss her outer thigh.

"Mine." I kiss her inner thigh, making her squirm and giggle.

"Mine." I kiss her hip and bunch up her top, revealing her toned stomach.

"Mine." I drag my nose downward over her skin to the top of her pussy, glad that she left her underwear off when she ran out to confront Owen.

"Mine." I cover her whole pussy with my mouth, licking and then kissing her clit, causing breathless gasps to leave her throat.

She reaches out to entwine our fingers together as she grinds her pussy against my mouth a few times, then grabs either side of my face, pulling me up to her smiling lips. "I'm yours."

"All mine." I kiss her lips, then her cheek, and move down her neck. "All of you. You belong to me."

Making my blood course through my veins like a rocket, she agrees, "My heart belongs to you, Jay."

My lips find hers again, and with slow, languid kisses, we lose ourselves in each other.

It's not long before our bodies demand more and my hand tightens in her hair, making her sense my need.

Feeling as desperate, Skye unzips my jeans with urgency, pulling my hard cock from my jeans, stroking me as I awkwardly remove the uncooperative fabric from my legs. I can't fucking think straight when she touches me. No longer a fantasy, I still can't believe how we got here.

She lets go of my cock, then traces her fingertips over the skin of my back, over our secret code words branded into the skin across my shoulders, up the back of my neck, leaving trails of goosebumps in her wake.

"I love you," she whispers against my lips.

My cock rests heavily against her hip as I pull back a little and lock eyes with hers. "You're mine forever. I made a promise to you to show you what true love felt like."

I brush her temple with the pad of my thumb, and she grants me the widest smile, making her whole face glow up.

"This is it," she says, her tone almost unbelieving but laced with contentment.

"We finally made it, Skye." My eager lips crash against hers again.

She pushes my shoulder with her hand, urging me backward.

"I need to taste you," she mumbles against my lips; I can feel her eagerness through her words.

Sitting up, all the while still kissing me, she moves onto her knees, turning us around as she settles between my thighs.

I pull my tee shirt she's wearing up and over her head, breaking our kiss for a beat, but it's enough to entice her to lay a path of soft kisses down my body until she reaches the weeping head of my cock.

Speechless, I watch as she kisses the tip first before licking me from my base to my throbbing head.

Without hesitation, she sucks me deep into her mouth, as she twists her tongue around my shaft not missing an inch. Her blue eyes lock onto mine. I take a mental photograph of this very moment.

Reaching down, I wrap her long silver hair around my hand to get a better view of her sucking me like I'm a fucking lollipop and the best thing she's ever tasted.

"Fuck, Butterfly. You're so fucking good at that." I almost growl when she sucks me deeper and harder, making my balls draw up into my body. The thumb of my other hand brushes her flushed cheek.

I thrust my hips, reveling in the feeling of fucking her mouth a few more times, before I reluctantly pull her off my cock and before she makes me come down her throat. I don't want that right now.

"Tastes so good." She kisses the tip again before I sit up and move her pretty lips to mine, tasting myself on her.

"Turn around. On all fours," I command, kneeling up, maneuvering myself behind her.

Once in position, I almost come at the sight of Skye, wiggling her ass and glistening pussy at me. She's caught me in her web of magic, and I'm so ready to start a life with her where we get to do this every day.

Hoisting her hips up, I cup her whole pussy from behind, making her arch her neck as she lets out a loud gasp.

I dip down and let myself drown in her folds, licking her

front to back, then plunging my tongue into her, fucking her with it.

"Jay," she gasps, then moans in disappointment when I stop because I need to be inside her.

I line the head of my cock to her entrance, edging her teasingly. "Are you wet for me?"

"Oh God, Jay, just fuck me."

"Why?" I demand more forcefully than I planned, her sweary bedroom talk making me so hard I can barely think straight.

"Because I need you." She moves her hand down to her clit as her breathing becomes labored.

"Why?" I question, softer this time.

"Because I love you."

I stop circling my cock at her entrance. "Wrong answer." But fuck me, do I love how those words fall off her lips.

She groans.

"Let's try that again. But get this wrong and I won't let you come. Why, Butterfly?" With my free hand, I remove her fingers from her clit, causing her to groan again.

She goes silent for a beat, then she says. "Because I'm yours."

"Right answer." With a rough thrust, I push into her from behind as she sucks me into her wet heat.

We both cry out. Skye dips the front of her body, giving herself to me, the position making her tighter, causing my eyes to roll back into my head.

"Holy fucking shit." I dig my fingers into her hips and then realize I don't want to give her any more bruises. Instead, I wrap my arm around her waist, pulling her up, her back to my front.

With her legs on either side of mine, holding her close, I thrust in and out of her, gently.

"You're holding back from me, Jay." She can read me like a book.

"I don't want to hurt you." I kiss her shoulder, then her neck.

Turning her head, she captures my lips and then says, "Fuck me like none of it happened. Give me back my power. Fuck me to remind me how strong I am and how I survived, Jay."

It all seems so surreal, and I almost have to pinch myself to remind me that she is mine. All mine, and begging for me to take her in ways I have dreamed about for so long.

I let myself go, giving her what she wants as I thrust into her, holding her close to me.

Wrapping my hand around her throat, I keep her lips sealed against mine as I fuck her faster.

"Come for me, Butterfly."

I rub her clit as her orgasm takes hold and I drive myself in deep. My balls pull up into my body as my own release builds.

I spank her clit, then rub, spank, and rub faster, driving her wild, which I can tell as her moaning grows louder. With one final spank and rub, she squirts all over my cock, her tight pussy milking me as her orgasm tears through her.

My thick cock explodes inside of her as she yells my name, telling me to keep fucking her harder.

I roar into her mouth as I come, and she flicks her tongue against mine, grabbing the back of my neck, ensuring we stay connected.

Resting back on my haunches, I bring her with me, holding her close, as my cock pulses inside of her. I pant against her lips, her inner walls contracting around me, making my sensitive cock tingle with pleasure.

Desperately trying to catch a breath, I feel like I've run a marathon as my heart hammers in my chest, so hard she must feel it against her back. Sex with Skye is fucking intense. I've never felt anything like it.

"I made a mess of the bed again. I don't know what you do to make me do that, but it's never happened before you." She stares at her arousal staining my bed sheets as if she's ashamed.

"It's the fucking hottest thing I've ever seen. I'd be happy if you squirted every time you came."

She twists her head back around to meet my gaze, her embarrassment replaced with a look of pure need. "Can we do it again?"

"Fuck, yeah." I rock my hips, my cock still inside of her, becoming hard again.

And just like that, the two of us become one, entangled in each other for the rest of the day, and if I have it my way, it will be like this for the rest of our lives.

35

SKYE

Three months later

"That, I think, brings everyone up to speed." I check the time on the wall clock. "Sorry I've kept you late. Come in half an hour later tomorrow." I look around the boardroom table.

"Thanks, Skye."

"Cool."

"See you tomorrow."

A chatter of gratitude and farewells fuse together as my team heads out of the office for the night.

It's almost Christmas and the dazzle of the snow douses a soft hue throughout the office.

We are off to pick up our Christmas tree I ordered this weekend and decorate it together. I can't wait to spend our first Christmas together. It feels super special this year and I'm so excited to wake up with Jacob in his beautiful house that he tells me I've to call my own.

The past few months have zipped by in a flash, and with

every day that passes, I fall deeper and crazier in love with Jacob.

After Kimmy and Jacob moved my stuff out of the rental, I moved in with my parents for a few weeks, but as I was spending more and more time at Jay's place, it made more sense for me to move in with him. So I did, and it's been incredible. I love living with him.

Traveling to work together, lazy Sundays reading, Saturday meals out, and, of course, the constant surprises of theater tickets and nights away.

He couldn't love me more if he tried.

I feel loved beyond anything I've ever experienced. He looks after me, making my breakfast and lunch. He bought me a new fancy e-book reader and filled it with hundreds of books, which must have taken him hours. He had my winter tires fitted to my car for the snowy months and, on a daily basis, he ensures I have everything I need to do my new job, which I interviewed terribly for. I was so nervous.

Even though I knew the job was mine, I still felt like I had to prove myself. Jacob reckoned my nerves got the better of me because it meant something to me and that I needed to prove that I didn't get the job because I am his girlfriend.

He was right.

He's always right.

It wasn't weird either when we announced at work that Jacob and I were officially dating. Everyone nodded their heads as if to say, *well, we always knew that was gonna happen.*

It felt so nice that they were all so happy for us. Except for some of the girls in accounts who are gutted that they didn't bag the hottest guy in the office and give me the evil eye. Those girls, I make sure I'm extra nice to.

A week ago, the police contacted me informing me that

Jules would be reviewed again under the Mental Health Act. It was reassuring to hear that he wouldn't be released as there was too much evidence against him. They also said that he would remain in custody until the court case, which is not until next summer. I am not looking forward to that one bit. However, my therapist, Dr. Burns, said that he would prepare me for questioning, ensuring I had the tools and coping techniques to deal with that. My lawyer also assured me that Jules will most likely be sentenced to life in a psychiatric hospital with zero chance of release, which is such a relief.

I have to admit the therapy helps; it's certainly making me sleep better. I'm no longer waking up screaming, covered in sweat. I'm so glad those days are over.

It helps that I've thrown myself into my new role at work to tire me out, and I have to admit, it's a good distraction, especially when I find my thoughts slipping into dark memories. The ones I want to completely forget.

Owen seems to be finding it less difficult to be around us the longer we're together. He even drops in every week to see us and we've even managed a meal out as couples, although Evangeline never did show up that night. The date for their wedding is set but Owen hasn't told us anything other than that.

It's the weirdest arrangement. I'm glad I'm not involved.

"Hey, beautiful."

I look up from my tablet, to find him looking all sexy, standing against the doorjamb, arms crossed, sleeves rolled up because I finally talked him into showing off the body art he's been hiding from everyone in the office.

I don't know how he manages it, but he gives my butterflies butterflies. He's so handsome.

"Hi." I close down my tablet, which I now only use for

notes... no more hand lettering for me. I'm not sure I will ever do any again. What a waste of a beautiful piece of equipment.

Sensing my tension, Jacob walks around the table to me.

"Come, stand." He full-arm beckons me to get up.

Rolling my chair away from under the huge table, I swivel the seat around and stand up.

"You look tired." He kisses my forehead and then rests his brows against mine.

"It's been a long day." I roll my stiff shoulders.

Reaching up, and like always at the end of every day, he unravels my two space buns, then massages my scalp.

"That feels nice," I moan with relief.

"Well, if you will insist on being involved in everything. That's what you have an assistant for." He massages his fingers into the back of my neck and then down to the top of my shoulders.

"She made three calendar errors this week." I throw my arm out to the side.

"Give her a chance. She's new."

"I'm sorry, I'm being grumpy."

"Yes you are, Ms. Grumpy McGrumperson." He cups my face and kisses me softly.

At every opportunity, Jay kisses me. We kiss way more than an average couple, I'm sure of it.

"Have I told you how beautiful you look today?" He kisses the tip of my nose.

At least fifteen times. "Not enough," I tease him, making him smirk. "Tell me how much you love me, though." Because I can never hear enough of that.

"Let me show you instead. Everyone has gone for the night." He pulls me in for a deep kiss, our tongues colliding, making us both groan. "I've switched the security cameras off in here." His fingertips dip under my pink and gray tartan skirt. "Let me help you relax, Butterfly. I know what my girl needs."

In one swift move, filling his large hands with my ass, he lifts me into the air and sits me down on the edge of the table.

"That's cold," I complain.

"I can warm your ass up," he mumbles, giving it a quick spank and I gasp.

"We've never had sex on the boardroom table before. Are we christening it tonight?" Excitement bubbles in my belly.

"I think it's the only room left."

He pulls my tiny G-string to the side and slides one of his fingers deep into my body.

"Always so fucking wet," he groans, adding another finger, stretching me in pleasurable ways.

"No squirting," he growls. "Or you will have to explain to the cleaner what the fuck it is," he chuckles.

"I can't guarantee that." I arch my head back when he rubs my clit with his thumb, working me into a frenzy.

Falling to his knees, he disappears between my legs, instantly flicking my swollen bud with his expert tongue, flattening it, covering my entire pussy.

Knowing what I love, he continues to finger-fuck me at the same time, building the pleasure... passion rising inside my core, through my thighs, and low in my pelvis.

He presses my clit, and I tilt my hips in such a way I know I'm going to end up doing what he doesn't want me to, but with him, it just happens.

The soft scruff on his face tickling my pussy lips, tantalizing me, adds to the pleasure.

Sparks turn into flames when he thrusts his finger into me faster again, fucking me into my orgasm, and I cry out, telling him I'm coming as a rainbow of stars flash behind my eyes.

With nothing to grip on to, I slap the table as I ride out my orgasm.

He laps up every drop from me, pushing his thick fingers into me as I come, drinking me down until I catch my breath again.

Kissing my inner thigh, my clit, then my tummy, he makes his way up my body; pulling off his now-soaked dress shirt up over his head, he wipes his bearded chin covered in my orgasm with it and throws it over his shoulder.

He bends down, kissing the base of my throat first, before covering his hungry lips over mine. "You're so beautiful when you come. I love you, Skye. So much. Words will never be enough." The strength of his lips is almost punishing as he delivers his confessions of adoration.

I feel his passion flowing into my bones, making my heart swell to the size of a helium balloon. He makes me feel weightless and I'm completely at the mercy of his never-ending love for me. Love, he shows me every day in so many different ways. From my morning coffee, to surprise book deliveries, to waking me up with him between my legs in the mornings. I simply can't get enough.

His belt buckle clatters off the edge of the table as he undoes it, his breathing becoming heavier, desperate with the need to fuck.

This is how we roll together. Instant fire burns between us twenty-four-seven and we can't get enough of each other.

He consumes me. My thoughts, my body, my heart.

When he pushes his cock inside of me, I nip at his lips to stop me crying out with pleasure.

He rides me, his hand clasping my ass to hold me steady as we rock together in perfect rhythm.

I lean left and right to take off my shoes, bend my knees up, and hook my toes around the lip of the table to give me leverage.

"So fucking tight." He thrusts, ramming his cock in and out of me.

Hands on my knees now, he pushes my legs back, and I gasp as my body stretches to accommodate how deep and hard he's driving into me.

His balls slap off my pussy, again and again, his breathing becoming labored with every deep hip thrust. He pulls out of me suddenly. "Get off the table, naughty girl," he commands and I lower my feet to the floor.

"Turn around."

"You know I will squirt again in this position?" I flick my hair to the side, looking over my shoulder at him.

He bends me over the table. "Well, at least this time, I'm not in the firing line," he says, making me giggle.

Both hands on my hips, he slips in from behind.

And then he really gives it to me.

I love it when we have slow and sensual sex, but when he goes feral like this, it's everything I didn't know I needed. When it's hot and aggressive, savage almost, I always come so hard for him.

He gathers my hair into a ponytail with one hand, and uses it like a set of reins to ram into me. With his other hand, he dips his thumb inside the top of my knee-high sock, fisting the fabric in his hand.

The kinky fucker loves those socks.

"Touch yourself, make yourself come for me," he shouts.

Reaching down to do what he asks, I rub my clit over and

over and the familiar sensation rises in my core, my orgasm dancing on the perimeter, flirting with me to rub harder.

"Oh Jay." I pant his name.

"Rub faster, Butterfly," he roars. "Pinch it."

The clatter of his belt, the sound of his balls slapping off my pussy and our animalistic sounds are all that can be heard through the quiet floor of the office.

I rub then pinch my clit and move up to my tiptoes to take him deeper. My pelvis tilts, the head of his cock hitting the right spot, and I come again, all over my hand.

I slam my eyes shut as the power of my orgasm takes control of my body.

"Squirt on my cock. Aw, fuck, I'm coming." He holds himself deep, bottoming out as he comes inside of me. "Skye," he cries. "Holy fucking shit." His fingers tighten on my hips as he loosens his grip on my hair.

We both come together, gasping and groaning in mutual pleasure. My inner walls stop clenching his cock as we descend.

"I'm getting too old for this." He rests his forehead between my shoulder blades, desperately attempting to catch his breath.

"Oh, God. I need to change before I go home," I grumble.

He slides out of me slowly and turns me to face him. "Don't fucking wash a thing off." He kisses me as he tucks his cock back into his boxers and re-zips his trousers before buckling his belt back up.

"But I'm covered in..."

"Your cum and mine. So fucking hot." He moves his hand between my legs and I moan when his fingers slide down over my swollen clit, then he pushes two of his thick fingers inside of me. "All mine." He kisses my neck, and I close my eyes, arching my neck to give him better access.

I'm too distracted by his tongue licking my sweet spot behind my ear when he says, "Open." My mouth falls open. "Taste us."

When he pushes his fingers into my mouth, I swirl my tongue around them.

The thing I love most about Jacob is that he has the ability to be so sweet and then so dirty. I've done so many more things with him in the bedroom than I have ever done before, as he pushes me to explore how pleasurable getting deep down and dirty can actually be.

I love it. This good girl's gone bad.

"You'll make me hard again." With hooded eyes, he watches me and I stare right back at him as I suck so hard I hollow out my cheeks. "I'm a lucky man."

I push his fingers out of my mouth with my tongue.

"Time to go home. You may even get lucky again."

"I hope so."

36

SKYE

Showered, fed, and then showered again because we fucked on the dining table after dinner, because, well, that's what we do and can't keep our hands off each other, I'm now seated in the corner of the sofa.

I look up from my book when he asks me the question I've been dreading.

"Have you given any more thought about starting up your hand lettering channel again?"

"Nope." I pretend to read my book again.

"You're letting him win."

"I'm not." I grip the pages harder.

"You're very talented."

"I don't want to hand letter again."

"You sure?"

"Yes." I slam my book shut and fling my head back against the cushions.

"You know I only want the best for you, yeah?"

"I know." I stare at the ceiling.

Jacob grabs my hips and pulls me onto his lap, making me squeal. He's so strong.

He makes me straddle him when he positions my legs on either side of his hips.

Playing with my fingers, I look down. I don't want to talk about this.

I'm wearing nothing but his tee shirt, which I sleep in. He tickles me with his touch, stroking his fingertips up and down my bare legs.

He ducks his head, so we are eye to eye, and grins at me.

"Stop it." I smack his shoulder playfully.

"I didn't do anything," he says innocently.

"You know I'm a sucker for your smile." I lift my head and he winks at me.

"Tell me what's going on in that pretty little head of yours." He holds my ankles.

"I don't want to do hand lettering again."

"Okay."

"However, I have given a lot of thought about doing an illustrated book for kids. How to stay safe online. Or something." I fill air into my cheeks then blow it all out. "It's a stupid idea."

"No, it's not. I think it's a great idea."

I widen my eyes. "You do?"

"Yes." He smiles, his caring eyes soft around the edges. "You could do one for adults too."

"I could do a whole series." I start getting excited. "And illustrate them all myself, hand-write them, as well as write the content, and a journal too. I've always wanted to design a journal. I could do all my doodle artwork, and maybe even a coloring-in book as part of the therapy to help people overcome anxiety."

"There's my girl."

"I can self-publish."

"Then do it."

I lift my shoulders to my ears in excitement and clap my hands together.

"I'd call it Castle in the Skye Publishing or maybe Skye Publishing or, oh, what about Skye McNairn Publishing?"

"Or what about SB Publishing?"

"Huh?" I push my top lip up in an Elvis curl, confused.

"What about Skye Baxter Publishing?"

I laugh. "That's your name, silly." My chuckle stops dead at the realization of what he's implying.

"Yeah, but it could be yours, too."

Smiling, I grab his handsome face with both hands. "Are you asking me to marry you, Jacob Baxter?" Butterflies swirl in my tummy and heart.

He nods. "Skye McNairn, will you marry me?"

I squish his cheeks together and smack a kiss to his lips.

"Ish vat a wesh?" he asks, *is that a yes?* between the palms of my hands.

I let go of his face. "Yes, yes, yes!" I squeal, throwing my hands in the air, then pulling them to my heart.

He rubs his jaw where I was holding him. "Christ, you have some grip." He moves his jaw side to side.

"I'm sorry, I'm excited." I place my hands on his shoulders. "Can we get married in Dubock Castle? The one at the end of the road?"

"Yes. Anything for you." His gigantic smile lights up my soul.

"In March with the snowdrops?"

"That soon?"

"It's a little over three months away, that's ages, and I would marry you tomorrow, Jacob Baxter. Oh, we have to celebrate, and call our parents. Your mom is gonna be so excited. My mom has the most beautiful tiara I can wear. Oh God, we're getting married?"

He chuckles, laughing at my reaction. "You're so fucking cute. I love you, Skye."

"I love you so much." My lips land on his and I take my time to remember this moment. He pushes his tongue into my mouth and I'm overwhelmed by how complete he makes me feel. Our kiss is slow and full of love and I melt into him when he threads his fingers into the back of my hair, pulling me closer. His lips work mine, hard, then soft, and I cup his face, running my thumb back and forth across his soft scruff I love so much.

Moving to the side of my mouth, he kisses my cheek, and then my temple before he whispers in my ear. "I'm so happy you didn't let me fall out of love with you."

I whisper back, "And I'm happy I fell in love with you, Jacob."

He lays his forehead against mine as if they're kissing one another.

"Do we have champagne?" I grin again. I can't stop smiling.

"Yes, we do."

"Let's video-call everyone."

"Do you not want to wait until you have a ring? We need to go shopping at the weekend."

"No, I need to share the news now, or I might burst." I fall to the side onto the soft cushions.

He smiles before lifting my ankle and kissing my tattoo.

"I'm getting married. To Jacob," I whisper to myself.

"And I am marrying the girl I've loved since the day I met her."

37

JACOB

Two months later

"I've found us the perfect house. C'mon," I say, running into the hall, and grab my keys from the sideboard.

"You have?" Skye asks. "I looked again this morning and there was nothing online. Are you sure?" Frowning with confusion, she picks up her phone to check the houses for sale app.

Sitting on the edge of her parents' couch, she looks up at me, where I lean against the doorjamb. Her big blue eyes are full of confusion. "There's nothing new on here." She shows me the screen of her phone.

"It's not on there. C'mon..." I clap my hands twice. "Let's go."

She pushes herself off the couch. "Okay, let me put my boots on. What's it like? Where is it? Is it nice?"

"It's perfect."

My eyes travel across the room, following her every move.

Stopping in front of the mirror, she checks her lipstick, then rearranges her short bangs.

A month ago, Skye decided to cut her long hair off into a short pixie cut. I thought it was a rash decision, however, her razor-sharp, short around the back and sides, with longer bangs at the front hairstyle makes her look even more beautiful now. Edgier too. She pulls off fun and glam, and I love how it highlights her bone structure and big blue eyes.

The best part is, she loves it too. She said it was a way to start again and I couldn't agree more.

I love her whatever, however, forever.

Looking cute today in her black dungaree shorts, thick black tights, and white tee, she moves into the hall and pushes her feet into her black winter moon boots.

I pass her the long white puffy jacket I bought her for Christmas to put on.

"Is it far, the house?"

"The only thing I will say is that it's five minutes away from here." I make for the front door.

"Give me three guesses."

"No."

She giggles. "Why not?"

"Because it's more exciting this way. C'mon, shoo." I hold the door open and beckon her to step out the door.

"Okay, big guy." She rolls her eyes, pulling the collar of her jacket around her neck.

It snowed overnight. Not much, but enough for it to leave a blanket over the ground. It's chilly today, but the sun is shining and it's already started to melt the snowfall.

Pulling into the entrance of Dubock Castle, I drive slowly down the orange gravel driveway.

"Oh, do we have wedding things to do?" From the passenger seat, she turns to look at me with a wrinkled brow.

"Not today, no." I pull up outside the arched entrance.

"You can't park here; you need to park in the visitors' spots around the back." She hooks her finger, instructing me to park around the corner.

I ignore her, click open the door and get out of my car.

She ducks down, looking at me through the gap of the open driver's door. "Jacob?"

I smile, close the door, and walk around to her side to usher her out of the car.

"What are we doing here? Why are you acting weird?" She takes my hand when I hold it out for her to take.

She mutters something under her breath I don't quite catch.

"Sorry, what was that?"

Sounding exasperated, she says, "You got me all excited. I thought we were going to look at a house first. To make a new fresh start together." She lets go of my hand and stands in front of the car.

"You're adorable when you're annoyed. Do you know that?"

She rolls her eyes at me again. "Whatever. Right, let's meet the wedding planner and do what we need to do, *then* view the property you want me to see."

I point at the castle, standing like a sandstone giant to my side. "This is it."

"What?" She cranes her neck to look up at the ancient structure.

"This is our new home."

"What?" she shrieks, snapping her head around to look at me.

"I bought Dubock Castle."

Her mouth falls open. She looks at the castle, then me, then back at the castle.

She shuts her mouth, but it falls open again. "Oh, my God, you're insane." She holds her hands over her heart. "You bought a castle for us to live in?" Her eyes pool with tears.

"Yes." I nod enthusiastically.

"But we have our wedding booked here? Was it for sale? What will we do now?"

I close the space between us and pull her into my arms. "Now, we have the wedding in *our* house. The owner decided it was time to sell. They don't want to do events anymore, and he can't afford to maintain or upgrade it without doing events. Our wedding was the last one he planned to fulfill and then he was putting it up for sale. I just happened to ask at the right time. It needs a little renovation to modernize it, but this is where we will live forever, together, married, in a castle and we're gonna have lots of babies."

"Just two. Not lots."

"Okay, just two. Girls? Little princesses?"

"Boys. Princes."

"Okay." I plant a soft kiss on her lips.

"Could you be any more romantic?" She grabs my face.

"I didn't know I was until I met you." I slide her hand off my face and kiss the top of her aquamarine solitaire engagement ring. The one the two of us picked out together. It's understated and smaller than I had planned, but Skye didn't want anything too big or too flashy.

She looks away, arching her neck back to take in our new home.

"Wow."

"Want to view your new home?"

"Do I ever? I've never been up the tower," she gasps, getting excited.

For the next hour, the two of us explore every nook and cranny of the five-bedroom, twelfth-century castle. Having been renovated in the nineteenth century, it's in need of a little tender love and care, which I am certain Skye will give it lots of.

While we explored the castle, she reeled off dozens of facts about its history. How it used to be a safe haven for monarchs and archbishops of the past and rendezvous for secret meetings between lords and their mistresses.

Buzzing with excitement, she went into detail about what she planned to do with the vaulted wooden ceilings, draping them in cloud-printed canopies to drop the ceilings in the bedrooms in an effort to make them cozier.

She has so many wonderful ideas.

"I have one more room to show you." I push open the door that leads to the towered corner on the farthest side of the castle.

She sucks in a breath as she steps into the magical space. "It's a library."

"Big enough?"

"It's enormous." In the center of the wall-to-wall book-filled space, she spins around with her arms in the air, making her long jacket look like a flared flamenco dress.

She comes to a standstill and skips across to one of the shelves. Running her finger along the spines, she hooks her finger into the top of one and pulls it out, flicks through it, and pushes it back in.

I watch on, fascinated by her fascination as she pulls another, and then another, from the shelves.

"The books are included in the sale." I interrupt her browsing.

"Some of these are first editions and look." She points up to the rolling library ladders that move back and forth along wrought-iron tracks. "I've always wanted those."

I know she has.

Moving over to the turret area, Skye reaches up and rests the palm of her hand against the crisscross leaded windows.

"This is really ours?"

"The sale went through at midday today." At one point I didn't think it would happen when the deed for the castle went missing. But like some kind of magical miracle, the owner found it.

"It's beautiful," she whispers, gazing out of the window.

Nothing makes me happier than seeing her happy.

I look up and down the shelves at the thousands of books we now own as I make my way over to her. I know if she ever goes missing in the house, this is where I'll find her.

"Look," she squeals, pointing at the window. "A family of deer. There's even a baby one."

"You might kill me with all of this cuteness." The weight of my stare makes her turn around.

Her face, now serious, falls into place as she looks back at the library in the circular turret we're both now standing in. "Do you ever get anything wrong? This is so..." Her eyes become glazed, and she looks overwhelmed.

"The only thing I ever got wrong was not asking you out on a date the same night I kissed you after that game of truth or dare."

"I don't think it was wrong."

"No?"

"I think it was perfect timing. We weren't in alignment

with one another then, but now? It's perfect. This is perfect." She spreads her arms wide. "We needed more chapters added to our story to get our happy ending. Perfect things happen in perfect ways. If we weren't getting married, would you have known the owner was selling? Or had I not worked that Saturday night all those months ago, would we have gotten together? Or if Frankie went in my place for your meetings in London and not me, would you have opened up to me and told me you loved me if your cousin Joanna hadn't told you to when you met up in London? It's all been down to timing." She drifts off thinking before she says, "Even after everything... the bad stuff... we're still here, together..."

"Forever."

"Yeah." She smiles as I cradle her face in my hands. "I love you, Jacob."

"I loved you when I was sixteen, and every year thereafter, now, always."

I slant my mouth over hers, and we kiss and kiss, tasting each other, connecting us in intimate ways I once never believed were possible.

Our kiss becomes rough and she bites my bottom lip. "Let's go home," she mumbles.

"We are home."

She lets out a sigh of contentment. "We're home."

Yes we are.

38

SKYE

A few weeks later

Earlier today we married on the grounds of our new home: a freaking castle. I still can't believe it.

The ceremony took place outside. It was freezing, but exactly how I imagined it. The last of the snowdrops still in bloom, fluffy white shawls, a castle, and fairy lights. Sheer perfection. Then we moved into the grand hall where we ate, sang, danced, and laughed until the wee small hours until there was just me, and him.

My husband.

Foreheads touching, chests panting, our lips ghost one another as Jacob makes love to me slowly.

His eyes are full of emotion, and with every thrust, I feel him, every kiss. He pours his love into my skin. With every taste and lick, he memorizes every part of me as I melt into him like liquid gold.

"You're so beautiful," he whispers, making my heart swell with warmth. "I love you."

With soft hands, my fingertips trace his inked skin, worshipping every inch of him.

He kisses me deep, then deeper again, licking his tongue against mine, making me shudder with his deep affection.

We rock together in perfect timing. Undulating his hips in waves, he breathes hard, moaning loudly as we move into a faster rhythm. My nipples pucker when his inked skin rubs against them, causing a wave of pleasure over my skin.

Our bodies are electric with desire for one another.

"I love you, Jay."

"I'll never get tired of hearing that. Not ever," he groans against my lips.

He pushes in further, the head of his cock rubbing my sweet spot, and I gasp when he tilts my hips at just the right angle. With every cell of my body tuned into his, we become one.

Holding himself deep and firm, digging his fingers into my hips, his pelvic bone teases my clit. My inner walls begin to clench; the pleasurable sensation burns in my thighs and between my pelvis.

He circles his hips, taking his time between thrusts as we both savor every moment.

Cupping my ass with his expert hands, the ones that know me so well, his cock flirts with my G-spot, once, and then twice and I come when he tells me to because I'd do anything for him.

Eyes locked as if he's looking deep into my soul, he comes too as we writhe and moan together. He kisses me, groaning as he pours himself inside of me.

It's this moment that bonds us together, not with a signed piece of paper, but with love and trust and, most importantly, true friendship, because we are partners in every way.

"I love you, Skye Baxter."

I can't stop smiling. "I'll never get tired of hearing that." I repeat back his heartfelt words.

* * *

The winter sun beats through the windows and I smile as happiness buzzes through my veins.

I'm so happy. Something I never thought I would feel again.

I started writing the books I had an idea for. Once I started, I couldn't stop. Fully illustrated, handwritten, and then digitally enhanced, I've written ten children's books so far.

Centered around a blonde girl called Blue with cute space buns, every book deals with sensitive topics like anxiety, stress, and anger, with simple tools kids can use to help and support them. All the things I have been doing myself that helped me.

Having kept in touch with Austin, the branding client from London, he put me in touch with one of his friends who owns a publishing house.

Two weeks ago, Jacob and I flew down to London for my meeting with AJNP Publishing to discuss a publishing deal. I only told Violet, because I was worried I wouldn't get it, but I finally got the news two days ago via email. Although I'm leaving Baxter and Bain, and will be sad to leave, I am also really excited about my future.

We've yet to tell our parents, but we're having them all round for Sunday roast today so we'll tell them then.

Then tomorrow we are off on our honeymoon in the Bahamas for three weeks. Jacob remembered everything from my vision board and I'm so excited about seeing those cute swimming pigs I've been desperate to visit. On our return, we begin the renovations, which I'm overseeing.

I pull myself up in bed and rest my back against the headboard.

Naked from the waist up, in only his luminous yellow and pink star-printed boxers, I can't help but lick my lips when Jacob, my husband, walks into our bedroom. I want to scream, *he's all mine*, but I don't.

He may be a tattooed devil in a suit, but he's an even sexier tattooed devil when he's naked.

"You look so tiny in that bed, Mrs. Baxter," he chuckles.

I look up at the wooden four-poster. It really is enormous. "Like the princess and the pea."

It's the biggest four-poster bed I've ever seen. Every move we make creaks like crazy, which isn't the best as we have so much sex and it causes us to laugh when we really get into it. It's ridiculously squeaky and we need to get a carpenter here to sort it out before we even think about having kids.

Laying a tray down on the bed with two cups of steaming coffee on it, he walks over to the sideboard and pulls open a drawer, lifting a pale blue present out of it with a huge silver bow.

"Is that a wedding present?"

"Yes, from me."

"I got you something, too." I lean down and pull his gift from between the sliver of space between the nightstand and the giant bed.

"I don't need anything. I have you; you're all that I need," he says, melting my heart.

He closes the heavy wooden drawer, which doesn't run as smoothly as it should. Yet another job to add to the list: wax the runners. It's never-ending owning a castle. Being a wannabe princess is hard work.

Being careful not to spill the coffee, he climbs under the covers with me and we exchange presents.

"You open yours first," he instructs.

Crossing my legs, I sit up, pulling the covers around my breasts, protecting them from the chilly air. Jacob lit the log fire before he went down to make our morning coffee, but it's still hissing and spitting away in the corner, gearing itself up to heat the room.

And there's another thing we need to upgrade: the heating system.

Being careful not to rip the aqua blue paper, I untie the silver bow first, then unfold the paper carefully and gasp when I pull out a copy of my favorite book.

"It's a special thirtieth anniversary illustrated edition," he says as I stroke the blue and gold gilded hardback cover of *The Princess Bride*.

"It's beautiful."

"Is it okay?"

"It's better than okay. It's wonderful." I grab his face and kiss him.

My perfect man is so perfect. Hard and fierce-looking on the outside and soft and squishy on the inside.

What more could a girl want?

39

JACOB

Skye's face lights up like a full moon on a dark night as she flicks through the pages of her book.

All I want is to make her happy.

"We should put this in a glass case and put it on display in the hallway," I suggest.

"Why?"

"Because it's special."

"It should be read and enjoyed; we need to put it in the library."

She scrunches her nose up, not agreeing with me.

"Your turn." She looks excited.

Unlike Skye, I rip the navy paper off in one go from my thin, twelve-inch square gift. Unwrapped, now I hold my hands on either side of the Crazy Town album I played over and over again when I was sixteen because it was always, always about her.

"It's signed." She points to the silver signature in the top corner.

"That's so cool." *Where the hell did she get this?*

"Do you like it?"

"I love it." I love her.

"eBay," she chuckles. "You get everything on there."

I wish that were true. If I could buy something to wipe away the memories of her horrific ordeal, I would. I lean to the side and kiss her shoulder. "Thank you."

I flip the twelve-inch vinyl record over in my hand to remind myself of the running order. So cool.

Laying her book on the bed, she leans forward, picks her mug of coffee and then mine off the tray, and passes it to me.

I take a sip and look around the house we've yet to make our home. I know with Skye's creative design skills she's going to make this place look incredible. "Will you be happy here?" I ask.

"If we get a better heating system installed, yes. Otherwise, I might freeze to death."

She's not wrong; the place is freezing. "What time is everyone coming today for Sunday dinner?"

"Early. They are all coming to help clean up."

Thank Christ, the place looks like a bomb site down the stairs. I'm now regretting the decision to host a small wedding and do everything by ourselves.

Both our parents, our grandparents, my brother, sister, and their spouses, along with their brood of children, are coming to the house today. Skye wants this to be our family tradition: everyone, every Sunday, comes to us.

My nieces and nephews love the house, and I can't wait to create so many new memories together as one big family unit.

"Do we have time for me to show you how big my sword is before they get here?" I slyly glance her way.

Without blinking, she replies, "Is it bigger than the heroes I read about in my books?"

"Much, much bigger." I grin against the lip of my mug, take a sip and place it on the nightstand.

"Show me," she challenges.

I take her mug from her hand and put it beside mine. Grabbing my phone, I scroll to find the song I'm after and hit play.

She bursts out laughing when the electric guitar strings play from "Butterfly" by Crazy Town.

"Oh my God, this song is so sexual," she says, still laughing.

"I know and I fucking love it." I climb on top of her as she sinks into the mattress and I start singing the words against the shell of her ear, making her giggle even more.

"You were so young; how did you even know what that meant?"

I nudge open her legs with my knees and move myself between her thighs.

"Oh, I knew." I don't tell her about the deeper meaning of the song for me, about how she makes me feel uplifted and free, like a butterfly, so I go with the filthy meaning of the song instead. "My wish for today is that you come all over my dick, but what do you wish for, m'lady?"

"I wish to be ravished." She gazes up at me.

"Done." I kiss her lips.

"I wish to be looked after." She wraps her legs around my hips.

"Done." I kiss her neck.

"I wish to be adored."

"Done." I kiss her lips again.

"I wish to be loved."

"Done, done, done, done, done." I kiss her all over, making her squeal.

Neither of us ever need to wish for anything again, because we have everything we want.

With each other.

It was touch and go and for a fleeting moment I didn't think we'd get it, but we did.

Our happy ever after.

Well... maybe...

Skye stops kissing me as she moves her mouth to the side. "Where's that sound of running water coming from?"

I lean away, propping myself up on my hands on either side of her face, and listen. "This fucking house." I roll my eyes.

Dick fully erect in my boxers, I jump out of the bed to go on a water leak search party.

"You love it, really," Skye shouts out to me as I run down the spiral staircase.

I love her.

My butterfly.

EPILOGUE
JACOB

Ten years later

I park my car in the gravel driveway of my house, well, my castle, and as soon as I open the car door, my three blonde-haired daughters fly out of the front door of the castle, screaming their heads off, dressed up in their princess costumes.

"Mommy is dying," Catherine, my youngest, shrieks.

Oh, dear God.

I sprint past Catherine, Elsa, and Aurora and into the grand hallway.

My heart beating faster than a freight train pounding down the tracks in my chest. I hear groaning from the kitchen and run as fast as I can in that direction.

Almost skidding across the black and white checkered floor in my dress shoes, I come to an abrupt halt, instantly relieved to see what the hell the girls were screaming about.

I hold on to the edges of the door and bow my head. "Oh, thank God."

Skye is lying on the floor fake-dying as she groans, pulling red silk scarves out of the bottom of her jumper.

"They gave me a heart attack," I laugh while trying to catch my breath and move into the room. Ten years in and I'm not sure the need to protect her with everything I am will ever go away.

"Shush, I'm dying. Play along," she whispers, then lays her arms out to the sides, against the floor.

With every day that passes, I can't help but love this woman more and more.

I'm standing over her now. Her tongue hanging out of the side of her mouth, she pops one eye open to look at me.

"Say the line?" she murmurs.

Fuck, what was it again? Oh, yeah, I remember. "Oh no, my queen. Who did this to you? Was it the evil prince?" I crouch down by her side, playing along, and peek up to see if I can see who I am looking for.

Skye pretends she's choking and croaks out, "It was the evil dragon." Then turns her head to the side, pretending to be dead.

I rise to my feet and say loudly, "I will slay this evil dragon. Where is he?"

I hear a tiny roar from the pantry and I wait.

The door opens gently and with his hands up, in claw-like shapes, out walks my cute-as-fuck two-year-old, William, dressed in a blue and purple spotty dragon costume with padded scales and wings. He looks adorable.

"What did you do to my queen?" I point at him, trying to be serious and stifle the laughter that wants to break free from my chest.

William snarls, trying to look mean, but all it does is cause his button nose to twitch, making him look even cuter.

"You killed the love of my life and now I will have to slay you, evil dragon."

William bares his teeth, snapping and snarling with intention. He knows the game better than me.

He moves over to me and pretends to breathe fire across my knees and thighs and I act out, falling to the ground. "Oh no, you burned my legs off. Now I'm going to die. Who will look after my queen and princesses? I will hate you forever." Then I fake my own death.

Everything goes quiet for a second before William clambers on top of my chest and whispers, "Please, Daddy, not hate me." *My sweet boy.*

I pop my eyes open, grab his sides and tickle him, making him instantly burst into a fit of giggles and squeals. My three girls run in and jump on top of me as they all try to tickle me back.

Skye sits up with a deep scowl on her face and says, "What about me, I'm the one that died. Where are my tickles?"

I give a knowing look to the kids with a cheeky smile, then I widen my eyes and shout, "Get her." They all spring into action and our kitchen becomes a ticklefest until none of us can breathe.

I pick up one of the scarves and wave it in the air. "I give in. I can't take it." All six of us lie panting on the floor. Even little William.

"That was so much fun. Can we do it again tomorrow, Mommy?" Catherine asks sweetly.

I sit up and look around at my incredible family. Three white-blonde girls, Catherine, aged four, Elsa, now six, and Aurora, nine; all princess names Skye loved. Having just turned two years old, William, also a proper prince's name, is going to be so well protected by his loving sisters.

Holding her out-of-breath chest, Skye looks at Catherine. "Absolutely. But I think William should be the knight. Dad didn't do a very good job, did he? He left you to fend for yourselves."

Elsa looks at me suspiciously. "I'll be the knight tomorrow. I will save the queen." She's such a serious kid.

"No, me, me, me." William struggles to his feet in his costume. When he stands up his dragon headpiece is covering his eyes, but it doesn't stop him running out of the kitchen in the direction of the playroom and the girls all race after him, calling dibs on who is going to be the knight tomorrow.

I move onto my side and prop myself up. "Well, that was fun."

Skye chuckles. "I'm reliving my childhood vicariously through our children." She loves this princess stuff and now she has William, who loves nothing better than dressing up as a dragon, knight, or a prince.

Positioning myself on top of her, I rest myself between her legs. She looks at me with warm eyes and smiles.

"Hey, Butterfly."

She gives me a small, almost shy "Hi" in return.

"I missed you today." I kiss the end of her nose.

"You miss me every day."

"I do. I should work from home."

"You wouldn't get anything done." She rolls her head against the shiny floor, causing her long hair to fan out across the tiles.

She finally grew her hair back, making her look exactly like she did in high school. Choosing to wear it down almost every day instead of her space buns, which she reckons she is too old for now, although I disagree, she still looks so much younger than her years.

Around five times a year, Skye travels all over the world delivering keynote talks about what happened to her, and how she's overcome her trauma. Her attack changed her life and career forever, but she used it to create a positive personal transformation. Going with her to every talk, I can see that she doesn't just engage the audience, she energizes and inspires them. She's a survivor.

It's coming toward the end of the summer break and Skye hasn't managed to write or illustrate one single thing. She said she didn't want to, choosing to be a full-time mom for every summer and school break. She's a wonderful, fun, and attentive mother.

"Two weeks then they go back to school and William starts daycare for a few days a week." I assure her she will get back to work soon.

"I don't want him to; I like him playing in my office while I'm working." Her face falls, looking sad. She's mentioned this a few times. She doesn't want him to grow up too fast. She thinks the girls have, and she doesn't like it one bit.

"But think of all the books you can write now. You have the next ten books to plot out."

Her face lights up. "I've already had a great idea for it. I want to do a princess series."

Of course she does.

"Right, Mrs. Clever Best-Selling Author, it's time to get ready for date night."

Every Friday or Saturday evening we go out, just the two of us, to the movies, or the theater, giving us a chance to catch up with family life but also remind ourselves that this is how we started, just me and her.

"I have a new dress." Her eyes shine and she looks excited to get dressed up.

"Good, now go and put it on..." I kiss her on the mouth. "... and forget the panties."

"Don't ever change; don't ever stop wanting me, Jay."

"Never."

* * *

"Why are we at the office?" Skye runs her hands over her aqua-blue silk evening gown as we ride up to the tenth floor of the Baxter and Bain building. The one my father gave to me not long after Skye and I married, when he handed me the reins of Baxter and Bain.

We've been out for a meal at Lincoln and Violet's Michelin three-star rated restaurant for the evening and my wife looks edible in her dress. Not wanting the evening to end, I thought I'd fulfill one of her fantasies.

"Did you forget something?" Playing along, she looks at me with a knowing eye.

"Yes, your panties." I step out of the elevator and make a beeline for my office.

"Are they along here?" she says sweetly behind me, knowing they are most certainly not.

As soon as she steps into my office, I slam the door shut and push her up against it.

"Good evening, Mrs. Baxter. Would you like to be fucked over my desk or up against the window this evening?"

"Over the desk," she says through hooded eyes as she stares at my lips. "But on this side of the desk so I can see your reflection in the windows. I want to watch."

I crash my lips against hers, diving my tongue into her mouth.

"Take off your dress," I demand, then step back, and toe off my shoes.

She slides her long dress up her thighs, revealing her black lace-topped stockings and nothing else.

I throw off my dress jacket, then undo my tie and top button of my shirt.

"Take it all off," she says, slipping her dress up over her naked body, letting it drop to the floor.

I know how much she appreciates my tattoos. It makes her wet for me. It always has.

Once I'm stripped to my waist, she walks over to me and puts her hand against my chest, prompting me to walk backward to the desk until I hit the edge of it.

"Have you been a good boy?" She smirks.

"Not even in the slightest."

"Do you know what happens to bad boys?"

"They get their cock sucked?"

Running her hands down my sides, over my body that's now covered in even more deep-blue butterfly tattoos, she drops to her knees, palms her hand over my now hard cock then proceeds to unbuckle, unbutton, and unzip my trousers in seconds, as if she can't wait to taste me.

"Can you remember what you said to me all those years ago?" I ask.

"I can't wait to taste you," she whispers, sliding my trousers down my hips. I lift myself up from the desk to help her pull them off and free my cock from my boxers.

Without hesitation, she pushes me back against the desk, then licks her tongue around the weeping head of my cock. Cupping my balls, she grips her hand around my shaft and begins stroking.

She's so fucking good at giving head.

"Suck my cock." I thread my fingers into the back of her silver locks, urging her to do what I ask.

She pulls me into her mouth, sucking me so deep I hit the back of her throat. Then she moves, fuck me, does she move, sucking, stroking, and licking her tongue around my cock.

She grabs on to my ass to pull me deeper into her mouth and I have to slam my hands on either side of my desk to stop my legs giving way.

"Aw, fuck." I slip my cock out of her mouth, pull her to her feet and plunge my tongue between her lips, tasting myself on her.

"Were you trying to make me come?" I move us around, then turn her to face the desk.

"Yes," she pants.

I slap her bent-over-the-desk ass, making her gasp. "When I come tonight, I am coming inside of this pretty pussy." I slide my cock between her folds.

Using my foot, I nudge her legs open. "Wider." I push her black patent stiletto-covered feet out again, causing her to arch her back and tilt her ass further in the air.

Fucking perfection.

"Now, Mrs. Baxter. I'm going to fuck you over this desk. Is that what you want?"

I glide my cock through her wet folds, teasing her entrance.

"Yes, do it now."

She pushes back as I slam into her.

"Jay," she calls out.

Watching us in the reflection of the windows, she never takes her eyes off of me.

"Touch yourself," I command.

She moves her hand to her clit and I watch her fingers move in slow, rhythmic circles.

"Now make yourself come for me, Butterfly." My hands dig into her hips, giving me the leverage I need to fuck her, burying myself inside of her, exactly the way she loves it. Hard.

My sweet girl might look sweet, but she fucks like a fucking stallion.

Her mouth, in the shape of an O, tells me she's about to come. I run my hands over the top of her lace and silk stockings, fucking her like my life depends on it.

"Come, baby, come," I call out.

Her moans and cries become higher, the sound of her coming on my cock, making me explode as I shoot my load inside of her.

Her walls clench around my dick as if she's trying to pull every last drop of cum from my body.

Not moving, not speaking, I trace my hand over the pale skin of her shoulders, as if tickling her back to reality as she pants against the surface of the desk.

I lay my body flat against hers and whisper in her ear, "Now back to your desk, or I may have to take further disciplinary action."

Her deep chuckle vibrates through me. I lean back, kissing a trail of soft kisses over her naked skin. She's fucking beautiful.

We dress in silence and I move across to the window to take in the view across the cove.

Warm arms slide around my hips, and I turn to welcome her.

"We have to go home. It's getting late and we need to relieve my mom and dad from babysitting duties."

"Just a minute longer." I plant a soft kiss on her lips.

"I love you, Jay."

"You'll always be my first love." I cup her face with my hands.

"And mine."

"My first kiss."

"And your last."

She'll always be my first and last everything.

And they all lived happily ever after... well, at least until the castle needed a new roof that winter... then they did... oh, but then there was the time William flooded the master bathroom and blew all of the electrics... and then, of course, Aurora smashed a lead glass window... do you know how difficult it is to source a glazier to repair a Grade A listed building? But, of course, Jacob found one; he always does... because he made sure his forever girl and their family were always happy... whatever, however, forever.

* * *

MORE FROM VH NICOLSON

Another book from VH Nicolson, *Owen*, is available to pre-order now here:

www.mybook.to/OwenBackAd

ACKNOWLEDGEMENTS

I hope you loved reading Jacob and Skye's story as much I have loved writing it. These two will live in my heart forever. I don't know what it is about these two beautiful souls, but I never wanted their story to end.

However, their story would not have been possible without the support network I find myself surrounded by.

To my incredible husband, Paul, who continues to feed me never-ending words of encouragement, thank you. I couldn't do this without you, babes.

To Carolann... my enthusiastic beta reader... thank you for taking the time out of your busy days and nights to read for me. You have been an enormous part of my author journey and your continued excitable energy for my books keeps me going.

To Lizzy, my beautiful alpha reader from across the pond. From your incredible development suggestions to your intricate edits, your passion for Jacob's story didn't go unnoticed. I cannot thank you enough for being in my world.

To my beautiful author friends, Elle Nicoll and Sadie Kincaid, yet again, thank you for always being there when I need you most. I love you girls. I love our regular three-ways—messenger chats, that is *winking face*!

To all of the book bloggers, Bookstagrammers and Book-Tokers, a huge thank you for all of your support and the beautiful graphics and videos you create; every day you blow me away.

A big shout out to a special group of talented Cygnet Authors I am proud to be part of. For the sharing and cheer-leading, I thank you all.

And to you, the spicy book reader, thank you for taking a leap of faith on a new-ish author; you have no idea how much that means to me, I am eternally grateful and without you, I wouldn't keep following my dream of becoming a full-time author. THANK YOU! Mwah x

ABOUT THE AUTHOR

VH Nicolson is a Scottish author of spicy romance fiction. She was born and raised along the breathtaking coastline in North East Fife. For more than two decades she's worked throughout the UK and abroad within the creative marketing and design industry. Married to her soulmate, they have one son.

Violet is up to her capers again... sign up to VH Nicolson's mailing list to find out what she does to Lincoln in an extended epilogue, and download the recipe for Yaya's secret moussaka recipe...

Visit VH Nicolson's website: www.vhnicolsonauthor.com

Follow VH Nicolson on social media here:

facebook.com/authorvhnicolson
instagram.com/vhnicolsonauthor
tiktok.com/@vhnicolsonauthor
bookbub.com/authors/vh-nicolson
pinterest.com/vhnicolsonauthor

ALSO BY VH NICOLSON

Lincoln

Jacob

Owen

Boldwood
EVER AFTER
X♡X♡

JOIN BOLDWOOD'S
**ROMANCE
COMMUNITY**
FOR SWEET AND
SPICY BOOK RECS
WITH ALL YOUR
FAVOURITE
TROPES!

SIGN UP TO OUR
NEWSLETTER

HTTPS://BIT.LY/BOLDWOODEVERAFTER

Boldwood

Boldwood Books is an award-winning fiction publishing company seeking out the best stories from around the world.

Find out more at www.boldwoodbooks.com

Join our reader community for brilliant books, competitions and offers!

Follow us
@BoldwoodBooks
@TheBoldBookClub

Sign up to our weekly deals newsletter

https://bit.ly/BoldwoodBNewsletter

Printed in Great Britain
by Amazon